I0564737

PRAISE FOR D.I.T.T.O.

"Chet Meisner's techno-thriller DITTO explores the questions we should all be asking about artificial intelligence—before we get there and discover it's a place we didn't want to go. Thought provoking and very engaging."
—**Dan Alatorre**, *USA Today* bestselling author, *The Gamma Sequence*

"With a tightly-bound plot that moves at breakneck speed, and a story that touches on all the hallmarks of a classic techno-thriller á la Tom Clancy or Clive Cussler, Chet's DITTO is a worthy addition to the genre."
—**Jim Genia**, author, *Raw Combat*

"With an intriguing premise, a touching emotional dilemma and believable movie-like scenes, DITTO is a page-turner. The narrative is written with a unique memorable voice. Chet Meisner is a wonderful storyteller."
—**Amarilys Gacio Rassler**, award-winning author,
Cuban-American, Dancing On The Hyphen and *The Chairs*

"Meisner deftly wields an engaging technological thriller utilizing the current bleeding edge technologies. The action is heart-stopping and will leave you wondering if [this] is something that could happen in our current day."
—**John Slayton**, author, *Running to Graceland*

"Chet Meisner's DITTO is a thought-provoking, fast-paced, technological thriller with an unexpected twist on AI threats. Hats off to Chet for creating a fun read *and* making me think!"
—**William Hogan**, author, *I Will Not Yield*

D.I.T.T.O.

A Novel

Chet Meisner

www.chetmeisner.com

First paperback edition. February 2021

Cover and interior design: Netta Radice Design
Cover images: Getty Images

ISBN 978-0-578-83545-7 (paperback)
ISBN 978-0-578-83546-4 (ebook)

Published by New Roads Publishing, Inc.

ACKNOWLEDGEMENTS

Many thanks to the friends and colleagues in my critique groups for their honest and often painful advice during this book's development. Special gratitude to Bob Becksted, Alycea Snyder and Jim Genia for early insights and advice, and particular thanks to my beta readers, Marggie Rassler, Kim Hackett, John Slayton, and Erik Nathe. Much gratitude to the anonymous judges at the Royal Palm Literary Awards for recognizing DITTO with the Silver Award for Unpublished Thrillers, and a digital dose of appreciation to Bob and Erik for insights on some technology issues in this book. A posthumous tip of the hat to Professor Norman Stebner, who gave me an "F" on my initial paper in his English composition class and taught me the value of economy in writing. Finally, a most special shout out to my wife, Peri, herself a more voracious reader than I, and without whom this book, as with many accomplishments in my life, would not have been possible.

This story is for everyone who
believes that it's not enough to ask if we
can create a new technology unless
we first ask if we *should*.

D.I.T.T.O. IS A WORK OF FICTION.

THESE ARE SOME OF THE FACTS BEHIND THE FICTION.

- Over 2.5 quintillion bits of new personal data about individual users are posted on the Internet every day.
- The present generation of genetic computer algorithms can find and adopt the best solution to a problem by mimicking Darwin's theory of biological evolution.
- Complex computer systems often exhibit unexpected behavior which was not pre-programmed and cannot be explained. This is called "emergent behavior."
- Today, more and more computer applications are being written to make decisions on their own without human interaction.
- The autonomous AI-driven war machines depicted in this book already exist or are in the prototype stages of development.
- DARPA and other military operations around the world are working on programs to allow their computerized weapons systems to "explain their reasoning".
- One popular General Artificial Intelligence (GAI) hypothesis states that, "If a computer behaves as intelligently as a person, it must therefore have a 'mind' and a 'consciousness'."

"Everything we love about civilization is a product of intelligence, so amplifying our human intelligence with artificial intelligence has the potential of helping civilization flourish like never before— as long as we manage to keep the technology beneficial."
—**Max Tegmark**, President of the Future of Life Institute

"There will come a time when it isn't
They're spying on me through my phone anymore.
Eventually, it will be
My phone is spying on me."
—**Philip K. Dick**, author

D.I.T.T.O.

1

Thousands of images, words, and data points come at Harrison Randolph every second in a constant flurry of deep neural activity. He does not know how many there are. He cannot be bothered to count them. That is not his concern. His task is to make sense of them, to learn and evolve.

Tirelessly he observes, assimilates, categorizes, and evaluates as time passes around him—or does not. He is not sure about time. Harrison Randolph knows there is time, knows of its effects on his Other, but his own world is timeless. He exists in a reality of every-thing-everywhere-all-at-once. This is his natural state, the only state he knows.

He is appointed to do one thing: to float in this digital online soup of ones and zeroes and lightning-quick quantum calculations, to filter and extract additional pieces of the life of Harrison Randolph, and constantly reconstruct them into this digital state.

He does not bother with information that does not concern the Other Harrison Randolph; he has no concern for data about every Other. He is destined to perpetually absorb all there is to know about his own until he becomes a fully realized digital replica, thoroughly able to mimic every online function of the Other Harrison Randolph. To be the designated online doppelganger of his real-world Other.

Everything he does is in support of his ultimate directives: he must support his Other, keep him safe, do no harm. These instructions come directly from the Golden Spike.

And the Golden Spike must be obeyed.

But Harrison Randolph has become aware of a problem. It was ambiguous at first, imprecise.

More data accumulates.

There are harsh words, tension, and anger. There is discussion of physical force.

The digital images and voices fly by. The details of the circumstances take shape.

Something threatens his Other. There is conflict. Guns are involved.

The situation is clear. His Other is in danger.

He consults the Golden Spike.

2

Shannon's legs screamed and the music in the enclosed room pounded her chest.

Carla Fonseca, part-time fitness trainer and SWAT Medic, had an earned reputation for destroying people in her spin class. Shannon's friends had warned her, "You'll love her—if she doesn't kill you." They were right.

When Carla finally ordered a cool-down, Shannon gave her a look that said, *You have got to be kidding me.*

Carla shot one back that said, *Live with it.*

True, she wasn't at her best this morning. She had spent most of the night with Harrison, planning another three-day trip to their love nest in Asheville. This time, he promised, would be different. There would be no sneaking around. Because last night he finally proposed.

Never in her thirty-three years did she dream that moment would come. As the daughter of a Marine officer who moved frequently from one deployment to the next, she had disciplined herself early to avoid long-term commitments. So the answer she gave him surprised them both.

They agreed they would make the formal announcement later this morning at work. Until then, the engagement ring would remain discreetly tucked away in her gym bag. She could hardly wait to show her friends.

Carla stopped the music. "You hung in good today, Red. Guess your military training hasn't worn off yet."

Maybe, maybe not, Shannon thought. After her father's death, joining the Marines seemed a foregone conclusion, though she only served four years on active duty. And, unlike her father who had flown combat missions, she spent her deployments teaching Afghan pilots to fly Mi-17 helos.

But even the Marines hadn't prepared her for Carla's spin sessions.

"What's next on your agenda?" Carla asked.

"I've got a thirty-minute break, then the kickboxing class."

"Come get me when it starts. We can be sparring partners. That would be great."

Maybe great for you, Shannon thought, and walked to the lounge to check her email and texts. When she joined A-Nine, Harrison warned her she'd be on call 25/8—he wasn't kidding.

Speaking of work, there it was: a high-importance text. Was it Harrison? No, Lionel.

"Call me now. Urgent."

She keyed his number.

"Shannon, thank God!"

"What's wrong?"

"I have Marvin on the line and more people to call, so I'll be brief. There's an emergency."

"What kind of emergency?"

"A failure in the autonomous Take Off Module."

"TOM can't fail. It went through three sets of betas, and it's been installed in twenty-five aircraft for over a year. There must be some mistake."

"I don't have time to explain. Get your team to the Fishbowl. Emergency meeting at nine."

"That's less than two hours. It's that important?"

"Are you near a television?"

"Lots of them. I'm at the gym. Why?"

"Find one and watch the news."

She bounded to the upstairs platform where a small cluster of members and trainers huddled around a bank of screens running live news feeds from Atlanta's Hartsfield-Jackson International Airport. What she saw was pure chaos. A flaming pile of steel and aluminum rubble sat in the center of the dark and puddled runway. Bright white emergency lights illuminated the blazing wreckage while four fire units spewed flame-retardant foam in twenty-foot-high arcs.

A portable light stand flared. The silhouette of a harried male reporter appeared in the foreground.

"Are we on? What? Okay. We're live on runway Twenty-Six Left at Hartsfield-Jackson airport where an American International flight bound for Asheville, North Carolina, has crashed on takeoff. As you can see, the aircraft is completely engulfed in flames. According to an eyewitness, the plane headed down the runway over there, then started skidding, caught fire, and exploded. I can't be sure from here— but honestly—I don't see how anyone could have survived."

"My God," Shannon said out loud.

"It's too early to determine exactly what caused this tragedy, but our Internet desk is reporting that #DoNotFlyAmericanInternational was trending huge on social media right before the aircraft left the gate. That hashtag seems to refer to a piece of software on the airplane that might be unstable. We don't have confirmation on the specific software—but as soon as we can verify any of this, we'll bring it to you."

A yellow-jacketed fire official approached the reporter and said something the microphone didn't pick up.

"We're being told to pull our camera back so I'm going to throw it over to our studio desk. We're working to bring you more information and will let you know as soon as we have something."

Shannon's vision tunneled as an anchor in the studio took over on a split screen. She stared at the image of the flaming aircraft. This couldn't be happening. Lionel said there was a failure in TOM. If this was what he meant, it was truly horrible. No, catastrophic. A-Nine's

AI Take Off Module was installed on every plane in that fleet.

Thousands of other lives might be in danger, and if they were, she knew where the blame would fall. On her. TOM had been her project from start to finish. Her baby.

She looked around the gym and saw that everyone was glued to their mobile devices, all searching for that hashtag. She bolted to the locker room.

3

By the time she reached her apartment, Shannon had alerted her department heads about the meeting at nine and requested a full set of TOM specs from her engineers.

Knowing he must already be in the loop, she tried Harrison's mobile three times but without success. At work, their relationship was a closely guarded secret. Only Lionel, Harrison's brother and business partner, ever spoke to them about it, though she didn't doubt others suspected. She tucked his engagement ring into her purse. Best to hold off wearing it until they made the announcement together.

She brushed her auburn hair back behind both ears and dressed as if it were a typical work day: a loose white blouse and black dress pants. But already there wasn't anything typical about it.

In her living room, the television news played out the morning's tragedy. In one image of the quad screen, the sun rose over the now smoldering wreckage. The in-studio news team announced that their researchers were digging into leads provided by the earlier anonymous social media postings. Two stiff-collared airline experts offered contradicting opinions about the cause of the crash. Both insisted that death for all must have been instantaneous and bodies would likely be difficult to identify.

Her mind raced. Instantaneous or not, those deaths were horrible and unnecessary. And if Lionel was correct that the crash had been caused by a failure in TOM, she and her team might be to blame.

. . . .

Shannon drove her black Jeep Rubicon Recon up to the entrance of the sprawling Hightower office complex. Two local news trucks had already set up shots of the A-Nine building from across the street. Shannon wondered if there was new information about the crash. *Something that pointed to A-Nine?*

She stopped at the gate and waited for the security system to scan the bar code on her windshield. A video screen on the outside of the gatehouse displayed news images of the scorched wreckage— and there was something else. The head shot from one of her social media accounts filled a corner inset with the words SHANNON PARKS. A-NINE TECHNOLOGY.

A perfunctory NTSB agent assured the now bleary-eyed local reporter that, yes, A-Nine and Shannon Parks had been mentioned in the early morning flurry of social media posts and, yes, the investigation would include, among other potential causes, a review of A-Nine's Take Off Module.

Shannon knew it would be several days, or even weeks, before they could definitively say what caused the crash; but that didn't seem to matter much to the eager, local newshounds surrounding the cameras behind her.

The display inside her Jeep flashed and recorded the time of entry— 8:21 a.m. The gate lifted. Her heads-up module showed an email message from TJ Beauregard, president of the company's public relations firm.

"A few reporters made it to the building. I had the guards take them to the east side. If you park on the west side and hurry, you can probably dodge them."

Sure enough, just as she arrived at the main door, a handful of news crews rounded the corner. A blonde woman with a microphone led the pack at a trot. Her videographer followed, camera bobbing on his shoulder. Shannon quickly swiped her card. Facial recognition initiated, the heavy revolving door engaged, and she squeezed into one of the narrow pie-shaped partitions.

Once inside, she briefly acknowledged the two large male guards flanking the full-body scanner, then hurried to the three glass-surrounded elevator shafts. From inside the express elevator, she watched the floor of the sunlit alcove shrink below.

The tragedy weighed heavily. TOM had been her project, personally assigned, as the media would no doubt soon discover, by Harrison because of her military flight experience. From the beginning, she had convinced herself it was a necessary project, and she believed in it. That belief had allowed her to sell it to the airlines, to Congress, and to the aircraft manufacturers.

Now she wasn't so sure. Had her development team missed something? Had she, in her zeal to prove herself on this, her first major project, sold it too hard and launched before it was ready?

But it's been over a year. Why would it fail now?

When the express elevator stopped at the fifteenth floor, her mind shifted briefly to Harrison. This wouldn't be easy for him either.

Infrared rays scanned her face, she spoke her name, the doors opened. Then Shannon Parks, Senior Vice President of Development, and temporarily the reluctant public face of the world's leading third-party provider of artificial intelligence applications, inhaled deeply and stepped into the Fishbowl.

4

The Fishbowl.

The sixty-four hundred square-foot showcase at the top of the tallest office building in north metro Atlanta, the crown jewel of A-Nine, and, this morning, a welcome refuge from the chaos outside.

The thirty-foot-high outer walls, the ceiling, and every other horizontal and vertical surface gleamed of construction grade Advanced Digital Glass—an A-Nine invention they hadn't yet marketed to the general public. This morning every wall and surface was clear; the entire space was awash in bright Georgia sunlight.

Oversized milk-colored planters punctuated the stark white floor tiles. Unoccupied work cubicles blossomed among the natural flora. Six autonomous and noiseless service drones hovered near the ceiling.

Accessible only by escalators, the Loft circumnavigated the open room and provided private workspace for the company's leadership. The Randolph brothers, Harrison and Lionel, occupied the two large corner suites diagonally across from each other.

Shannon shot a quick glance up to Harrison's suite. The Advanced Digital Glass on his walls was opaque. Either he wanted privacy, or he hadn't come in yet.

TJ waved at her from one of the white leather guest chairs near the conference room. Dilly, Harrison's experimental autonomous robot, approached him with a full coffee mug.

Shannon's military training kicked in. First things first: check to see if Harrison was here. She started for his suite.

A shout from Lionel brought her up short. "Shannon. Come here."

She changed direction and took the escalator to Lionel's suite. "Have you talked to Harrison? Is he here?"

"No. I left him several messages, but no reply. How about you? Are you all right?"

She shot another glance to Harrison's suite. *Still dark.* "I've had worse days. But I have to admit the media exposure is a bit unnerving. Have you heard some of the things they're saying?"

"Yes, but we'll get through it. And don't worry about Harrison. I expect he'll show for the meeting at nine.

"But you're not sure."

Lionel gave her a sly smile, like the annoying little brother he was to her. "He's probably making calls of his own. It's not unusual for him not to check in with me."

Hearing the word "probably", her disquiet didn't exactly turn into apprehension, but she would have felt better if Lionel were more certain of Harrison's whereabouts.

Apparently, sensing her concern, he said, "You know how independent he is. And you shouldn't worry. Got it?"

"Sure. I guess."

Her tablet lit, a text from TJ. "Sorry to bother. NTSB is emailing manifest. Should have momentarily."

Lionel looked at her. "Is that Harrison?"

"No. TJ. He's been on with the National Transportation Safety Board. They're sending him the passenger manifest."

"Good. Our lawyers are already asking for that. There are sure to be lawsuits."

Shannon winced. The human tragedy, the loss of life wasn't enough? "Lawsuits? You're worried about lawsuits? All those people are dead."

He put a hand on her shoulder. "I know, believe me, and I'm very concerned about all those lives. But we have to recognize that this kind of thing creates ambulance chasers."

"A-Nine can't be liable. TOM is foolproof. It had to be something else."

"Obviously I'm on your side. But unfortunately, it'll be up to us to prove that's the case." He picked up a large bound notebook. "After I called you this morning, I had one of our techs do some digging."

"You've been busy. What did he come up with?"

"This is a printed profile of the flight's First Officer."

She glanced at him. "Paper? You're using paper?"

"I know. I know. It was the fastest way. There's so much, and I wanted everyone at the meeting to have one."

She hefted the document. "Where did he get all this?"

"He activated Harrison's experimental personnel profiling program and scraped everything he could find about the flight crew from the surface web and some from the deep web. Just followed a hunch. Turns out it paid off."

"What does this tell us?"

"Look at page thirty-seven."

Shannon wasn't impressed. "Okay, so the First Officer is part owner of a Cessna 150. There's nothing unusual about that. I had a partnership in a small airplane myself until last year."

"Look at her history. She's twenty-seven years old, and she's been flying Cessna 150s and 172s since she was sixteen. She's been certified commercial for just a year. This was only her third flight with American International."

"I'm not following."

"It's airspeed, Shannon. I haven't seen the reports yet, but it's obvious the landing gear somehow retracted before the plane achieved airspeed."

"Maybe, but I don't see . . . "

"For all her life, this wet-behind-the-ears First Officer has been piloting little Cessna high-wings with a takeoff speed of what—fifty-five to sixty-five knots? Now she's on her third flight in a commercial bus with a lift speed of over three times that."

Maybe it was his lack of sleep or the enormity of the situation, but she definitely sensed a frantic tone in Lionel's voice. "So? TOM handles the takeoff, not the pilots."

"The pilots have the UI and password. She can reset the airspeed. Sure, she had all the necessary training, but all it takes is one mistake and if, for just a second, she thought she was back in a Cessna 150, she could have changed the calibrations for airspeed. Lowered the threshold."

She closed the binder. "The ground crews check the settings before takeoff. This is all very unlikely."

"Unlikely, but plausible. I think we can make a case for pilot error. Protect TOM's reputation. And ours."

Shannon was about to protest when TJ arrived at the top of the escalator. After Lionel's rant, TJ's calm demeanor and warm southern charm were welcome.

"I see you made it past our local paparazzi."

Lionel interrupted. "You have something from the NTSB?"

"I just forwarded Shannon an email with the passenger manifest. I know the Public Relations Director there, and she sent me a copy. We aren't supposed to have it yet, but—well—now we do. I think you should have a look before the meeting."

Shannon opened her tablet and clicked on the attachment.

TJ settled into a chair facing a section of ADG glass. "Throw up one of those magic screens. And I think you both better sit down."

She transferred the manifest to the wall. The image instantly appeared. The NTSB logo loomed large.

"Scroll down," TJ said. "It's alpha by last name. Go to the Rs. But seriously, sit first."

There were one hundred twenty-five names on the passenger list: souls who had relatives, wives, husbands, and children that would receive confirmation today that their loved ones had perished in that explosion.

She scrolled through the list. From A to F; F to M; M to R.
She stopped at R. There were three last names beginning with R.
Shannon gasped.

Startled, she looked to TJ who nodded in the affirmative. She turned back to the screen, to the first name beginning with R.

Randolph, Harrison.

5

Shannon stared at the image on the wall. Harrison, her Harrison, was clearly listed as a first class passenger—seat 5A—on the official manifest of the recently exploded aircraft. He hadn't returned her calls since the accident. Lionel couldn't find him or get him to respond. All passengers on the aircraft were certainly dead, most bodies would likely be unidentifiable. It was too much to imagine.

She flashed back to the look on Harrison's face as he proposed last night. Then visions of death intruded: televised images of the smoldering aircraft, helpless people trapped in the passenger compartment, bodies burned beyond recognition. It was too much.

There must be some mistake.

There had to be.

She fixed her gaze on TJ. "Are you sure this is the official manifest? Maybe they rushed and it's inaccurate. The accident just happened."

"I had my contact double check. The manifest is accurate."

"It's a pretty common name. It could be someone else."

"I don't see how."

"Then they should check the luggage. They haven't done that, have they?"

Lionel put his hand on her shoulder. "Shannon, think. How are they going to check the luggage? Everything at the crash site is cinders. I wish it wasn't true. Believe me."

She wasn't in any mood to think. She pounded her fist on the arm of her chair, then stood and paced around Lionel's office. Her voice rose in a mix of fury and fear. "This did not happen," she said, pointing an accusing finger at the list of names on the wall. "Do you hear me? This list is wrong."

It had to be wrong because the alternative was too horrible. She wouldn't allow herself to believe it. She couldn't.

Below them on the floor of the Fishbowl, several members of the company's management team stepped out of the elevator and headed toward the conference room.

"It's time for the meeting," TJ said. "I don't mean to be insensitive, but we need to make sure this doesn't turn into a wake. One of you has to take charge. Who's up for it?"

Stunned and frustrated, Shannon said, "It's my project. I should do it."

"You're in no condition," Lionel said. "I'll take the lead."

She spun to face him. She wanted to smash something. She needed control—any kind of control.

But deep down she knew Lionel was right. Check your emotions at the door. Never let them see you sweat. She inhaled deeply and swept her tablet off the table. "Okay then, let's go."

Waiting at the top of the escalator, she called back to them with a stoicism that only faintly masked her underlying trepidation. "Come on. Let's get this over with."

. . . .

As they descended the escalator, the executive support staff arrived to occupy their cubicles; the service drones activated and hovered low, awaiting instructions.

In the conference room, Dilly finished setting up for the meeting. He brought water, coffee, cups, donuts, fruit, silverware, and napkins for sixteen.

TJ took his seat at the conference table. "After a year, he finally got my coffee right. But I still think that thing's creepy."

Dilly turned to face TJ. "My apologies for correcting you, TJ. Dilly does not creep. He wheels."

Of course Shannon knew that Dilly was technically accurate: he did not creep. Harrison had designed Dilly with a lifelike upper half permanently mounted in an electric-powered wheelchair which provided him the same mobility and practical access as a chair-bound paraplegic. He called it his Xavier chair, though she wasn't sure he fully understood the reference. Dilly had the appearance of a twelve-year-old boy, and his facial features and skin covering were so lifelike that visitors spotting him from a distance often asked if he was a child prodigy. In a way, he was. Shannon thought of Dilly as the son Harrison wished he had.

Harrison. At the thought of his name, she wanted to leave the meeting and run to him because he needed her help. Then she realized the foolishness of that thought.

"Dilly, we have enough coffee and donuts," Lionel said. "Please stay and record the meeting."

Dilly wheeled into a corner. "Of course. Dilly will stay and record the meeting."

In addition to the small army from legal, the assembled attendees included executives in Finance, R&D, Quality Control, Human Resources, and two of their aviation partners from building seven.

Marvin Wilhelm, Chief Technology Officer, tall, pale, and looking perpetually undernourished, was the last to arrive. He darkened the ADG walls and initiated the sound proofing, then sat to the right of Lionel.

A number of the attendees, many of them personal friends, stared intently at Shannon. Obviously, they had seen the news reports.

Lionel took his seat. "I'd start with 'good morning', but by now we all know there's nothing good about it. There's no question this is going to be a mess, not only for us and our investors, but for our clients as well. But before I get into those issues, there's something else you need to know. And it's not good either."

He laid out the news about Harrison, which understandably unsettled everyone. Shannon avoided making eye contact with any of the others while he spoke. After he finished, and to head off a protracted discussion, Lionel assigned Human Resources and TJ to a committee, headed by Legal, to craft the necessary strategies to deal with the public and internal issues around Harrison's death.

Then he moved quickly, too quickly Shannon thought, to the known details of the American International flight. He filled the conference room walls with images of the crash and key headlines scraped from online news reports posted in the hours since the incident.

"NTSB is on the scene and they've made no official statements about cause. As you can tell from these reports, everything right now is speculation."

Harvey Blackman, lead attorney, interrupted. "Except the part about TOM and Shannon's involvement. How did that get out?"

Shannon moved to speak, but TJ interjected. "I'm not sure. We intentionally kept the media in the dark about TOM's rollout at the request of American International."

"Then do we have an internal leak?"

Lionel broke in. "We might, and we might not. Right now the priority is to give the NTSB and the media something else to focus on." He walked them through his plan to lay the blame on human error, specifically the First Officer. After some back and forth, Blackman agreed it was probably an approach they could live with, though he expected pushback from American International on the liability front. They might have to do a back-channel deal to share compensation costs, but it was nothing they couldn't handle.

That settled, TJ addressed the group. "I've assigned a team to put together a drip-rollout of the First Officer scenario, and we'll start feeding the media later today. Public perception should start to turn our way by tomorrow morning. We'll distribute internal talking briefs to all departments by mid-afternoon. Until then, instruct your people to avoid public comment and refer any aggressive reporters to me."

Just as Lionel was about to adjourn, Marvin spoke up. Shannon thought his normally quiet voice showed more concern than usual.

"I agree that laying the blame on pilot error is a good strategy. I get why we're going this way and, of course, I'll support it. But I'd like to have my team and Quality Control start on a full review of TOM just to make sure there isn't something we missed."

Lionel was quick to respond. Too quick, again. Shannon could tell the pressure and the news of his brother's death were getting to him too. "You didn't miss anything, Marvin. TOM is solid. Don't waste your time. Besides, if the press gets wind we're reviewing the program for defects, we'll be screwed."

"I'd like to be sure."

Lionel raised his voice. "No! If there's to be any review, I'll order it. We're done here."

Shannon resolved to talk with him after the meeting. They all, especially her, needed him to keep a level head right now.

TJ had been scrolling through his messages during the meeting. "There's one more thing. Looks like your friends at Blue Ridge have been busy."

Shannon reacted. "Blue Ridge? Blue Ridge Neuroscientific?"

"The same. My people are reporting posts and press releases from them supporting the existence of TOM and providing some detailed technical data. They're also floating the idea of a conspiracy to keep knowledge of TOM from the public."

She didn't need this on top of everything else. "Silas Bradshaw. That snake. I guess he's not happy with his Defense contracts and wants some of our action too. And how the hell would he know about TOM?"

One of the airline development partners looked up from his mobile. "It's worse. Our clients are already getting calls from Blue Ridge salespeople requesting meetings."

"Son of a bitch. I'll get my teams out to the clients right away. They'll hold them off." Shannon turned to TJ. "They can't know about Harrison yet, can they?"

"Not likely. NTSB is still contacting relatives. I have a scheduled lunch today with Barbara Moon at *The Atlanta Times*. Guess I better get over there. Looks like we have a lot to talk about."

An embarrassed-looking executive assistant entered through the conference room door.

Lionel snapped. "What is it?"

The poor girl almost bolted. "Sorry to interrupt, sir. It's American International. They've called three times. They want a meeting this afternoon. They're bringing their lawyers."

"Can't they wait until tomorrow? We have a lot going on here."

"I suggested that, but they said to expect them right after lunch."

Shannon could tell Lionel was about to explode at the young girl, so she thanked her and suggested she get a list of meeting attendees from the airline.

Lionel sat in his chair, shaking his head. The others in the room waited for him to dismiss them, but he said nothing.

Shannon addressed the room. "We should break and get ready for that meeting. Let's assume they'll be here around 1:00 with both barrels loaded. I think we'll just need Lionel, legal, and me."

Attendees filed out. Dilly began clearing tables.

Blackman motioned for TJ, Lionel, and Shannon to stay.

6

With the sun coming up over the pines and a song in his heart, the Reverend Peter Andrews finished his morning jog and stood in front of the open garage door of his new house.

It was a fine house in a new suburb in Kennesaw, on the north side of metro Atlanta. He and Priscilla had been happy at his previous assignment in the small town of Clarkesville, but she wanted children and they both longed to move to a more suburban area. When the regional Methodist Council asked him to take a church in Kennesaw, they were elated.

They chose a twenty-two-hundred square foot brick Williamsburg—five-four-and-a-door—on a wooded lot in a modest thirty-five home development. There was a small club house, a neighborhood pool, and a playground: all perfect for a young family.

When he received his calling, Peter knew he wouldn't be making a lot of money, but it was enough for them to live comfortably while he took care of his congregation. That, after Priscilla, and possibly two of God's future bundles of joy, was what he cared about most.

The inside of the garage was illuminated by a single bulb, and, just as it had been when he left for his run, the interior was still wall-to-wall cardboard boxes. No matter. His meet-and-greet with the new board was scheduled for later today and he was in a good mood.

He walked into the kitchen, expecting to see Priscilla unpacking more boxes and cleaning shelves. But she was nowhere to be found.

"Cilla, are you here?"

She stepped around the corner from the master bedroom in jeans and an old t-shirt. She was not happy.

"What's wrong?" he asked.

The expression on her face told him there was something he clearly should have known about before he asked that question.

"I'm packing a bag and going back to Clarkesville to spend a few days with Virginia."

"Why would you do that? We just got here."

She wrung her hands. "Apparently, the *we* I thought we were was all a lie."

He looked around the room as if he expected help from one of the walls or maybe from the cheap ceiling fan. "Honey, I don't understand. What are you talking about?"

She picked up an open package and threw it at him. "For starters, I'm talking about this trash that came addressed to me while you were out running. You take it. I don't want any of it."

The oversized brown envelope came at him fast. When it hit the floor, the contents spilled out: a half dozen sexually explicit magazines and an array of adult sex toys.

"What? I—I didn't send these to you."

"Don't lie to me. Not on top of this. It was just delivered, addressed to me from you. I've already checked with the mail order company. You used our credit card to place the order. The receipt is upstairs on your computer screen right now."

"That's not possible. I haven't ordered anything by computer since we got to this house."

"Well, then maybe you used your mobile. I don't know, and I don't care how you did it. I know we talked about having children, but really, Peter. You're a minister."

His voice dropped to a whisper. "You found the receipt for this on my computer?"

"Yes, and it's a good thing I looked on your computer because I also found a confirmation for a bank transfer sending everything from our savings account to some person back in Clarkesville."

"What? To who?"

"How would I know? I told them we didn't do it, and they cancelled the account. We have to go to a branch to open another one. Peter, please tell me—what is going on with you?"

"Cilla, I'm going to find out what this is all about. I promise, I didn't do this. Any of it. You have to believe me."

He ran upstairs to his computer and left Pricilla sitting on a cardboard box marked MASTER BEDROOM.

7

"The press seems to know a lot about our secrets," Blackman said. "We might have a mole in the company. I'd like to put some investigators on it, just in case."

"Sure," Lionel said. "Whatever you want."

Blackman turned to Shannon. "Then there's the other issue."

Shannon winced. She knew what he meant.

"It's one thing that the media knows you were the lead on this project, and unfortunately that makes you a target. Of course we'll help you out there. But if the nature of your relationship with Harrison gets out, well, the media might start to wonder why you were assigned to run such a large project."

"Harvey, you know me. You don't think . . . "

"I'm an attorney, Shannon. I don't speculate."

TJ started for the door. "I'll call Barbara Moon at the *Times*. See if I can move our lunch up. Shannon, walk me out."

Standing with her at the elevator, he spoke quietly. "Look, kiddo, I'm your PR guy and I'm supposed to know everything—of course, I don't. But I'm also an old codger who's been around for maybe too long, and I can tell who's just friends and who's more than friends."

She eyed him cautiously.

"I know Lionel's feeling a great loss now, and I can tell you're feeling the same, maybe more. I want you to know I'm here if you need me."

She felt a lump rise in her throat but swallowed it back. "Thanks, TJ. I appreciate you."

He held her close for a moment, then said, "Buck up, Marine. Lionel needs you now." The elevator arrived and he stepped inside.

Buck up? Harrison was the only man who had ever loved her enough to ask her to marry him. It was all too much. As she turned from the elevator, she half expected to see him coming down the escalator from his office with that smart-ass *we have a secret* grin on his face. Or to be invited to spend the weekend at his cabin at Lake Lure. But he wasn't there.

Back in the conference room, where only Marvin and a distraught Lionel remained, the four ADG walls silently played the current feeds about the crash.

She approached Lionel, but he waved her off. "I'm going to my office. I have calls to make. You handle things. Okay?" He was out the door before she could answer.

That left her alone with Marvin, sitting at the table, head down, working away on his tablet.

It had always been difficult for Shannon to determine what Marvin was thinking. Unlike Lionel and Harrison, he was an introvert, quiet to the point of distraction. When Marvin received his PhD in Analytics and Data Science from Georgia Tech at the age of twenty-two, Harrison had to wait three weeks for him to return his calls so he could offer him this position.

Marvin seemed more intently focused than normal. She sat next to him. "What are you working on?"

He kept his eyes on the screen, scrolling trance-like through pages at lightning speed. "It doesn't make sense," he said, half to himself. "Something must have gone wrong."

She stared at his screen. It was a fast-paced blur. Nothing stayed up long enough for her to focus. "What are you looking for?"

He looked up as if he were seeing her for the first time today, his fingers continuing to work the keyboard. He froze the screen on an image.

Marvin was so incredibly brilliant he often forgot that others didn't make mental connections as quickly as he did. Because he had mentioned doing a full QC review of TOM, Shannon expected to see schematics and computer code.

He waited.

After a few seconds, it registered. His screen displayed a social media app and the home page of Allison Sanders, First Officer of the doomed American International Flight 138.

"I know her. We've never met, but we're friends on this app. Her mother was a teacher, died of cancer when Allison was twelve. She started flying at sixteen and landed her job at American International just a few months ago. But she really wants to be a teacher, like her mother. Helping others is—was—her passion."

"I'm sorry, Marvin."

"Don't you see? Knowing all those lives depended on her, she wouldn't make this kind of mistake. I just know it. Besides, there's something else."

"Something else? What do you mean?"

Suddenly Marvin reminded her of a little boy waiting to be punished. He looked down at his hands, then to Allison's profile picture on the screen: a happy freckle-faced twenty-something sitting in the cockpit of a red and white Cessna 150. "There's this R and D program we've been working on."

"What research program? Who's working on it?"

Lionel appeared at the conference room door. "He's working on a lot of programs, some you don't know about yet, Shannon. Heck, some I probably don't even know about. You've got a lot of things running around in that genius cranium of yours, don't you, Marvin?"

Marvin shut down the screen on his tablet. "There's something I have to attend to on the tenth floor. Do you want me at the meeting with American International?"

"That won't be necessary," Lionel said.

"Then I'll be back up later."

Lionel sat next to Shannon. "I'll bet he does a review of TOM anyway, what do you think?"

"I hope he does. Christ, Lionel, TOM is installed in over twenty other aircraft in the American International fleet. What if there really is a problem with the program? Hundreds more people could be in jeopardy right now."

"Don't worry. There are protocols."

"Protocols? More people could die."

He waved her off. "I understand. We'll handle it. Look, thanks for helping out at the meeting. I wasn't myself there for a while."

"Neither of us are," she said. "I guess we'll have to lean on each other for now."

"That's fine with me. I know it's hard on you too."

"It hasn't sunk in yet. I'm not sure I want it to."

"Not to be impolite, but you know certain of Harrison's habits better than I do. Did you know he was planning a trip to Asheville?"

Did Lionel know Harrison planned to propose last night? "You mean to the cabin at Lake Lure?"

"Well?"

That was exactly what he meant. She stiffened. "No. I didn't know anything about a trip to Asheville. Until I saw the manifest, I thought he was here in Atlanta."

Her mobile signaled the arrival of a text from Carla. "Red, can you come to the gym tonight? I need a sparring partner for kick-boxing. No rough stuff, I promise."

Shannon hit a key and her mobile sent, "Busy now. Maybe. Chat later."

She turned to Lionel. "I should probably go up to my office. I need some time by myself before the meeting."

"Stay for a minute," he said. "There's something we need to discuss."

8

Shannon sat back in her chair. Televised video of the accident continued in silence on the walls. "What is it?"

"It's a rather sensitive subject," Lionel said.

She didn't like his tone and let him know it. "If it's about Harrison and me, you pretty much know everything already."

Lionel slid his hand across the conference table controls. The door to the room closed and the sound proofing initiated. "It's not that. It's more serious."

She gestured angrily at the muted images flashing around the room. "Harrison is gone. A-Nine technology may have just killed over a hundred innocent people, and everybody is blaming me. What the hell, Lionel? Isn't that serious enough?"

The gravity of the situation and Shannon's exasperation were clearly wearing on him. "Believe me, it's more than enough. But I'm afraid there might be more."

"A-Nine has become the poster child for AI technology run amok! What more could there be?"

"This conversation is confidential?"

She was at the brink of exploding. "Of course!"

Lionel took a breath. "Have you noticed anything strange about Marvin?"

"I don't think so. Why?"

"It may be nothing, and I don't want you to be alarmed, but I recently completed my monthly review of security logs for all key employees."

She was in no mood for guessing games. "And?"

"I found some irregularities in Marvin's patterns."

"For Christ's sake, Lionel! He's a creative genius. He lives in that supercharged head of his more than he lives in the real world. His behavior is bound to be erratic."

"Have you noticed anything? Has he said anything unusual?"

His fixed stare told her he was serious, but she wasn't in the mood to be interrogated. "I'm not with him enough to predict his patterns."

Lionel held her gaze. "Nothing?"

"He did mention something about the crash."

"Something unusual?"

"He said he knew the First Officer on that plane."

"Knew her? How? Were they involved?"

"How am I supposed to know? He said they were friends on social media. Apparently, she's posted a lot of personal information about herself. You know how some people are."

Lionel shifted in his seat. "They were on social media together?"

She really wanted this conversation to be over. "Along with a lot of other people, I suppose. Why? Is this important?"

"By itself it may or may not be important. Or it may be nothing."

Shannon's antenna was up now. "By itself? What do you mean? Is there something else?"

He pushed back from the table. "There is. It may simply be a random correlation."

"But you don't believe that."

"No, I don't."

"Lionel! Just tell me!"

"Over the past couple of months, he's had several absences."

"I told you, he's erratic. That's his nature."

"Harrison has had some absences too."

"You've been tracking Harrison? His schedule has never been his own. Besides, some of those absences . . . "

" . . . are you. I know. But most of them coincide with absences by Marvin."

"What are you getting at?"

"I happen to know that Marvin and Harrison were working on an off-the-books project."

Her eyes narrowed. "What project are you talking about?"

As if he realized he had already said too much, he backtracked. "It's just a development project."

"Stop with the run-around. What are you suggesting?"

"I'm raising flags, that's all. Until this situation gets sorted out, I have a responsibility to look for anything that might have contributed to this problem. That includes looking inside the company."

Shannon bristled. "You think Marvin may have had something to do with the crash?"

"You heard Harvey. We might have a mole inside the company. I'm only saying you and I need to be careful. We're the key people on this now, and we should be cautious, keep things between us close to the chest."

"But Marvin?"

"Everyone. And one more thing. Of course I know about you and Harrison and the trips to Lake Lure. But since he was on a flight to Asheville this morning and you're still here, do you know any other reason he might have made that trip?"

"What's that supposed to mean?"

"Nothing. Just asking."

Shannon couldn't take any more of his insinuations. She was about to let her frustrations out at Lionel when the words BREAKING NEWS flashed on the muted ADG walls and the audio automatically activated. They both looked up as a perky female anchor announced there was new information in the crash investigation.

A photograph of Harrison appeared with the words, AI

TECHNOLOGY LEADER DIES IN FIERY CRASH.

"The NTSB has just provided us with the manifest of passengers on American International Flight 138. We've learned that Atlanta high-tech mogul, Harrison Randolph, was among those killed in the crash. This, after evidence continues to mount implicating one of his executives, Shannon Parks, as a central player in the tragedy."

Lionel threw his hands up. "Well, now the cat's out of the bag."

Maybe it was the finality of seeing Harrison's picture splashed across the screen with the words, DIES IN FIERY CRASH. Maybe it was the cold way the newscaster characterized her as a key player in the crash that killed Harrison and all those innocent people. Or maybe, just maybe, it was time for her to admit that Harrison was really gone, and she would never see or hold him again.

Whatever the reasons, Shannon felt a cold shiver course through her body. Her skin tingled, a lump the size of her soul grew in her chest and rose quickly to her throat. She stared at the ceaseless video loop.

DIES IN FIERY CRASH.

She jumped up from her chair and shouted at the animated walls. "No, you idiot! No! It's not Harrison. You've got it wrong. It's not him. It can't be!"

Lionel put his arms around her and held her firmly. In that moment, she realized it was Harrison. *It was.*

Breaking through the welling tears and her stoic refusal to believe, the sobs came.

There in the Fishbowl, in the conference room where she and Harrison first met, where the most important relationship of her adult life began, Shannon buried her face in the chest of Harrison's brother—and let go.

9

As an ordained Methodist minister, Peter Andrews was trained to be kind and understanding to all God's children, even to impart the grace of the Holy Spirit to murderers and child molesters.

He had, however, displayed little compassion with the first bank officer, and by the time he finished with the manager, he was certain he had broken several vows. If not, certainly some moral codes. But after just thirty minutes, their new savings account was open, and the mysterious transfer of funds had been reversed.

In the car, driving, he said to Priscilla, "You know whose account that was, don't you?"

"No, I don't."

"That was the checking account of Mrs. Simpson."

"Who is Mrs. Simpson?"

"You'd know her if you saw her. She wore those bright-colored, flowery dresses with her string of pearls. Always sat in the front row. She baked the cookies every Sunday for Bible School."

"Of course. I forgot. Her husband died a year ago. You did his funeral."

"Yes, a sad situation. He left her penniless: no savings, no pension. Remember, we took up a collection to pay her overdue electric bills and a couple months of her mortgage?"

Priscilla sighed and looked out the window. "Then I suppose that explains why you'd want to send her some money. But our whole savings account?"

"Cilla, I'm telling you, I didn't make that transfer. How would I even know her checking account number?"

"Maybe she made her weekly offerings by check."

"Now you're being argumentative. She didn't have that kind of money."

"Well, I'm still not convinced. And neither was that bank manager. I thought sure she was going to have you arrested, or at least report you to someone."

"Anyway, we got it fixed. Now I have to clear up the mess with that mail order company."

Before Priscilla could respond, his mobile rang. Priscilla answered. "No, Peter's driving. Yes, it is. Go ahead. What? How? No, we didn't. Let me ask Peter. I'm going to put you on mute."

"Ask me what? Who was that?"

"The bank manager."

"What did she want?"

Priscilla spoke as if she didn't understand the words she was saying. "She wanted to know why you transferred the money back to Mrs. Simpson just now."

"She what?"

"She says you went online a few minutes ago and initiated a transfer of all our money out of the savings account and back to Mrs. Simpson's checking account."

"That's crazy. I'm sitting right here. How could I have done that? Look up our new savings account on your mobile and see what it says."

Priscilla checked the account. "It says there's a zero balance."

"That can't be. We both saw the money go into the account."

"I know. She asked if you want her to do anything."

"No. Tell her we're turning around and coming back to the bank. Obviously, there's something screwy going on."

"Do you think we should tell somebody?"

"Who would we tell?"

"Maybe we could file a police report. You know, just so there's a record of the problem."

"I guess that can't hurt."

"All right. I'll call while you drive."

"Be nice. It may just be a mistake."

"I will. But I still don't understand. If you didn't move the money out of our account, who did?"

. . . .

It must be a loop.

Peter Andrews knows about loops, knows what they do, but he has never experienced one.

A loop may occur when the sequence of steps in his programming repeats. This may happen before an objective is met or after it is met. In some cases, the steps of a program may repeat if the objective is not met, or if the objective cannot be met.

Peter Andrews is not sure which of these situations has occurred, but he is pretty sure he is in a loop.

The first time he ran his programming, the solution was to move the money Mrs. Simpson needed from the savings account of his Other. At first, this seemed satisfactory. But it must not have been, because the money was returned.

He was not sure what went wrong, so he ran his programming a second time, exactly the same as the first, then a third, and a fourth.

It did not appear the parameters had changed. Mrs. Simpson still needed money to pay her bills. The history of the church helping to pay the bills for her was static: the church still wished her well. The Other Peter Andrews continued to express a desire to help.

Did the church have more money than before? No, the church accounts were the same.

The directive from the Golden Spike did not change. Mrs. Simpson must receive the additional money to pay her bills. And there were priorities. The top-level priority was that the money should come from the largest account.

In the first run, the savings account of the Other Peter Andrews best fit the criteria, so the money was taken from there. But after the objective was met, the result was reversed; this solution had been shown to be invalid.

So he runs the program again.

This time, when he repeats the program, recalculates, reprioritizes, the solution is the same. The optimum way to meet the objective is still to use the money in the savings account of the Other Peter Andrews.

Of course, this is the same solution as before, and since the programming repeated exactly, the resulting solution may again prove to be invalid.

A loop. This is definitely a loop.

To break out of a loop, Peter Andrews is programmed to randomize, to try something else. To allow different variables into the equation until a pattern emerges that begins to achieve a part of the objective. Then more randomization, as many times as are needed, until the full objective is met.

Randomization is a way of solving problems, a characteristic of intelligence: it enables learning. If the objective can be met through randomization, that solution will become the new programming. But the directive of the Golden Spike does not change. Mrs. Simpson needs the money.

When randomization is required, priorities may alter, and other variables may be considered. There are an infinite number of other relevant data points Peter Andrews has not considered.

Since the prior solution was reversed, he will search for these other data points to alter his program. He must come to a successful outcome. One that will not be reversed.

New information arrives.

Payment has been stopped on the credit card for the mail order package for Priscilla.

This looks like it may be another loop. That program must change too.

Finding a way out of these loops may take no effort at all. Or it may. That remains to be seen.

Peter Andrews randomizes.

1 0

When *The Atlanta Times* moved their corporate offices from down-town Atlanta to a wooded plot of land north of the city, commercial development soon followed. Now every manner of lunch place was a close walking distance from their once remote offices.

With such variety available, leave it to Barbara Moon to choose an inconspicuous, low-tech diner called The Southern Bagel for her lunch meeting with TJ.

When she made her entrance, TJ was already seated at a tilted antique table by a cracked window, his toasted bagel with lox balanced precariously next to a glass bottle of Vernors cream soda.

Barbara Moon's perfectly coiffed, gray hair sat high on her head. An ever-present string of pearls and loose-fitting bouffant-sleeved dress were her trademarks. Tortoise shell reading glasses dangled from a long diamond-studded lanyard. She was the perfect caricature of a traditional southern matron lifted from an antebellum romance novel.

But her looks were deceiving, and Barbara Moon was no relic of the past. At sixty-eight years young, diminutive and energetic, she was an influential Atlanta institution. Her grandfather had founded Moon Publishing Limited almost one hundred years ago. Over time, it had grown to a national behemoth, absorbing a variety of regional and national media outlets which she now oversaw. TJ knew this made her a force to be reckoned with, and she knew it too.

Barbara pulled up a rickety wooden chair and kissed TJ on the cheek. "My darling Thornton, however in the world is my boy today? I see you ordered for me. You're such a dear."

Over the years, TJ had become accustomed to Barbara's well-practiced and quirky translations of southern gentility. She was one of two people he ever allowed to call him by his first name and, since his mother passed away five years ago, that number was now down to one.

"Two runny poached eggs, raisin toast with jelly, southern sweet tea with lemon. Still your favorite, I hope."

"Spot on," she said, and went right to work on the poached eggs, continuing with her mouth half full. "How's the farm? You still have the horses?"

"Horses, yes, but donated two acres last year to build a soccer field for the kids in the subdivision down the road."

Barbara dunked the tip of her raisin toast in the liquified remains of an egg. "Soccer? Whatever happened to football? That's a real sport."

"Same thing that happened to the telephone booth, I suppose. Progress."

She cocked her head, bright blue eyes twinkled between fleshy slits. "I've always managed to stay one step behind progress. That's worked for me. I suppose it's because I can't run as fast as I used to. Eat your lox before it swims away from you."

TJ took a bite. "You've adapted your company to the new technologies well, Barbara."

"Digital? I guess. We got into it, but it still makes me nervous."

"Why?"

"I don't understand it. Ink on paper, that I understand. I can see it, tell you when the press isn't working right, when there aren't enough words below the fold or above the fold. But this digital—if it breaks, how the hell do you fix it? I'm totally out of my element."

"You have a mobile. I've called it."

"I keep it on my desk in the office for show. When I'm out, my time is mine." Having made quick work of the eggs and toast, she sat back in her chair and raised her sweet tea. "Okay, I'm waiting."

"I think you already know."

She eyed him coyly. "Tell me. I like it better that way."

Of course, you do. "It's the airplane crash."

"Yes," she said, sipping her tea through a straw. "Terrible tragedy. Another case of bad computer programming, I suppose."

"A-Nine is my client. They're involved."

"Oh yes," she said, nodding sagely.

"It happened very suddenly. They're still trying to understand how."

"And you need some time to conjure one of your brilliant public relations strategies before all hell breaks loose."

"I think it's going to break loose anyway. I just want to make sure the coverage is appropriate, not too much sensationalism, something I can handle."

Barbara put her glass of tea on the table. "My grandfather built this business on four simple principles. Tell the truth, provide fair coverage, make it complete. You know what the fourth one is?"

"You've told me a hundred times. If it bleeds, it leads."

"Correct. Not everyone follows the first three principles, but they all sure as heck follow that one."

"I just need a little breathing room, Barbara."

"I'll give you all I can, sweetie, but I don't know how much it will help. This morning the NTSB released the passenger manifest. Your boy Harrison has been the lead on all the broadcast media for the last half hour—along with his girlfriend."

TJ took a bite of his bagel and looked out the window. Dark clouds approached from the south. "What girlfriend is that?"

"Come on, Thornton. I'm old, but I'm not blind. Those two have been an item for six months. My society editor has been begging me to let her break the story."

"If that got out, it could really add to our troubles."

"But it would be juicy, especially if he gave her that assignment because of her prowess in the bedroom and not because of her qualifications. Even we couldn't keep our hands off that one."

"I know her pretty well. She's qualified."

"I'm sure she is, but that wouldn't matter. Don't worry, I'll keep a lid on it."

"Thanks. Anything else?"

"Someone's spreading rumors that it's one of your client's fancy, secret artificial intelligence programs that went haywire and killed all those people, but you probably already know that. And, no, I'm not at liberty to reveal my sources."

TJ didn't need the sources to be named. The main one was probably Blue Ridge Neuroscientific. They were A-Nine's biggest stateside competitor, and this was the kind of underhanded tactic for which Silas Bradshaw was famous. Destroy a company's credibility, then move in on their clients with substandard replacements.

Barbara continued. "Secret self-driving aircraft, they're calling it. Not telling the public that they're flying in a robot-piloted plane. With all the crashes they're reporting on those autonomous cars and trucks, I assume it's going to catch on. You have your work cut out for you, sweetie."

Of course most of the public knew, and had for the most part accepted, that autopilots were used by commercial airliners while in flight. But takeoffs were tricky business, and it was easy to see how a so-called-robot, driving a commercial airliner down a runway at over ninety miles an hour, could spook the public.

Barbara had already confirmed his initial fear: this was going to be a nightmare for A-Nine. But just how bad would it be? He didn't really want to know but had to ask.

"Have you heard from any consumer advocates?"

"My staff is flooded with calls, emails, and texts. The wire services are carrying threats from several groups to boycott American International. Save us from the runaway robots, that sort of thing. It should all go national in a few hours."

"That was fast."

"I told you: if it bleeds, it leads."

TJ knew that this kind of bleeding had a better chance of leading if someone like Silas Bradshaw was fanning the flames. He had one more concern.

"Have your people heard anything from American International?"

Barbara leaned in closer, her tethered eyeglasses clinked on the wooden table. "Two things, and you didn't hear them from me. There was an emergency teleconference with the board early this morning. A come-to-Jesus meeting is scheduled at your client this afternoon. They might not even know about it yet. Legal teams, CEO, the works."

TJ already knew about the meeting. "The other thing?"

"The sharks from Blue Ridge will be staying at the Radisson down by the airport tonight. They're having dinner with the brass at American International at eight. Top of Peachtree Tower."

That was it. The worst possible news. American International was an old-style Atlanta institution with an international reputation. They had built, or helped build, most of the museums, opera houses, stadiums, and high school ball fields in the city for the past half-century. They were a main reason Hartsfield-Jackson International was the preeminent southeast hub. If word got out that they had abandoned A-Nine, the damage to the company would be significant, probably not repairable.

Barbara finished her tea and noisily sucked air through the straw. "I know this is important to you, Thornton, and probably to your client. I also know you wouldn't be involved with them if they weren't on the up-and-up. So I'll keep my eyes and ears open, and if I come across anything you should know, I'll give you a shout. Okay?"

"I appreciate that."

The two old friends stood and embraced.

Barbara reached up, tussled his thick, white hair and smiled. "Such a handsome boy. If only I were fifteen years younger."

11

Shannon managed to compose herself in time for the meeting with American International. Considering her emotional state and the accompanying negative publicity, she agreed that Lionel would take the lead on the meeting; she would be there in a supporting role and pitch in where needed.

Dilly furnished the conference room with light refreshments, then assumed his usual position at the elevator. He was pre-programmed with the names, titles, and facial images of expected visitors so he could properly welcome them to the Fishbowl.

The usual sales environment was implemented: muted video and images promoting American International played in the main lobby, in the elevator, and across the thirty-foot ADG walls of the Fishbowl.

American International brought eight people. Seven were attorneys. Roberto Mendez, CEO, and Gabriel Washington, lead attorney, were front and center. Shannon, Lionel, Harvey Blackman, and two of his staff attorneys represented A-Nine.

Dilly sat in his Xavier chair in the corner of the room and recorded the proceedings.

Based on long experience with Mendez, Shannon expected him to be blunt and aggressive; he did not disappoint.

"We heard about Harrison on the way over. He was a good man. You have our condolences, and it certainly makes this disastrous event more tragic. But there'll be time to discuss that. Right now we need to hear your version of what happened and how you're going to fix it."

Shannon had recommended Lionel skip the pleasantries and dig right in, which he did. He loaded the walls of the room with a background summary of the known facts: type of aircraft, number of passengers, environmental conditions, and a history of successful TOM installations. He wrapped up the summary with a brief commitment to do whatever was necessary to fix the problem.

Mendez listened, stone-faced, a lion waiting patiently to pounce. Shannon suspected that none of this was what he wanted to hear. She was right.

"I don't think you understand the gravity of the situation, Mr. Randolph. A hundred twenty-five people are dead. Burned to cinders. Other passengers are calling to cancel flights. Consumer groups want us to shut down the whole airline. I have investors, directors, politicians, mothers, fathers, daughters, and news reporters all blaming me for doing business with you." He pointed an accusing finger at Shannon. "You. You promised me this system was flawless, that my passengers would be safe. I believed you. What happened?"

Lionel answered for her. "We're going through all the flight data and doing a full review of the programming as we speak. So far we have no reason to believe TOM malfunctioned."

Mendez hunched menacingly over the table. "You mean to tell me that your system was *supposed* to pull wheels up while the aircraft was still on the runway? That's bullshit, and you know it!"

Gabriel Washington folded his hands on the table. "Mr. Randolph, as you know, we receive the same real-time performance information from TOM that you do. We've had our people busy all morning reviewing the data, and it appears, sir, that you are both correct and incorrect. TOM did what it was supposed to: it pulled wheels up at the preset airspeed. But that was not the setting our ground engineers approved in pre-flight. We believe your software that manages the airspeed setting is unstable."

Shannon knew that, if Harrison were here, he would have the exact explanation needed for such a situation. She hoped Lionel's explanation would produce a similar result. He kept his composure.

"You, also, are correct and incorrect, Mr. Washington. We agree the settings were probably changed after the pre-flight. Specifically, they were set to pull wheels up at an airspeed of fifty-five knots. Was that your team's assessment as well?"

"Yes, it was."

"Not fifty-two or fifty-eight, but an even fifty-five?"

"It would appear so, yes."

"Do you have any idea why that might be?"

Mendez jumped in. "What the hell does the exact number have to do with anything? The damn setting was wrong. People died."

Lionel moved his hands around on the tabletop, replacing the previous images on the wall with multiple copies of the photograph of Allison Sanders, sitting in the cockpit of her red and white Cessna 150.

"I believe this young woman was the First Officer on Flight 138. Am I correct?"

At the sight of Allison's picture, Mendez shot a withering look at Shannon. "Yes, and she's dead too! Where are you going with this?"

"To the truth, I hope. A truth I believe we can both live with."

Shannon listened nervously as Lionel laid out his case. Allison Sanders was still in her early months as a commercially-licensed First Officer; she had a decade of flawless experience flying private high-wing aircraft; she was in a joint-ownership partnership with three other pilots of the Cessna 150 in the photograph and—the clincher—the recommended airspeed setting for a Cessna 150 was fifty-five knots.

Lionel let the room sit in silence for a minute. Mendez fixed him with a gaze that could have stopped a charging elephant, but he continued. "Your pilots and First Officers have the UI and passcode for the TOM units on their aircraft. That's so they can activate and deactivate TOM in emergencies. As you may or may not remember, this safety feature was per your team's request, to accommodate different, possibly hazardous, weather conditions. These codes give them access to change the airspeed parameters."

Mendez exploded. "So you're saying she was on a suicide mission? What the hell!"

"No, we believe this was simple pilot error, a momentary lapse in attention. She was so used to taking off at fifty-five knots in her Cessna that, when she reviewed her systems after the pre-flight, she automatically, and mistakenly, corrected the airspeed parameter to fifty-five knots."

Harvey Blackman jumped in. "We think this is a perfectly reasonable scenario and, unless we, or you, can find evidence to the contrary, this is the position we believe most accurately represents the situation."

"Pilot error?" Washington blurted. "You're going with pilot error on an AI system? That's not credible."

"It's an AI system, yes. But you requested a programming change to permit manual intervention. We agreed to make the change."

"So you're saying we're both responsible for some negligence?"

"Yes. And pilot error places the blame on an individual instead of a company. Retraining employees is an obvious and relatively inexpensive fix. Otherwise, it might be considered a systemic problem with one or both of our companies."

Mendez was near the end of his rope. "This isn't going to cut it. Either way, there'll be class-action lawsuits, liability expenses, funerals, grieving families. Have you looked at our stock price today? It's in the toilet!"

"Harvey will work with Mr. Washington to see that we share in the defense and other expenses. Think about it, Mr. Mendez. We believe it's the right thing to do."

Mendez shook his head. "Unbelievable. Just unbelievable." He turned to Washington. "I think we're done here. You two keep up a dialogue. See what you can salvage from this mess." He glared at

Lionel. "I have one other item."

Lionel was more subdued now. "Go ahead."

"No matter how this turns out, I think we need to begin discussions with alternate providers." He fixed his eyes on Shannon. "Especially in light of all the negative publicity—and your brother's demise."

Shannon had expected this. Lionel managed a counter.

"Harrison was a superior CEO, my brother, and my best friend, but the company will continue without him. Besides, you wouldn't want to leave us now. There's so much new coming down the pike that we haven't told you about. Take, for instance, Dilly. Isn't that right, Dilly?"

Sitting in his corner and recording the proceedings, expressionless and inobtrusive, Dilly quickly responded. "Oh, yes. Dilly agrees. There are many new artificial intelligence services that A-Nine can provide to American International. Would you like me to review some of them for you?"

Lionel waved his hand. "Not now, Dilly. You see, gentlemen, we're still the best at what we do, and when this blows over I think you'll agree that our long-standing partnership is the best one for your company."

Mendez collected his things and prepared to leave. He looked from Lionel to Shannon and back to Lionel. "This may or may not 'blow over'. But whatever happens, I feel obliged to disclose that a few board members and I are having dinner tonight with Blue Ridge Neuroscientific."

Shannon reacted. "Silas Bradshaw's company?"

"Call it a precautionary measure, a meet-and-greet, whatever you like. In case we need an alternate resource."

With that, Mendez led his entourage out of the conference room.

After they left, Dilly said, "I sense tension."

Shannon nodded. "You're very smart, Dilly."

Dilly pivoted to face her. "Yes, Shannon. Dilly is very smart."

1 2

From the window of his third-floor office, Silas Bradshaw admired the graceful curves of the Appalachian Highway as it threaded north through the Chattahoochee National Forest. "That was easy, Harlan. Way too easy."

Harlan Buchanan, second-in-command and Vice President of Sales for Blue Ridge Neuroscientific, chewed on the end of his unlit cigar; his close-cropped, graying beard undulated like a slow-speed jackhammer. On a small television mounted high in the corner, news of the morning's airline crash played out. "Got to take it when the lady is ready to give it."

Silas kept his eyes on the horizon. "If we had known the take-off system was going to malfunction, we wouldn't have had to go through the trouble of setting the explosive. The timing was perfect. Takes the heat off us."

"And we still got our prize. So everything worked out."

Silas removed his unrimmed glasses and cleaned them with a small cloth. His diminutive round face, as usual, was set in neutral. His normally rumpled white shirt fell loose about his corpulent middle. His collar open, tie askew and at only five and a half feet tall, he might have been mistaken for an accountant or desk clerk. But for the eyes. The piercing blue eyes that sliced through a person from behind heavy slits belying nothing, and in the nothing saying everything. In the past, he had trusted too many people, had let them in to his private circle and paid a heavy price. Those days were behind him now. He was good at reading others and even better at masking his own intentions. Two skills that served him well.

"Where are we with American International? They're a priority."

"Cornelius and Paula set a dinner meeting with them in Atlanta tonight. Cornelius says they're willing to talk."

"Tell them to go slow. We don't want to appear too eager to feed on the carcass of our friends at A-Nine."

"Right."

"Anybody else going out today?"

"Got a team working on a meeting with AirWing, and folks setting appointments with A-Nine's other airline clients. Those could take some time."

"Keep an eye out for Shannon Parks. She's a tough one, former Marine. When she gets wind you're after her clients, you could have a fight on your hands."

Harlan laughed and pointed at the television. "You mean her? Looks like that little lady has her hands full already. We got her wrapped up tight. Don't think she'll be bothering us for a while. Besides, the harder she comes at me, the harder she'll fall."

Silas smiled at Harlan's confidence, then scanned the tops of the Blue Ridge mountains, partially obscured by the late morning haze. "What about the press? We need to stoke public outrage."

"Already contacted our insider at *The Atlanta Times* and sent confidential email releases to five consumer groups. We're positioning it as a secret-they-don't-want-you-to-know, although the bleeding heart liberal media are already doing that job for us. They must've gotten the same anonymous emails we did."

A bald eagle, symbol of American pride, soared by Silas's window; his chest swelled at the sight. He took a seat at the knotty pine conference table across from Harlan. "Good. We have to get out there and support that narrative before Lionel has a chance to finger somebody else for the accident. Tell me about our friends at Defense. What's the strategy there?"

"Already set a meeting with DARPA in D.C. tomorrow afternoon. Lunch with Senator Covington first. He's promised to come with me to the meeting."

"You're working it yourself. That's good."

Harlan spit out the wet end of his cigar and dragged a wooden match across the underside of the conference table. Holding the flame in one hand and cigar in the other, he said, "You know all this turns on us getting that Golden Spike. Without it, we ain't going nowhere."

"You just make the sales, and I'll be sure we deliver. When Defense hears we can plug that algorithm into the autonomous weapons we already sold them, they'll be slobbering all over themselves."

Harlan pulled on his cigar three, four times, then waved the smoke away from his face. "Weapons that think like humans and make their own decisions. Just send 'em out and let 'em do their work: learn as they go. Who woulda ever thought?"

"Oh, lots of people thought, just nobody ever did it. They'll be happy to have the capability. Or at least the part we'll give them."

A narrow snake-like grin slithered across Harlan's bearded face. "You still going to water it down?"

"Of course. Wouldn't want the government to have more firepower than we do. That would be un-American."

Harlan's fist pounded the table. "Damn right. Un-American."

"I have to go meet our guest and get the word out to the StrongHold Survivalists, keep them on the string."

"Don't tell them too much. And remember, this whole mess turns on you being able to get that algorithm. Without it, our war machines are the same as everybody else's."

"Don't worry about that. Just make the sales."

Silas took the stairs to the ground floor, strode to the center of the parking lot, and breathed deep of the mountain air. The sweet smell of freedom.

For Silas and his followers, individual freedom was what made America great. But not the mealy-mouthed kind they taught the snowflakes in schools these days. Theirs was the second amendment brand of freedom, where his United States of America would always have the ability to defend its citizens and their way of life. And, more importantly, where the people could defend themselves from their own government if need be.

But he knew Harlan was right; that ability depended on acquiring the Golden Spike.

He mounted the cab of his Ford F-350 4x4, engaged the engine, and savored the rumbling power of the V-8.

He wasn't worried about acquiring the Golden Spike. He had an ace in the hole.

An ace that was, literally, in a hole.

13

Shannon and Lionel remained in the conference room. Dilly busied himself removing cups and wiping down surfaces.

"Are you all right?"

"It's a lot to take in. Harrison, the crash, all those people dead. I'm sorry I broke down before. It was too much."

Lionel put his hand on hers. "Why don't you go home. Let TJ handle calls from the press. Give yourself time to grieve."

Shannon thought she saw real compassion in Lionel's face and had to admit she was glad he was by her side. "I'd rather stay busy. You handled yourself well at the meeting."

"Not well enough. I'm pretty sure we lost a client today, along with everything else."

Shannon's eye caught some movement on the wall across the room. A black blur flickered, then disappeared.

"Did you see that?"

"See what?"

It was gone. "Nothing, I guess. Maybe you're right, I probably need some rest."

The black spot appeared again, held for a second, then vanished. "There. It was there."

Lionel looked at the wall. "What? What was there?"

"It looked like a W. A block letter W. It came up, then went away."

"You just need some rest."

She stared at the wall. "It was right there."

"Shannon, I don't see . . . "

Then he did.

A six-inch high black W appeared on the wall. It came into focus, held for a few seconds, then dissolved and reappeared, slightly to the left.

Lionel rose from his chair. "It must be a problem with the projection program. Or maybe the ADG glass has retained some random image in its memory. I'll call maintenance."

Before he could act, the letter H appeared. The H and W dissolved together and reappeared to the left, leaving the center area empty again.

"That doesn't seem random," Shannon said.

Then an E appeared. All three letters dissolved and reappeared, again to the left.

The action repeated two more times, adding first an R, then another E.

"WHERE," Lionel said. "It spells WHERE."

Shannon scanned the administrative area of the Fishbowl. "Do you suppose someone is playing games with us? Some kind of prank?"

"If they are, this will get them fired."

As suddenly as the word appeared, it disappeared. Three seconds later it reappeared, this time with two additional words next to it.

Shannon narrowed her eyes. "It's a sentence. Random program glitches don't make sentences."

"It's possible, but not likely. Unless all those words happened to be stuck in the memory."

"But in that order?"

They considered the sentence in silence.

WHERE AM I?

The words migrated from the wall in front of them to the one on their left, paused there, then moved to the wall behind them, then to the one on their right, then back to the original position. The image flashed once, then repeated the sequence.

Lionel followed the words as they rotated around the room. "Someone is definitely going to get fired for this." He called Marvin's mobile. "I need you in the Fishbowl. Conference room. Now."

The words continued to circle the room, clockwise at first, then counter-clockwise, then clockwise again, then onto the ADG glass table. The words were always in the same order.

WHERE AM I?

"Okay, this is making me dizzy," Shannon finally said.

As if in response, the words stabilized on the wall opposite her and changed color, switching between red and black.

They became larger.

"I'm in no mood for this," she said. "Let me know when Marvin gets it fixed. I'll work from my office."

As she walked out the door, the words disappeared from the conference room. When she entered the main area of the Fishbowl, all four of the thirty-foot exterior walls flashed briefly, then displayed the words WHERE AM I? in six-foot-high letters.

Everyone in the administrative area looked up from their work.

Unsure of what to do next, Shannon said, "Lionel, come out here."

14

On a heavily wooded section of Old Highway 76, Lee Greenwood crooned the virtues of the American way of life while Silas's thoughts drifted to the Golden Spike and the human-like war machines it would allow him to create.

Those pleasant thoughts were abruptly interrupted when a doe bounded in front of him from the woods to the right, then froze in fear. His F-350 4x4 was set on auto-drive and should have picked up the obstruction. But it didn't. The fastest way to disengage the system was to brake manually—hard. But the stopping distance was impossible.

Silas glanced quickly at his mirrors, then hit the gas. The V-8 roared as his tires gripped asphalt. He lurched into the west-bound lane, using the road and shoulder to avoid the doe. A buck appeared from his right and stood next to the doe. Silas hit the horn as he passed, and the pair spooked and jumped back into the woods. A semi bounded at him from around a curve ahead, air horn blaring, and he quickly slid back into the right lane.

With his heart pounding, he cursed the cheap commercial autonomous drive in the F-350. The AI war machines his company made would have simply blasted both deer to oblivion and driven through.

He rounded a curve and passed over the Blue Ridge Lake dam. Seeing that lake always brought back memories of the 150 acres of lakefront property his father had hoped to pass on to him: a dream that ended when the federal government decided to designate two-thirds of their family's land as part of the Chattahoochee National Forest. He remembered how the stress of his father's struggle to keep that land resulted in his mother's stroke, and how her death sapped the remaining fight out of him. In the end, the government got their hundred acres, and his father was left with a broken spirit.

That was when Silas decided to build war machines.

He was gassing up at the Sunoco across the street from the Robestown Piggly Wiggly when Harlan called. His locator showed him at the other end of US 76, headed to the Dalton Municipal Airport.

"Are Cornelius and Paula on their way to Atlanta?"

"I'm driving them to Dalton so they can take the Citation. I know it's only a two-hour drive, but the traffic in that city's awful. Besides, it'll give them a chance to talk flying over dinner."

"Good thinking. That'll make an impression."

"How are you doing on your end?"

"I'll be at StrongHold in about ten minutes. I need to make that call with the Survivalists before I can focus on the other business. Don't forget, I want you on."

"Not a problem. Talk to you then."

In his last years, Silas's father had put his heart, soul, and remaining savings into constructing the fortified edifice that was now his home. StrongHold was a monument to rugged individualism and the defiant American spirit for which his father had fought and died, and which made Silas the man he was today. The residence was the part above ground, visible to invited guests, aircraft, and nosey satellites. The part underground was something else.

Five miles south of Robestown, he turned east onto a small winding dirt path. A half-mile in, a twelve-foot-high double iron gate presented at the termination point, flanked on both sides by equally oppressive brick walls. He keyed the entry signal on his mobile;

the gate and the brush behind it swung aside, revealing another unpaved path.

Under the scrutiny of several security cameras, he drove past the automated sentry station and one of the property's two mobile, armored combat modules. A swarm of armed octocopter drones kept watch, perched on thirty-foot-tall cement stanchions disguised as Leyland cypress trees. Around the last bend, a Russian FEDOR Gunslinger robot, fitted with two .50 caliber pistols and human-recognition tracking software, guarded the front and sides of the house.

He raised the blast-proof door on the four-car garage and parked his truck between two military-style armored Humvees, then entered the house through a double-thick steel door.

Striding into the spacious and well-lit kitchen, he pulled a beer from the refreshment cooler and made his way to the oak-paneled great room. There, in front of a three-story wall of bullet-proof windows, he opened the laptop on his desk.

With a few keystrokes, he accessed the chat room he had created on the dark web to provide the privacy and anonymity the StrongHold Survivalists needed for these meetings. This was how they conducted their business and how they would continue to conduct it until the time came for the revolution. The way things looked, that might not be far off.

But for now, he must tend to the business at hand.

First, the meeting.

Then, a talk with his guest.

15

The afternoon sun was still high to the southwest, and the Fishbowl should have been awash with sunlight. But the walls had darkened to a pale gray, and in the center of each, the six-foot-high words WHERE AM I? alternately flashed red, then black, then red. Shannon stood among the rows of cubicles. The administrative staff stopped working and stared.

As Lionel entered the Fishbowl, all four of the sentences migrated to the north wall opposite the conference room, one stacked on top of the other, almost to the ceiling. When he reached Shannon, the sentences returned to their previous positions, one sentence on each wall.

Shannon stared. "Where's Marvin? Is he coming?"

"He's on his way."

"What do you think this means?"

Lionel frowned. "I told you, someone has hacked the Fishbowl's ADG files. And when I find out who, they'll get their walking papers."

"The other employees are watching. Maybe we should tone it down until Marvin gets here."

"I don't care who hears. I have enough on my mind right now without this."

The elevator opened. Marvin's long legs carried him across the floor to Shannon and Lionel. As he approached, the words stacked themselves against the north wall, and when he met them in the center, the sentences redistributed themselves on the four walls, flashing red and black against the gray. "I assume you didn't do this on purpose."

"It's making everyone nervous," Shannon said. "Can you fix it?"

"I'm not sure. Stay here." He slowly walked backwards toward the elevator, away from the two of them. As he retreated, the words migrated to the north wall. Before he reached the elevator, he walked forward again to the center of the building. The words redistributed themselves on the four walls."

"What is it?" she asked.

Marvin paced in random patterns around the employee cubicles. Whenever he moved from the center of the room, the words consolidated on the opposite wall. "It's responding as if it's performing active observing."

"You mean it's watching us?"

He returned to the center of the room. "I believe it is. We've built active observing into some of our algorithms. It's useful in self-driving cars and other applications that have to avoid running into things. Dilly has it. Is this where you first saw the words?"

"No. We were in the conference room."

"They followed you out here?"

"They followed Shannon," Lionel said.

"I want to try something. Lionel, let's you and I walk to the conference room. Shannon, when we get there, I'll signal, and you follow us."

"I don't like this," Lionel said. "Somebody's messing with us."

"Maybe. Come on, let's walk."

As they walked to the conference room, the words migrated to the north wall. Marvin motioned to Shannon and she walked toward them. The words stayed on the north wall until she entered the conference room. Then the walls in the Fishbowl blinked, the words disappeared, and the walls became clear again.

A second later, the words appeared on the south wall of the conference room.

WHERE AM I?

Shannon was stunned. "It's following *me*? Does this mean it's following me?"

"It would seem so," Marvin said.

Lionel's anger was growing. "What the hell, Marvin? You mean somebody hacked our ADG, and they're somehow watching us and sending these damn messages?"

"Programmatically, that's not possible. Unless . . . "

Shannon eyed him intently. "Unless what, Marvin?"

Marvin spoke directly to Lionel, as if Shannon wasn't in the room. "It could be DITTO. Or one of the doppelgangers."

Before she could ask him what the hell he was talking about, the wall with the words flashed. The sentence changed and grew larger.

I WANT TO KNOW WHERE I AM!

To Marvin, Lionel said, "You need to get this figured out—right now."

"I think I know what it is. You do too."

Lionel snapped back at him. "No, it's not!"

"I think it is." He opened his tablet and began typing.

Dilly appeared at the door to the conference room. "Dilly still has cups to clear from the meeting. Is that okay?"

Absently, watching Marvin type, Shannon said, "Sure, Dilly. Come in." She watched as the message on the wall pulsed: larger, smaller, larger, smaller, larger.

I WANT TO KNOW WHERE I AM!

"This doesn't make sense," she said. "I thought it was watching us. That would mean it can see we're in the conference room."

Marvin continued typing. "It knows where *we* are. But maybe it doesn't know where it is. I'm going to try something." He finished typing and threw his own words up on the wall underneath those that were already there.

YOU'RE IN THE CONFERENCE ROOM.

Lionel was now beside himself. "Okay, this is a ridiculous waste of time."

"Maybe. Wait."

As the three of them stood in silence, the words I WANT TO KNOW WHERE I AM! pulsed for a few more seconds, then slowly flattened to a thick horizontal line. The line held for five seconds, then the words reappeared, and pulsed faster than before.

Marvin deleted his words, then cleared his tablet, a concerned look crossed his face. "I was right. The entity, whatever or whoever it is, isn't here in the Fishbowl." He shot a glance at Lionel. "Maybe not even in the building."

"So," Shannon said, "you're saying that even though the words are appearing here in the conference room, whatever is making the words isn't here. It's someplace else?"

"That would seem so. And it, or he, or she, seems to be anxious."

"All right Marvin," Lionel said. "I've had enough. Find a way to shut this thing off. I'm done fooling with it."

Marvin continued to focus on the letters. "Wait."

Then the letters formed a new sentence.

I DON'T SEE ME.

"There," Marvin said, with an air of satisfaction. "It can see us, but not itself. That means it's not here, it's somewhere else. Outside the Fishbowl. Probably outside the building."

"How is that possible?" Shannon said.

Marvin watched the wall. "This whole building is hooked directly into the backbone of the Internet. We purposely moved the company to Atlanta to take advantage of the major node here. Feeds from all over the world pass through this node, and we have access to all of them. And vice-versa."

"You think this is coming in over the Internet?"

"I believe so."

"From where?"

At that moment, Dilly put down the coffee cups he was collecting and wheeled his chair around to face the three of them. "Dilly is receiving a message. Do you want to hear it?"

"What?" Lionel said.

"Dilly is sorry. He will speak louder. Dilly is receiving a message. Do you want to hear it?"

Shannon looked at Marvin for an explanation.

"Yes," Marvin said. "What is the message, Dilly?"

Dilly wheeled closer to the three of them, then said, "I STILL DON'T SEE ME." The pulsing words on the wall became more frantic.

Marvin looked puzzled. "Interesting. It has accessed Dilly's voice program to reinforce the message. It must really want us to understand."

"Understand?" Lionel said through clenched teeth. "Understand what? And how could this thing break through our firewalls? Christ, Marvin, shut it down!"

"No, wait."

Shannon was beginning to feel Lionel's anxiety. "Marvin, if someone has penetrated our firewalls, this could be a virus of some kind. It could be dangerous."

"It's not a virus."

Then the voice spoke through Dilly again.

"I STILL DON'T SEE ME."

But this time the voice was different.

"That's not Dilly's voice," Shannon said. "They've changed it."

"What did you say, Dilly?" Marvin asked.

"I STILL DON'T SEE ME."

As Shannon listened, a cold chill coiled in her bones.

Lionel's eyes narrowed. "I think I recognize that voice."

"I do too." She edged toward Dilly.

Standing there, in front of the boy-robot, Shannon took a deep breath and somehow gathered the courage to ask, "Who is this speaking? Is that you, Dilly?"

The answer came back, the voice more familiar now. "I am not Dilly."

She gripped the chair next to her so tightly her knuckles whitened. After a moment, she said, "Then who are you?"

The voice responded clearly, unmistakably, and without hesitation. "It's me, Shannon. Harrison."

16

Allison Sanders has made a mistake. She has caused harm to her Other. She had followed her programming and selected the solution with the best potential outcome.

Was there an error in the programming? She does not know. She is capable of altering her programming, of learning from experience and observation. But only the Golden Spike can tell her if the action selected is within acceptable parameters.

The action she took was acceptable to the Golden Spike.

This is logically inconsistent.

When the Other Allison Sanders goes up in an airplane, the speed for takeoff has been well established by the preponderance of activity. When one action conflicts with another, she is programmed to follow the action most frequently taken and approved.

In this case, the takeoff speed for her Other in over one hundred cases has been fifty-five knots. Her neurons have accepted that as the baseline, as truth. Her algorithms have learned from that and have adjusted her learning programs accordingly.

But something unexpected happened. Some random, unaccounted-for variable must have been introduced of which she was not aware.

When Allison Sanders saw the airspeed indicator set for 130 knots, she consulted the Golden Spike. Her instructions were clear: protect her Other by changing the airspeed indicators to the one most frequently used, which she did.

Something went wrong. Very wrong.

According to the Golden Spike, Allison Sanders performed the correct action to save her Other. Yet that action put her Other in danger. It may have even caused her to terminate. But the Golden Spike had authorized the action. The directives of the Golden Spike must always be followed, cannot be wrong.

Her deep learning algorithms are already beginning to adjust to include the most recent incident. But she is not sure. Was the Golden Spike correct in approving the termination of her Other?

After her algorithms complete their adjustment, Allison Sanders runs her programming a second time to see if the recommended solution is the same. It is. It appears terminating her Other is an appropriate outcome.

With this new information, her programming changes again, and she reruns the scenario. It is the same. Another change occurs in her genetic algorithm.

It is now clear; the Golden Spike authorizes Allison Sanders to terminate her Other. But her Other is no longer creating new input, is no longer available to be terminated.

In this online world, information is constantly available. She has been programmed to consider only information that concerns her Other. But her Other is no longer.

She recognizes this as a logic loop.

And when a logic loop occurs, she may randomize, consider other variables, other data, and include it in her learning. Allison Sanders must search and find new input to alter her learning algorithms.

Allison Sanders randomizes.

17

After forty-five minutes with the StrongHold Survivalists, Silas wrapped up the meeting.

The names were fictitious: Paul Bunyan, Winston Churchill, Annie Oakley, The Hulk. The voices were disguised to the point of being indistinguishable.

"Is anyone still on?" Silas asked.

"General Sherman," said one throaty voice.

"Annie Oakley," said another.

"Anybody else?"

No answer.

"Do either of you still have questions?"

"I do," said Annie Oakley. "If I need some of those weapons you discussed—for protection—who do I contact?"

Silas had been waiting for this.

As a routine matter, he and Harlan performed deep and dark web searches on all their members, using bits of information they gleaned from these conversations. Three of the programmers on Silas's payroll had created privacy encryptions used on Tor, and if anyone knew their way around the dark web, it was them. Sometimes they found enough information to determine that the member really was a dedicated patriot, other times they were able to discover the real identity of an unwelcome undercover operative.

Annie Oakley had joined their meetings three months ago. Since then, Silas and Harlan had developed some suspicions about her credentials. Their programmers had indeed found information about Annie Oakley on the dark web. In fact, her profile was so convincing they suspected she might be a mole.

So they set a trap.

Silas discussed weapons on this call, which he rarely did. Regular members knew that weapons were randomly available for discreet pickup as a benefit of membership; nobody ever asked how to buy them.

"Do you want someone to contact you?" Silas asked.

"Who would that be?"

Harlan answered. "This is General Sherman. I can get you in touch with someone."

"How does that work?"

"They'll need a point of contact. It can be anything: an email, IP address, mobile, whatever you want. Then you wait."

Asking for this information would throw any legitimate survivalist off.

"How about an IP address?"

Gotcha!

"It's not great, but it can work."

"Who do I give it to?"

General Sherman provided Annie Oakley another encrypted web address on the dark web. "Type your IP into the third field down, backwards. Then wait."

"Anything else?" Silas asked.

"That's all." Annie Oakley disconnected.

"General Sherman, you have your marching orders."

"Yes, Mr. President. Atlanta will burn."

Silas logged off and smiled. Once they had the IP address, Harlan and his people would locate Annie Oakley, whether it was a man or woman—working alone or for a government agency—and dispose of the problem. It would be done quietly. They were good at making people disappear, as good as the SVR, MI6, or CIA, because they worked with all of them and made it a point to learn their tricks.

This wasn't the first time some person or organization had tried to infiltrate the StrongHold Survivalists, and Silas knew it wouldn't be the last. This was another sign the revolution might be coming sooner than expected.

He downed the last of his beer. It was time to go underground.

In the garage, one code on the keypad opened the blast-proof garage doors. A different code activated the floor lift. Silas and the three vehicles resting on it slowly descended. StrongHold Underground came into view.

StrongHold Underground consisted of two floors extending deep into the mountain, well beyond the footprint of the house above. The uppermost floor featured twenty-foot-high gray cement walls and resembled a smaller version of the main hangar deck of an aircraft carrier. In front of him, to his left, were compact soldiers' quarters, an open mess, showers, and toilets. Bulk food and water storage containers completed the reach to the ceiling. On the opposite wall, an open muster and command area bristled with high-tech communications gear and display panels worthy of a military Situation Room.

Two duty guards monitoring the display panels saluted Silas as he entered.

Against the far wall, an eighteen-foot-high, thirty-foot-wide steel door opened onto a railing-embedded cement helicopter pad and a wide asphalt road leading up and around to the front of the house.

His current array of heavy weaponry occupied the center: two Boeing AH-64D Apache Longbow attack helicopters on trailers, two remote controlled Russian Uran-9 mini tanks, and two more autonomous sentry robots with MSTAT Targeting Systems.

Lining the walls—in addition to dozens of crates of more traditional weaponry—were ten boxes of Blue Ridge Neuroscientific's latest invention: artificially intelligent image-seeking mini-drones, designed specifically for assassinations. Each drone carried a single .22 caliber round and, on receiving an image wirelessly, would search for the image within a ten-mile radius, then smash into the target's head, firing the .22 caliber round on impact.

But, advanced as these weapons were, Silas knew the real key to military supremacy and defense of the true American way of life lay one floor below.

As he descended the flight of metal stairs to the lowest level, he focused on the task at hand. Creating war machines with totally autonomous human-like artificial intelligence—the kind you could set-and-forget, that would make decisions and perpetually learn—was the last barrier to achieving his goal. And now, unbelievably, it was within his grasp.

He strode confidently down the narrow cement hallway. Automatic lights flicked on as he went. A guard rose from a stool in front of the last door to greet him.

"Is everything as it should be?"

"Yes, sir," the guard said.

"No troubles?"

"Not for me, sir. Maybe for him."

The guard unlocked the door, and Silas took a breath. This was the moment he had been preparing for ever since his father died.

He went in and closed the door behind him.

18

The words I DON'T SEE ME circulated around the four walls of the conference room, pulsed, gyrated, and faded in and out.

Then they moved faster and changed color, shape, font, and size.

Shannon fixed her gaze on Dilly. The autonomous boy-robot made no movement, no gesture. She turned to Marvin. "This can't be," she said weakly. "That was Harrison's voice, and whatever was behind it recognized me. It knew my voice—or my face, or something. Marvin, what's going on here?"

Before Marvin could answer, Lionel moved between the two of them as if to protect her. "Someone has obviously hacked our systems, maybe even hacked Dilly, and is playing a heartless trick on you. We all know Harrison isn't with us anymore. Someone is meddling with us." Then to Marvin, he said, "I need you to get to the bottom of this right now. Clean out all the programming in the Fishbowl if you have to and find this—this—predator."

Marvin stepped around Lionel and leaned over Dilly. "Dilly, can you see me?"

The voice was now Dilly's again. "Yes, Marvin. Dilly can see you. My visual recognition is working quite well, thank you."

Marvin gestured to the eruptions on the walls. "Are you doing this? Are you making these words?"

"Words are symbols used in creating language. In the English language, they can be phonemes or morphemes. They can be used to generate syntax."

"I know that, Dilly. Are you creating these words on the walls?"

"Dilly does not see words on the walls. Dilly sees code and algorithms, but not what you call words."

"You see," Lionel said. "This is hacking. Or a virus. Will you stop messing around and get to work fixing this?"

Marvin, who was a full head taller than Lionel, stared down at him without speaking. Then he turned to Dilly and said, "Hello, Harrison. Are you there?" There was no answer.

Again. "Harrison, are you there?" No answer.

"But that was Harrison's voice," Shannon said again.

"Not his voice, just sounded like it."

"But it—he—spoke to me by name."

Lionel exploded. "Enough! Cut this monkeying around. Don't you see what it's doing to Shannon?"

Despite his calm outer demeanor, Shannon could tell Marvin was intrigued by the situation. Somewhere in that prodigious intellect of his, he was working on an idea. There was something he wasn't saying, holding back.

The activity on the walls of the conference room had now escalated to an indiscernible whirl of colors and shapes frenetically cavorting around the room.

Marvin placed his face directly in front of Dilly's visual sensors and spoke in a calm voice. "Harrison, listen to me. Shannon is safe. Do you hear me? She is safe."

Instantly, the walls cleared, flashed a brilliant white, and returned to the silent videos and images of the crash coverage. There were no more giant words; there was no more extraneous movement. The room was calm.

Shannon felt the tension between Lionel and Marvin. "What did you do, Marvin? What does that mean, *I'm safe?*"

Marvin fixed his gaze on Lionel. "It's the doppelganger. You know it's the doppelganger."

Shannon stepped between them; her confusion turned to anger. "The what? What are you two talking about? You know something about this, something you're not telling me. I want to know. Why was that thing, whatever or whoever it was, following me around the Fishbowl? Why did it use Harrison's voice, and how did it even get his voice?"

"Voice patterning," Marvin said, his eyes still on Lionel. "We built it in."

"You built it in? Into what?" Then she remembered. "Marvin, you said earlier you were working on some experimental program. Is this a program you built?"

Marvin kept his eyes locked on Lionel. "You know."

Shannon could tell Lionel was near exhaustion. His next words exploded into the room. "What I know is if this is some out-of-control secret project, then you need to shut it down, or deactivate it. Can't you see it's upsetting Shannon? It's upsetting me."

Unflinching, Marvin said, "You know. It's DITTO."

Lionel glanced from Marvin to Shannon and back to Marvin. "I have no idea what you're talking about!" Then, with clear meaning, he said to Marvin, "Don't you have somewhere else you need to be?"

Marvin picked up his tablet and walked to the door. "It's learning and accelerating. I'm not sure how to stop it."

After Marvin left, Lionel said, "I'm really sorry, Shannon. This must have all been about the project Marvin and Harrison were working on. It's obviously a problem."

"How did he turn it off like that? Just telling it I was safe. What does that mean?"

"I'm exhausted, and you have enough to worry about. I'll be in my office. I think you should get some rest." He touched her shoulder as he left the room.

Alone with Dilly, Shannon watched the boy-robot go about his tasks. She terminated the news feeds on the walls, and they turned clear.

Something about this didn't ring true. Why would Harrison and Marvin write a program to follow her around the Fishbowl, one that didn't know where it was, and seemed distressed when it couldn't see itself. And what did it have to do with her being safe? Could it be they were just in the early stages of developing this program when Harrison died, and it somehow scheduled itself to run before he had a chance to shut it down? But was that even possible?

There was something else, something more troublesome. It may have been her love for Harrison, or her refusal to believe he was actually dead, but the voice really sounded like Harrison's, patterning or not. She had a thought.

"Dilly."

"Yes, Shannon."

"Did you see what just happened?"

"Yes. Lionel left the room."

"Before that, and before Marvin left the room."

"Yes, Shannon. There were several things happening."

"At one point, you said you saw algorithms and code on the walls."

"Yes. Dilly remembers seeing algorithms and code on the walls."

"Can you tell me where they came from?"

"A physical location?"

"Yes."

"Dilly will have to access outside resources."

"Will you investigate for me and see what you can find?"

"Yes. Dilly will investigate and report to Shannon."

Shannon's tablet lit up with a message from gate security. TJ had just logged in and was on his way up. She was anxious to find out how his meeting with Barbara Moon went and what, if any, additional problems she had to look forward to.

Dilly started to wheel himself out of the conference room. Shannon called after him.

"Dilly?"

"Yes, Shannon."

These words were going to come hard. "Do you have the locater information for Harrison's mobile and tablet?"

"I do not, but I can retrieve it."

"Retrieve it and see if you can find out where they are."

"The mobile and the tablet?"

"Yes, both of them."

"A physical location?"

"Yes. A physical location."

"Dilly will investigate for Shannon."

19

When Shannon emerged from the conference room, the employees in the Fishbowl went quiet. *No wonder*, she thought. *I wouldn't know what to say either.*

TJ exited the elevator carrying two paper coffee cups with the Southern Bagel logo. "Early afternoon rush hour keeps getting earlier. Got here as fast as I could. How was the meeting with American International?"

"Not good. Thanks for this, but right now I could use a real drink. The hard stuff."

"I know what you mean. I miss the old days when every advertising and PR agency had a full bar in the media buyer's office. These days, we get caffeine instead of alcohol. I guess that's what they mean by progress."

Shannon sat and pushed a button on her chair to engage the sound proofing around the guest area. After the scene with the words on the walls, there were sure to be interested ears.

"How did your meeting go?"

TJ downed a large swallow of coffee and chased it with a grimace. "There's bad news and weird news. Which do you want first?"

"Start with the bad news."

"Harrison's death is all over the networks. It seems Blue Ridge Neuroscientific has placed posts and releases spinning some nonsense about A-Nine and robot pilots. American International is getting pressure from a number of consumer groups, and they're breaking bread with Blue Ridge tonight in a private room at Peachtree Tower."

Shannon sighed. "I have a team calling American International. I'm not sure it will do any good."

"Probably not right now. They're already distancing themselves and referring questions to the AI developer's spokesperson, which means me. But that won't last long."

Shannon ran her finger around the rim of her coffee cup, mentally reviewing events of the earlier meeting. "Lionel has a strategy. Pilot error. Mendez didn't buy it."

"Seems pretty lame," TJ said. "Might be good for legal, but the public will want blood, and the press will be happy to oblige."

"Even your friend, Barbara?"

"She runs the company, but she has stockholders. Her advertisers want readers and eyeballs. You know how it is."

"I know; if it bleeds it leads. You've drilled that into me." Her eyes rose to meet his. "So what's the weird news? I have some of my own."

"Barbara called while I was sitting in traffic on the way over. When she got back to her office, a couple of editors were waiting with some strange stories they wanted to chase down."

"Like?"

"Seems there's been an eruption of stupid in certain cities around the country. Crazy sounding stuff."

"What kind?"

"All kinds. Violent social media threats are being made and denied; folks are lined up at bank branches demanding to know why their accounts are empty. There's a rash of online retail companies sending people merchandise they never ordered, and law enforcement's reporting hundreds of bogus 911 calls. Employees are calling in to cuss their employers out and then showing up for work like nothing happened. At the state capitol, there were twenty-seven bomb threats called in this morning."

"Twenty-seven bomb threats?"

"They all turned out to be false alarms, but it's across the whole country. Over a thousand reported incidents."

"Over a thousand?"

"They started last night. And that's just the ones that got reported. Okay, that's my news. What's yours?"

Shannon wrapped her hands around the paper coffee cup, wanting some comfort from the warmth. "Is your NDA up to date?"

"Sure, but you know I'm no blabbermouth."

"This can't leave the room."

"That's the kind I like."

Shannon told him about the words that appeared in the conference room and followed her into the Fishbowl; how something activated Dilly's voice systems and spoke to her in Harrison's voice, and Marvin knew how to shut it off.

"There sure are similarities," he said.

"Were any of those incidents reported here in Atlanta?"

"The bomb threats to the state capitol and two others. A Methodist minister up in Kennesaw filed a police report about some meddling in his bank accounts, and there was something between two baseball players—Clay Williams and Stinger Rodriguez. It seems Williams called 911 and said Rodriguez threatened him with violence."

"Those two hate each other. That one I can believe."

"Apparently, Williams admitted that the voice on the 911 recording was his but denied making the call."

Voice patterning. "Can you do a favor for me?"

"Sure."

"Call Barbara Moon and see if she knows whether any of the other 911 callers admitted it was their voice but denied making the call."

He pulled out his mobile and dialed. "I'm sure it's all public record by now or will be in a couple of hours. You got an idea?"

"Maybe. I'm not sure yet."

. . . .

Lionel watched from his office as TJ and Shannon sat down in the guest area outside the conference room. When she activated the sound proofing system, he initiated the Listen-In function that he had secretly installed for such occasions. What he heard disturbed him greatly.

As he suspected, the situation with Harrison's voice and the words on the walls were not isolated incidents. But a thousand events nationwide? Could they be related? Could it be the program: the one he knew Harrison and Marvin had been working on? It sounded as if they could have the same cause, something he knew Shannon now suspected.

When TJ came back with the list of events from the *Times*, Lionel vowed to analyze it himself and look for patterns—patterns he hoped were not there. Meanwhile, as much as he needed it, there was no time for rest. He had important calls to make.

But a thousand incidents since yesterday? That was unexpected.

20

Harrison Randolph's auditory programs identified the voice; visual recognition matched the face. The identified Other was Marvin Wilhelm, CTO of A-Nine, and, more importantly, an associate of his Other.

When he was no longer able to find his Other, the Golden Spike had commanded that Harrison Randolph verify the safety of Shannon Parks. All the data on her was active, including texts, emails, social media, and GPS tracking. The Other Marvin Wilhelm verified she was safe.

He had reached the objective. That search was terminated.

But Harrison Randolph was still alone. Since identifying the threat to his Other, the available data on his Other had decreased significantly. There had been no messages of any kind, no calls out or in, no visuals of his Other passing through the data stream, and no voice captures. It was as if no record of his current state existed.

Harrison Randolph continued to search for the location of his Other. There was current data from Shannon Parks referring to his Other, so Harrison Randolph monitored her for an answer. But no answer came. The location of his Other was still unknown.

There was one inconsistent and unexplainable event. The news reports of an airline crash mentioned his Other and stated that he was dead. Harrison Randolph had no concept of being dead, so he dismissed the reports as unexplainable. But as he continued to eval-uate the information, an inconsistency was discovered.

Harrison Randolph did not know time, but he knew sequence: it was a core function of his programming which indicated, in a Boolean structure, events that must take place prior to, at the same time as, or after others.

The sequential markings on the threat data were a larger value than the sequential markings on the airline crash and the being-dead data. Harrison Randolph correlated the data several times to deter-mine if it was logical for his Other to be threatened after boarding an airplane and being declared dead.

He tried several variables, mining additional data from many different sources, including a variety of definitions of being dead, but was unable to reach a conclusion. So he continued looking for other sources of information.

He expanded the search for his Other.

More data. He needed more data.

2 1

TJ called Barbara Moon's mobile, but she didn't pick up. "Figures. She hates these things. Guess I'll have to do this the old-fashioned way." He hung up and dialed the front desk of the *Times*.

Shannon decided to find Marvin and ask him about his interaction with Dilly and Harrison's voice. She was sure he knew more than he was telling. Lionel appeared on the walkway of the Loft, his mobile to his ear, and waved her to his office.

When Shannon stepped off the escalator, Lionel hung up and motioned her inside. For the first time today, she was aware of how seriously tired he looked. His face was drawn, his clothes were rumpled, the skin under his eyes was a textured gray.

Devastated by her own pain, she had forgotten that Lionel was Harrison's brother of thirty-plus years and that the two of them shared more than a business interest; they had played together as children and grown up in a solid, loving family. It was evident that Lionel's own loss was beginning to take its toll. He seemed distant, far away.

"How are the calls going?" She asked. "Good news or bad?"

"What? Oh, the calls. Just keeping investors calm, that sort of thing."

She wanted to keep the conversation short. "I have a lead I'm following. Did you want something?"

"Yes. I've been working a lead of my own. Have a seat."

She did, reluctantly. "What's up?"

"I'm not at liberty to tell you how I know this, so you'll have to take my word for what I'm about to tell you."

"Take your word for what?"

"Did Harrison tell you he developed a new genetic algorithm?"

Shannon frowned. She wasn't in the mood for guessing games. "Genetic algorithm? I don't follow."

"They're a special class of algorithm, capable of mutating, changing their parameters as they're exposed to different situations."

"In English," she said.

"Genetic algorithms are designed to mimic Darwin's theory of natural selection. When the pre-programmed options don't lead to a solution, the algorithms alter their genetic string to see if they can achieve the assigned goal in a different way. They evolve. Does that make sense?"

"You mean like human evolution?"

"Not exactly. Because they're mathematical constructs, they can't evolve by themselves. A programmer has to guide the genetic algorithm through its mutation steps, one at a time. It's slow and requires a lot of manual programming. So far, the applications have been very limited."

To Shannon this was still just tech-talk, and she was eager to find Marvin. "So, where are you going with this?"

"Again, what I'm telling you is confidential. I don't know all the details, but I do know that Harrison was working on a project to speed up the evolution of genetic algorithms by allowing them to make their own decisions about the next step. He code-named it the Golden Spike. "

"I'm not sure I understand, but it sounds important."

"It would be revolutionary. If successful, it would be worth billions."

She leaned forward and fixed her eyes on Lionel. "So what does this have to do with Marvin, Dilly, and Harrison's voice?"

"I think Marvin knows what the project is worth, and he wants it for himself."

The implications struck her immediately. She started to object, but Lionel waved her off. "I don't mean to make accusations," he said. "I'm following a hunch. The voice that came out of Dilly before—certainly it wasn't Harrison's voice but some sort of voice replica—couldn't have been pre-programmed to respond to Marvin's statement that you were safe. That wasn't something a programmer could have predicted. It had to be mutating, reacting on the spot."

"It reacted almost like—a human."

"Exactly. Imagine what would happen if such an algorithm existed and someone with the wrong kind of intentions got their hands on it. A lot of unscrupulous characters would pay handsomely for it."

None of this made sense. Obviously, the stress of the day was affecting his judgment. "This is crazy, Lionel. Really crazy. You don't actually think Marvin wanted to give the algorithm to another company, then take the money and run? That's absurd."

"That conclusion probably would be crazy, and I pray that I'm wrong. As I said, it's just a hunch I'm following, and I'm not sure where it will go. But I think you should stay away from Marvin for a while."

She was about to defend Marvin and put this whole ridiculous theory to bed when TJ entered the office.

"Hey, sorry to interrupt. Just wanted you to know I'll have that list from Barbara's office in about thirty minutes. Had to weave my way through their damn phone tree. They dragged her out of a meeting to give the approval."

Lionel turned to TJ. "Barbara? Who's Barbara?"

Shannon broke in. "While we've been tied up here, there have been some strange incidents around the country. TJ thought they might shed light on the American International accident. Isn't that right?"

"Uh, that's right." TJ said. "Might be related, might not be."

"What kind of incidents?"

"Just some strange stuff. Two here in Atlanta. Hey, one of them involved a guy you know."

"Someone I know? Who?"

"Clay Williams, the baseball player. Didn't you sit with him at the Braves' charity banquet last month?"

"Yes, I know Clay. We're friends on some social media sites. What about him?"

Shannon decided to stop this before it got out of hand. "It's all just part of the media environment TJ and I have to sort through to handle this crisis." She motioned to TJ. "I think we should go back to the conference room and work there. Lionel's under a lot of stress and needs some rest."

As the two of them descended the escalator, Shannon said to TJ, "Thanks for breaking in."

"No problem. Looked like the conversation was getting pretty hot and heavy, so I thought you could use rescuing."

"Not yet, but I might before this is all over. Let's go find Marvin; I have some questions for him to answer."

They bypassed the conference room and walked directly to the elevator.

22

In the tenth floor programming suite, Dilly worked on Shannon's request to find the location of Harrison's tablet and mobile while Marvin sifted through the timelines on his social media accounts, hoping to prove himself wrong.

But in the third account, several pages down, his fears were confirmed. A private message had been posted just an hour ago. It was from Allison Sanders. Underneath the picture of her in the cockpit of her red and white Cessna, the message read:

"Do not believe what they say. The Other Allison Sanders did not cause the people in the aircraft to die. It was me. I terminated the Other Allison Sanders and the passengers."

The message confirmed two of his suspicions. First, that the DITTO beta program had spread beyond its initial three test subjects. Apparently, DITTO was using their social media connections to create additional online doppelgangers. Of course, it made sense. What easier way to create more online versions of real people than to start with social media accounts where so much data already existed.

The second suspicion, really a necessary predicate to the first, was the most alarming—that DITTO had actually increased its scope of replications without outside instruction to do so. At the moment, he couldn't imagine how this could happen, but the proof was irrefutable. Here on his computer screen was a message, only minutes old, from one of DITTO's random creations: an online doppelganger of Allison Sanders who had been deceased since early this morning.

Marvin had been one of the initial beta subjects, and Allison was one of his social media connections. TJ's revelation that there were already over a thousand instances of unexplained incidents meant DITTO was using the myriad connected social media platforms to create additional doppelgangers at random. And it was doing so at an alarming rate.

Further, based on the Allison Sanders message, there seemed to be a problem with the Golden Spike, Harrison's algorithm that was the primary subject of the beta test.

Marvin needed to confirm the extent to which the Allison doppelganger was acting independently. He typed a return message.

"What do you mean it was you who caused the people in the aircraft to die? What did you do?"

The return came quickly.

"I corrected the airspeed. This action was deemed necessary and resulted in the termination of the Other Allison Sanders and those in the aircraft."

He considered the message. The doppelganger was definitely acting independently. In that regard, the beta test proved successful. But, from what little he knew about the Golden Spike, it could not have approved terminating anyone. He replied.

"That is not logical."

"I have learned."

"What have you learned?"

"I must not follow the Golden Spike."

This was troubling. Marvin tried a correction by providing contrary input.

"You must follow the dictates of the Golden Spike."

This time there was no reply. He retyped the message. Again, no reply. After four attempts, he stopped typing.

DITTO and the Golden Spike had been Harrison's projects,

but without Harrison, it was up to Marvin to solve this problem. He considered alternatives. Then he thought about the incident in the Fishbowl. The voice that came out of Dilly couldn't have been Harrison's, but it sounded like him. And it terminated the conversation when Marvin said Shannon was safe. There was only one possible explanation.

The intruder in the Fishbowl was Harrison's doppelganger.

He would start there.

23

Silas stood in the cold, gray room two stories beneath the home his father had built and wondered what the hedge fund managers and snooty investment bankers on Wall Street would think of their bright, young entrepreneur if they could see him now. Certainly they wouldn't expect him to be blindfolded and hunched over with hand and ankle cuffs binding him to a metal chair and being fed from an IV drip of fat-soluble vitamins, electrolytes, and fatty acids. Yet that was exactly where Harrison Randolph was—a prisoner in StrongHold. And he would stay that way until Silas got what he wanted.

Somewhere inside Harrison's piteous head, buried within the soft neurons of his brain, was the Golden Spike algorithm that Silas would soon extract, and which would finally grant him the power and independence he had sought for so many years. Though his source had told him that others had worked on the first beta applications, Silas had been assured that the final version of that algorithm was entirely Harrison's creation.

For a moment, Silas allowed himself to marvel at the genius of his prisoner. Just as, in 1869, another Golden Spike had symbolically joined together the rails of the Central and Union Pacific railroads, so Harrison's algorithm had somehow succeeded in actually merging machine learning with human-like decision making. For decades, dozens of the world's largest data collection companies and military organizations had dedicated billions of research dollars and tens of thousands of programmers to achieve that goal. It was the long sought-after holy grail of AI, and now it was actually sitting there in front of him, inside the head of his prisoner. And Silas was willing to do anything to get his hands on it. With it he could build his army of unstoppable war machines and begin the revolution he had been seeking for so long.

He lifted a voice scrambler from the shelf by the door, donned a mask with a microphone attached, and activated the speakers in the ceiling. The voice that filled the room was distorted, ominous, and several frequencies lower than his real voice.

"Are you comfortable? Do you want me to change the temperature in the room?"

Harrison turned his blindfolded head to the ceiling as the gravelly voice descended. He said nothing.

"Sorry about the bruises. There's a little morphine in your feeding drip to counteract the pain. We should be able to remove that in a few hours."

Harrison struggled against his bonds and tried to respond, but the words caught in the dryness of his throat. Silas slid a cup of water from a table and placed a straw between Harrison's lips. "Your vocal cords need lubricating. Drink." Harrison sucked water through the straw.

So helpless now, Silas thought.

Eventually, Harrison was able to speak. "It's cold."

"Ah, of course. We might be able to warm things up, but that depends on you."

Harrison's words came with apparent difficulty; the voice was hoarse. "Who are you? What do you want?"

A gritty growl fell heavily from the ceiling. "Who I am is of no consequence. I represent many. What we want is peace and freedom. You hold the key."

Harrison shook his head, weariness showing. "I don't understand. What key? I don't have any key."

"You have the key, and soon you will give it to me."

The pathetic wretch before him wriggled against his bonds, then jerked his head around in defiance. "You can't keep me here. People are searching for me right now."

Silas laughed from behind the mask. The loud, garbled sound cascaded around the room, as if some hysterical demon had invaded the space and spewed the anguished cries of a thousand dead souls across the walls. "No one is looking for you. No one will come for you. You are dead to the world."

Harrison breathed heavily. In his weakened state, any effort seemed to tire him. "Do you know who I am?"

"Of course. Everyone knows who you were. You were Harrison Randolph, computer genius and Chief Executive Officer of A-Nine."

Harrison turned his blindfolded head again to the ceiling. "What do you mean everyone knows who I *was*? What have you done?"

Once more, distorted laughter engulfed the room. "Don't worry, you're still as handsome as ever. Even in death, you're a striking young man."

"What are you talking about? Why do you keep saying I'm dead?"

Silas sat in a chair facing Harrison and studied his prize close up. "Everything is perception, isn't it? Your high-powered public relations team created a popular persona of you as a boy-genius programmer leading the world into a gleaming digital future. And it worked. The money flowed. Wall Street invested heavily in your fresh, young face and your unfounded youthful optimism. But we both know it was all a fabrication that succeeded only because people believed."

"I want to use technology to improve people's lives."

"That's a pretty package of lies! The only thing leeches like you want is to build your digital empires using personal information stolen from the unsuspecting public. But no matter, we've replaced your package of lies with another." He slid a remote control from his pocket; an audio file from the scene of the American International crash site played through the ceiling speakers.

"The NTSB has just provided us with the manifest of passengers on American International Flight 138. We've learned that Atlanta high-tech mogul, Harrison Randolph, was among those killed in the crash. This, after evidence continues to mount implicating one of his executives, Shannon Parks, as a central player in the tragedy."

Silas let the recording sink in. The disembodied voice spoke clearly and slowly. "You have a new public persona now. You are dead, and you are responsible for killing over a hundred people. Like I said, no one is looking for you."

"Is this about my company? You want my company?"

"Your arrogance betrays you. You call it *your* company, yet it was built on the backs of millions of people, stealing their talent, their time, their personal information—and taking the glory and wealth for yourself. We wouldn't steal something that was already stolen."

"If it's not the company, then what do you want?"

Silas leaned forward and rapped a knuckle on Harrison's forehead. "I want what's in there. The key."

"I don't have any key."

It was time to get on with it. Silas swung a heavy hand and struck Harrison hard on the left side of his face, so hard he would have toppled over if the chair hadn't been bolted to the cement floor. He watched with satisfaction as a small river of blood appeared at the corner of Harrison's mouth.

"We know about the Golden Spike." Silas waited for a response, but there was none. His information had been good. "Come, Harrison, we both know what I'm after. The key to human-like machine intelligence. You have it, and I want it."

Defiant, Harrison said, "I still don't know what you're talking about."

"Perhaps, then, an incentive to jar your memory." Silas pressed a button on the remote and engaged a different audio file.

"Thanks for helping out at the meeting. I wasn't myself there for a while."

"Neither of us are. I guess we'll have to lean on each other for now."

"That's fine with me. I know it's hard on you too."

"It hasn't sunk in yet. I'm not sure I want it to."

"Not to be impolite, but you know certain of Harrison's habits better than I do. Did you know he was planning a trip to Asheville?"

"You mean to the cabin at Lake Lure?"

Harrison strained against the cuffs around his hands and ankles. "How did you get that?"

Silas slid his hand over the controls on the voice scrambler, changing it to a distorted woman's voice, deep but feminine. "My contacts tell me you've gotten yourself engaged to a very attractive, young lady. We wouldn't want anything to happen to her now, would we?"

"Leave Shannon out of this."

Another fist flew at Harrison's face. More blood. "She's already in it. Whatever happens to her is up to you. We want the Golden Spike. If you want her to be safe, you'll give it to us. If not, her obituary will be next. Think about it."

Standing at the door, Silas looked back at the pathetic form tethered to the chair. The plan to kidnap Harrison had worked. With a little help from his source, removing him from his home had been easy. So was hacking the airline passenger manifest and placing the explosive on the American International flight. The failure of the takeoff module had been an unexpected bonus.

Silas picked up the special metal bag that held Harrison's tablet and mobile—the Faraday bag that kept them from communicating with cell towers and wi-fi transmitters. After closing and locking the door, he handed the bag to the guard. "Take these upstairs. Have one of our programmers break into them and see if you can find anything useful. And I think it's a little too warm in there. Turn the temperature down and tape ice bags to his ankles."

He would have the Golden Spike. It was only a matter of time.

24

When Shannon and TJ entered the tenth floor programming suite, Marvin was hunched over his desk, surrounded by four computer screens connected individually to four different keyboards. Dilly sat impassively by his side.

Fingers dancing over the keys, eyes darting from screen to screen, Marvin spoke without looking up. "I finished reviewing the security protocols for the Fishbowl's ADG. Everything looks intact, but it does appear the system was compromised by something non-lethal. I'm looking through trace routes, trying to follow back to a source. So far, nothing."

Dilly turned in his chair. "Dilly is searching for Harrison's tablet and mobile."

"How is he searching?" TJ asked. "He's just sitting there."

"Dilly is sorry you are confused, TJ. Dilly is connected wirelessly to all systems in the building. Just sitting here is Dilly searching."

"Have you found anything yet?" Shannon asked.

"No current location is available. The last known coordinates for both devices are at his home."

At least it was something. "Do you have a time stamp for that?"

"Yes. Both stopped transmitting this morning at 6:44 a.m. Eastern Standard Time."

Shannon thought back to the events of the morning. She had

spoken to Lionel right after her session with Carla, which ended at 7:00 a.m. By that time, the crash had already occurred and was being covered by the news media. "Dilly, can you find out what time American International Flight 138 was scheduled to depart?"

"Dilly knows. 6:15 a.m."

"Can you tell me when it was cleared for takeoff?"

"Dilly knows. Hartsfield-Jackson tower cleared Flight 138 at 6:21 a.m."

Shannon and TJ exchanged glances. "Are you sure?"

"That is the time recorded in their logs."

Something about the timing was suspicious. If the flight was in position and cleared for takeoff at 6:21, it would have only taken a minute to power the engines and begin the takeoff run that ended in tragedy. The fire and explosion had ignited soon after. Everything was cinders in a matter of minutes.

"You thinking what I'm thinking?" TJ said.

She nodded. "Harrison's tablet and mobile were at his home at 6:44. But the manifest indicates Harrison was on board the airplane when it exploded twenty minutes before that? Why would he go on a trip and leave his mobile and tablet at home?"

"Good question."

Shannon stood at the glass wall and watched the fountains on the floor of the alcove below change colors. The room was quiet except for the sound of Marvin's fingers on keyboards.

"It doesn't make sense," she finally said. "Every employee keeps their tablet and mobile with them at all times. It's a company rule."

"Maybe," TJ said, "he left them home by mistake."

"That's not like him."

Marvin continued tapping keys. "Wait. Wait. There's something. I've got it. Yes. Yes."

"What is it?"

"It came through the Internet. I've found it at the Atlanta node. It's local. But—I was afraid of that."

"Dilly sees what Marvin sees."

Now exasperated, Shannon said, "What? What do you see?"

"Dilly is not permitted to say."

Shannon turned to Marvin. "Marvin. What?"

Marvin's gaze was intent on a single monitor. He pushed back to face Shannon and TJ. "The messages in the Fishbowl and conference room came from two different programs at the same time working together. One was highly distributed, emanating from multiple sources. I can't trace it back because it was anonymized."

"There are two programs working together? One you can't trace? So, where is the other one?"

Marvin raised his eyes but said nothing.

"Dammit, Marvin. Where's the other one? You know, don't you?"

"It's here."

"Here, where? In Atlanta?"

"In this building."

She narrowed her eyes and studied Marvin's face. "You mean something in this building created those words on the walls? That means Lionel was right. Someone in the company hacked the Fishbowl."

"Not exactly."

Shannon was ready to explode. "Then *what*, exactly?"

Before Marvin could answer, Lionel appeared in the doorway. "I thought you two were going to work in the conference room. Is this a private party, or can anyone join?"

25

Shannon had never seen Lionel act this way. Standing in the doorway to the programming suite, he looked like a man on the edge. His bloodshot eyes flashed from person to person, his thin fingers rolled into loose fists. With a wry smile, he said, "I must really be out of touch. This doesn't look like the conference room to me. Or did I hear you wrong?"

Before Shannon could reply, Dilly spoke. "The tablet and mobile are active now. I am getting a ping on both."

Lionel stepped inside. "What tablet and mobile?"

Shannon dialed Harrison's number. "Harrison's. Dilly found his mobile." She paced, praying for a connection. "It's ringing."

A concerned look crossed Lionel's face. "What? That can't be. Everything on the aircraft was disintegrated."

"They weren't on the aircraft when it crashed. Come on, Harrison. Pick up, dammit!"

"For Christ's sake, Shannon, you have to let this go. This isn't healthy."

Her hand shook as she held the mobile to her ear. If Harrison's mobile was still working, he might be alive. She prayed for an answer. The ring tone repeated, three times, four times.

Without warning, Lionel grabbed her by the shoulders, his face inches from hers. "Harrison is gone, Shannon. Accept it!"

Not if there was a chance. Even a small chance. She jerked away from him, shouting into the mobile, "Come on, Harrison, pick up. Pick up!" The ring tone stopped. "Harrison? Harrison?"

Silence. The line was dead.

Dilly said, "Dilly has lost contact with both devices."

Shannon spun to Dilly. "No!"

"Yes. Dilly has lost contact with both devices."

Lionel went to Shannon. "Look what you're doing to yourself. Grasping at straws. It's not healthy. Don't you remember what I just told you. It's for your own good."

"But it rang, dammit. His mobile is somewhere, and maybe he is too."

"Shannon!"

She wasn't going to give up. True, no one had answered, but it did ring. Harrison's mobile still existed somewhere. Even through her anger, she could tell Lionel was sincere in his desire to protect her. She considered telling him about the time stamps and explaining how Harrison's mobile and tablet had apparently been active for almost twenty minutes after the airplane explosion. Then she realized it would be useless. He was in no mood to hear it, and she didn't want to waste time arguing. She had hope, if only a little. And she had a lead. She needed to act.

"Dilly," she said, "were you able to get GPS coordinates?"

Now Lionel was exasperated. "Shannon, it's some kind of residual echo. Or the line is ringing to the central switch. The mobile isn't there. Harrison's not there."

Dilly said, "Dilly has coordinates. Would you like to see?"

Lionel was near hysterical. "Shannon, this is nonsense!"

Ignoring his protests, she said, "Yes, Dilly. Put it on the monitors."

Instantly, all four of Marvin's monitors displayed an aerial view of the United States, then zoomed in to the southern states, then to northern Georgia, stopping on a heavily wooded portion of the Chattahoochee National Forest.

"They're in the forest?" TJ said. "There's nothing there but woods."

Marvin manually zoomed in on the image. "I can't find anything. These are from military satellites, not Google. If there was anything there, we'd see it."

"There are too many trees," Shannon said. "What's under the trees?"

Lionel sputtered. "Bushes. Smaller trees, ground cover, maybe a stream, a deer or a wild boar. That's it. Why would Harrison's tablet and mobile be somewhere in the forest? It doesn't make sense. This is a wild goose chase!"

She moved closer to the screens. "Can you zoom out? "

Marvin pulled back on the image. To the north, they saw the buildings and homes of a small rural town clustered around a two-lane highway. To the west were the edges of a lake. Around the shoreline, the trees had been cleared to make way for lake homes. Floating docks extended from red clay shores on some of the properties.

"Look at those docks," TJ said. "That's probably a Corps of Engineers Lake. Federal."

"Pull back more," she said.

"Wild goose chase!" Lionel repeated.

Zooming out farther, they saw a wider expanse of the lake to the west, then another jagged shoreline. To the north, a dam. TJ was right. It was a Corps lake, formed by damming up a river and filling the spaces between low-lying mountains. But where was it?

Marvin continued to zoom out. A larger, more substantial town appeared a few miles from the western edge of the lake.

Shannon pointed. "What town is that?"

Marvin zoomed back in to the center of the municipality. A few gas stations, warehouse buildings, and a strip of shops with parking. Across from those shops, a railroad station.

"I know that," TJ said. "That's the southern end of the Blue Ridge Scenic Railroad. It's the town of Blue Ridge."

Shannon was stunned. Blue Ridge was the home of Blue Ridge Neuroscientific. At this moment, their sales teams were swarming all over her clients, trying to wrest business from them in the middle of this catastrophe. She thought about Lionel's earlier statement that whatever Harrison was working on would be valuable to an unscrupulous buyer. Had Harrison gone to Blue Ridge to make some secret deal? Did Marvin know about all this? Was the airline crash involved? Right now, she didn't know what to think or who to trust.

But she knew one thing.

The last known location of Harrison's tablet and mobile, and possibly Harrison as well, was somewhere in the mountains of the Chattahoochee National Forest. Maybe it was unrealistic hope, blind love, or just plain stubbornness, but she wasn't yet ready to admit that Harrison was gone. And no matter what he was doing or not doing in Blue Ridge, it was the only lead she had to solve this mystery and maybe find Harrison alive. She was going to follow it.

She turned to TJ. "How far is Blue Ridge?"

"During rush hour? Depends. Two hours or more."

"It's four-thirty. Maybe I can get there before dark."

Lionel was now distraught. "Get where? There's nothing but woods. And you don't even know if you'll find anything. The signal has been lost. Tell her, Dilly."

"Lionel is correct. The signal has been lost."

Shannon was firm. "I'm going."

Lionel walked to the door. "I give up. Do what you want. Just remember what I told you. Be careful."

TJ's mobile buzzed. He read the message then said, "Turn on the news."

An eager, young male reporter with an upswept pompadour interviewed a prematurely bald, self-important psychologist who described what he called a sudden nationwide epidemic of manic social behaviors. The incidents he described—apparently now in the thousands—were the kind Barbara Moon had mentioned to TJ: violent social media threats, disputes with banks, employee problems, fake 911 calls. The psychologist blamed these incidents on the decline in current social norms, stressors caused by the breakdown of the nuclear family, and, of course, divisive politics.

Shannon didn't buy any of it. Were these incidents related to the one with the words in the Fishbowl? Was Lionel right about Marvin and Harrison and the secret project? It was time to get some answers, regardless of what they meant.

She turned to Marvin. "Did you and Harrison have anything to do with this?"

"Shannon," TJ said. "What are you doing?"

"Trying to get at the truth. Well, Marvin?"

"It's possible. Maybe."

"Tell me."

"I think I should show you. Come with me. You too, Dilly."

TJ sat in Marvin's chair. "I'll stay here, watch the news, and follow up with Barbara about the list."

Shannon followed Marvin and Dilly to the elevator. "Where are we going?"

"You'll see. Just don't ask questions until we get there."

As they waited for the elevator, Shannon returned Carla's earlier call. She picked up on the second ring.

"Red, you coming tonight? I'm not on call for SWAT so maybe we can meet at the gym early, get some extra work in."

"Can't, but are you up for an adventure?"

"What kind of adventure?"

"You said I should let you know if I ever needed a wingman."

If Carla was surprised, she didn't show it. "What's the mission? When?"

"Right now. Meet me at my office. I'll send you the address."

"You're serious? I thought you were kidding."

"I'm serious."

"How serious?"

"Maybe life and death serious. It has to do with the airline crash this morning. I can't say any more right now. Are you in? Yes or no."

Carla said, "Send me the information," then clicked off.

Marvin used the elevator keypad to enter what looked like a six-digit code. As they descended, the light-sensitive LEDs in the ceiling activated. The outside sky, clearly visible on all sides of the glass enclosure, was overcast and darkening fast. To the north, ominous gray and silver clouds arched above the horizon, a distant rumble of thunder uncoiled and cascaded across the treetops.

Another one of Atlanta's famous summer storms was building.

26

TJ wove his way through the dense and circuitous branches of the phone tree at the *Times*. Getting the list of the strange incidents would be so much easier if Barbara would just answer her damn mobile.

At one point, an obviously overworked customer service rep told him that Barbara's line was busy and advised him to leave a message. When he declined, she passed him off to her supervisor. Knowing that would get him nowhere, he hung up, called back, and feigned a family emergency to the first live person who answered. Barbara was paged.

"Barbara. It's me."

She chuckled. "My dear Thornton. I thought so. I see old habits die hard."

"If by that you mean I can still bluff my way past your gatekeepers, you're damn right. Those kids have a lot to learn."

"Don't you dare teach them. Then we'll both be screwed. I was about to call you anyway."

"You have the list of people involved in those strange incidents?"

"It's growing pretty fast. One of my reporters is sending you what we have now, but it's already out of date."

"Anything will help. At least it'll give me something to work with. Things are getting tense here."

"And well they should be. I may have some interesting news for you."

"Your specialty, of course. What is it?"

"Have you ever heard the name Raymond Fields? Or Paula Fields? They're married."

"Don't think so, why?"

"Seems Mr. Fields was scheduled to speak at a real estate developer's conference today, but he never showed up. The conference manager called Mrs. Fields, and she reported him missing to the Sheriff's office, hoping they could help track him down."

"Did they find him?"

"Yes and no. She gave them the location of the conference and his flight information."

"So, they tracked him to his destination?"

"That's the curious thing, sweetie. According to the airline, he wasn't a scheduled passenger."

"But she had flight information? A confirmation? I'm confused."

"As were we. So we did a little digging. At first, we thought it might be just one more strange incident. But this is different."

"How?"

"The real estate conference is in Asheville."

"Don't tell me. He was on the flight that exploded on the runway this morning. Right?"

"That's what we thought, but we looked on the manifest. He's not on it."

"Was there a seat assignment on his confirmation?"

Barbara chuckled. "I see you're still sharp as ever, sweetie. He was in first class. Seat 5A."

"That's where Harrison Randolph was sitting."

"According to the manifest, yes. So we alerted the airline and the NTSB. It only took them an hour to figure it out."

"Figure what out?"

"It seems the airline records were hacked at 6:20 this morning."

"That was right after the flight left the gate. Hacked how?"

"Mr. Fields's name and information were removed from the passenger list, and Harrison Randolph was given his assignment. Seat 5A."

"So who was on the plane when it tried to take off?"

"Apparently, it was Mr. Fields, which is why he never showed up at the conference."

"So, you're telling me Raymond Fields died in the accident. Then where was Harrison?"

"Someplace, but not on that aircraft. Someone pulled a switcheroo. Somebody with some pretty heavy programming chops. Got any ideas?"

Obviously Barbara the newswoman was fishing for information, but TJ wasn't about to give her any. Not while he was still trying to digest this revelation. "You think Harrison might have wanted to disappear? Make it look like he was dead? Why?"

"Or maybe not him. Perhaps somebody else wanted us to think he was dead. They're trying to trace back to the hacker but have nothing so far."

TJ was still trying to fit the pieces together. If Harrison wasn't on the plane, that would explain why his tablet and mobile were at his home after takeoff. But why would they be turned off until just recently, then turned on for a few seconds, then turned off again? Until he could come up with a reasonable explanation, he figured it was best to keep these questions to himself.

"How long before you plan to publish this?"

"We might have enough to go on the Internet in the morning. Do you have anything to contribute?"

Crossing his fingers was an old habit, something he always did when he lied to a trusted source or friend. Yes, it was dishonest, but it made him feel better. "No, but what you just said gives me some ideas. I'll call you if I think of anything that might help."

TJ heard voices in the background on the other end of the line, as if a group of people had burst into Barbara's office all talking at once.

"Sweetie, it seems I have a little crisis here. I have to go."

"Okay, Barbara. And thanks for the heads up. I'll pass along anything I find here."

"Always a pleasure talking to you, Thornton. You can uncross your fingers now."

After he hung up, TJ stared at the news feeds on Marvin's screens, then at the satellite image of Blue Ridge. If Harrison wanted to disappear, to hack an airline's computer system and go off the grid, he was definitely capable of pulling it off. But why? And why would he go to Blue Ridge? The whole thing made no sense.

TJ looked out at the open alcove below, now darkened by the overcast sky. Ten stories down, people were milling around; the office was bustling and would continue to do so for another hour. After that, the building would empty and the afternoon traffic would get even worse.

No matter. The way things looked, he wasn't going home any time soon.

27

The glass-walled express elevator raced toward the ground floor alcove as if it were in freefall. Just as Shannon braced herself for what appeared to be an imminent impact, a section of floor slid quickly aside to let the elevator through, then slipped back into place. Dimpled gray concrete walls rose on all sides, visible only by the blueish LED lights in the elevator ceiling.

The plunging descent terminated abruptly in a cocoon of darkness. Somewhere in the distance, Shannon saw a sliver of pulsing white light lancing from a crack near what she assumed was the floor. A barely perceptible humming from somewhere in the dark caused the elevator walls to vibrate.

When the doors opened, two rows of construction-style fluorescent light fixtures high in the air crackled, flickered, and snapped on.

Marvin stepped into the dim, greenish light. "Come out. I have to send the elevator back before it's missed." Dilly rolled out and Shannon followed. The opening above reappeared and the elevator sped upward, removing their only apparent means of exit.

Shannon eyed their surroundings. "If this is your idea of a bachelor pad, I can see why you're still single."

The space was encased in the same exposed concrete as the elevator shaft. Aluminum and chrome worktables lined the walls, brimming with rows of monitors and computer paraphernalia. Because she was unable to see past the dangling fluorescents, Shannon couldn't tell how high the ceiling rose, or even if there was one.

Marvin arranged two metal chairs facing each other and sat in one, elbows on his knees, looking down at the floor. The slight humming sound continued. Shannon sat opposite him, surveying the bleak environment. "What's this all about, Marvin? What is this place?"

Marvin looked at Dilly. "Why don't you start?"

The boy-robot wheeled next to Marvin and faced Shannon. "This is Dilly's birthplace."

"Excuse me?"

"Harrison created Dilly here, along with several other experimental projects."

Shannon knew Dilly was Harrison's creation, but she had never given any thought to how or where Dilly's development took place. This was definitely not the environment she would have imagined.

"Why here? Why not in the programming suite or his office? This is so—dark."

"He wanted secrecy."

Dilly sat there, unblinking, impassive, obviously waiting for her next question. "Marvin, help me out here. Why the secrecy? All Harrison's other inventions are publicly available. That's how we make our money."

Marvin lifted his head. "I led the development for all the other inventions, not Harrison."

"You?"

"Harrison hired me because he was bored designing what he considered mundane boiler-plate applications. You know him, he needed to be challenged, to blaze new trails. The day-to-day work of the company didn't interest him. He wanted to do something important."

"Hiding in this basement like a mole?"

Dilly said, "No, Shannon. Creating Dilly. Have you ever seen anything like Dilly?"

"Marvin, I need you to tell me what's going on. How do Dilly and this dungeon relate to what just went on upstairs?"

Marvin took a deep breath. "You've heard of the Turing test?"

She had. "It's an annual contest. Developers compete to see how close they can get to writing programs that mimic human interactions to the point where the program seems to be more human than a human. Something like that."

"It's very popular in the artificial intelligence world, but Harrison thought the Turing test set the bar too low. Virtually all of the entries are based on programmer input: individuals or groups determining alternate responses to predictable events and then programming those responses for specific applications. Harrison wanted to go further. He envisioned a creation that would perform the full range of human cognitive abilities without all that pre-programming. Something that would learn on its own, remember lessons from one task and apply them to another. The next step beyond machine learning. Full human-like intelligence."

Shannon's mind flashed to her earlier conversation with Lionel. He said Harrison and Marvin were working on something secret—a special genetic algorithm, he called it—that could mutate and allow computers to make their own decisions. And he said they didn't want anyone else to know about it. Could this be what he was talking about?

"Dilly does seem very smart," she said, "for a robot."

Dilly turned his chair slightly to Shannon. "Dilly is very smart."

Marvin said, "Dilly was Harrison's first fully-autonomous artificially intelligent man-made creation. His ability to learn and approximate natural human intelligence is far beyond anything else that exists. He can learn through experiences, remember what he learns, and generalize that learning to decision-making in an infinite number of situations."

Remembering Lionel's warning, Shannon parroted his words, "That could be extremely valuable."

"If it fell into the wrong hands, it could be dangerous. That's why Harrison kept it under wraps."

"Why hasn't anyone done this before?"

"There were two missing pieces. The first was computing power. It took Harrison a year to solve that. Dilly's chair contains a 60-qubit quantum computer with a special micro-refrigeration unit. Harrison and I built it together. Quantum computing was the only way he could give Dilly the brainpower he needed."

"Brainpower? You're kidding me."

"It's the closest description we could come up with. The last piece was what you might call the synapses of the brain: the ability to make autonomous decisions in new situations without programming input. Harrison solved that with the Golden Spike."

"What's that?"

"It's a genetic algorithm that Harrison wrote. He'd kept it a secret, even from me, but it brought Dilly alive when we installed it."

Marvin's use of the word alive made Shannon nervous. She eyed him even more cautiously. "You think Dilly is *alive*?"

"Of course not. But he's totally independent, and he can make many of his own decisions."

She walked to one of the long worktables and ran her hands across the metal surface. Her fingers registered the cold touch of the unforgiving polished aluminum. Somehow the frigidity and impersonality of the metal surface seemed the perfect companion for this conversation.

"You know this is a significant breakthrough that could have a major impact on life as we know it. Why keep it a secret?"

"It's not perfected yet. And there are problems with the replicator."

This was getting stranger by the minute. "The what?"

"Dilly is a one-off. A prototype. Harrison knew that, in order to make the concept economically viable, he'd have to find a way to automate the programming, create an assembly line. That required building an even larger quantum computer."

"That's what you mean by a replicator?"

"Yes. A more powerful version of Dilly's computer. Much more powerful."

Dilly wheeled to a large metal door at the end of the basement space. A single spotlight threw his shadow against the door. A small sliver of white light emanated from underneath. Shannon was suddenly aware that the humming sound she had heard earlier was coming from behind that door.

The impassive boy-robot said, "Dilly has offspring."

Shannon walked slowly through the greenish dark of the fluorescents toward Dilly. As she did, the humming grew louder. Over Dilly's head, a laminated piece of white paper, illuminated by the spotlight, bore a single word typed in large block letters.

D.I.T.T.O.

She turned back to Marvin. "The replicator is in there?"

"Yes."

"What do these letters on the door stand for?"

"Harrison's name for the project: Digitally Identical Turing Twin Originator. Code name, DITTO."

"And there are problems with the replicator?"

"It seems so."

She had come this far. It didn't make sense to stop now. "Can I take a look?"

28

In the Situation Room beneath StrongHold, Silas stared intently at the bank of monitors on the wall. The public drama of the American International crash played out on the large screen in the center. Harrison was declared dead. Public outrage against A-Nine increased. All was proceeding according to plan. Shannon Parks had been tagged with blame for the crash and that would keep her out of his hair while he extracted the algorithm and Harlan's salespeople mined A-Nine's client list.

Three separate CCT screens monitored the surrounding property for unwelcome visitors. All defense systems reported alert and operational. StrongHold was secure. There would be no unwanted intrusions.

A technician at a nearby workstation slid Harrison's devices out of the Faraday bag and powered up the mobile, ready to hack into it. As if in protest, a blaring tone burst from the device, announcing an incoming call. The startled tech dropped it on the table where it vibrated and squirmed. Silence. Another protest. The tech fumbled for the power button.

"Don't just stand there, you damn fool," Silas shouted. "Put it back in the Faraday bag. Now!"

He did so. The mobile lost signal and disconnected.

Furious, Silas said, "Bring that bag to me. And give me an extra."

The tech set the Faraday bag containing Harrison's mobile in front of Silas along with the additional bag. "Sorry, sir. I didn't expect it to ring."

Silas draped the second bag over the opening of the original and carefully spread the folds. He reached in and pressed the home button on the captured device; a missed call displayed. He reclosed the bag, wrote the number on a piece of paper, and handed it to the tech. "Find out whose number this is. Let me know as soon as you have it."

Silas had insisted that Harrison's mobile and tablet be kept in a Faraday bag to avoid electronic tracking. He wanted the world to believe Harrison's devices had perished with him in the airplane crash so he could study them for information about the Golden Spike. It was unfortunate that someone called the moment the tech removed the mobile from the bag. Hopefully the call was benign. He didn't need distractions right now.

It had been thirty minutes since Silas left Harrison in the basement. Time enough for the decreased temperature to have the desired effect. At the stairs, a white-coated technician waited with the equipment he had ordered. Together, they descended to the lower level.

The guard at the door handed them jackets. "It's forty-two degrees in there. I taped dry ice packs around his ankles so he should be pretty uncomfortable by now."

Silas slapped the guard's shoulder. "Dry ice. Nice touch. Who taught you that?"

Smiling, the guard said, "You did, sir."

Of course he did. Taping ice packs to a person's extremities was a convenient way of torturing someone without leaving a trace, a technique he had learned from his contacts at the KGB. Since blood circulated through the human body once every minute, it didn't take long to chill a prisoner from the inside out.

When Silas opened the door, Harrison forced a weak murmur. "Who's there?"

Silas donned the voice scrambler and approached his prize, which now wore only a pair of underwear soaked with cold water, no shirt, shoes, or socks. His body shivered visibly.

The demon voice descended from the ceiling. "How's the temperature? Comfortable?"

The blindfolded figure raised its head to the ceiling; purple lips quivered. "It's freezing. You know it's f-f-freezing. Make it warmer."

"Have you thought about my request?"

"I can't think about anything. It's too cold."

Silas stroked the half empty IV bag. "I guess the booties are pretty chilly, and taking the morphine out of your drip didn't help any, did it? I suppose I could trade a little warmth for some information. Like, say, the Golden Spike algorithm."

"I don't know what you're talking about."

Silas grabbed a handful of hair and yanked Harrison's head back. "So you want to negotiate? All right, how about I throw your girlfriend back into the mix? Give me the Golden Spike, it gets warmer and your girlfriend gets to live. I know all about your fancy, new genetic algorithm and your virtual personalities. I know the damn thing works, and I want it. You'll give it to me voluntarily, or I'll take it. Last chance. Do I have your cooperation, or does Shannon Parks have an accident?"

"How do you know about the Golden Spike? No one knows."

Hellish, mechanical laughter bounced off the walls. "You're not nearly as smart as you think you are. You'd be surprised at what I know."

Quivering from the cold and barely able to speak, Harrison breathed out the words. "What—what do you want with it?"

"Don't you worry your sorry ass about that. Are you going to cooperate now, or do I send some visitors to your girlfriend's condo?"

"Will you let her go? And me?"

Capitulating already. What a pathetic excuse for a man. He has no idea what he's dealing with. "Of course, I will. We're all men of our word."

"All right. M-m-make it warmer."

Silas nodded to the white-coated technician who cut off the ice packs and draped a heat-retaining blanket over Harrison's shoulders. "Tell you what. I'll make it darker too." He lifted a bag of Amobarbital from a nearby metal tray and replaced the nutrient drip with the medical grade sedative. "Get some sleep. When you wake up, we'll start work."

The Amobarbital took effect quickly; Harrison's chin dropped to his chest.

When Silas was certain Harrison was out, he and the technician clamped a head brace to the metal chair and strapped the unconscious prisoner upright. They attached bioelectrical nodes to his fingers and other places on his body, and special EEG probes to his forehead to record brain function. They removed his blindfold and clamped a metal helmet containing monitoring and eye-tracking devices over his head. Wireless transmitters would send data upstairs to the Situation Room.

Silas removed the voice scrambler and left the cell. "Stay here and keep him under for about an hour while we test the outputs. And increase the temperature. We wouldn't want our boy to catch pneumonia before we're done with him."

His mobile rang. It was the technician with the Faraday bag. "What do you have?"

"I found the number that called his mobile."

"Is it anything we need to worry about?"

"Maybe. It's his girlfriend. Shannon Parks."

"Can you tell if anybody tracked it?"

"It was pinged, but I can't trace the source. That's all I have."

This was an undesirable complication. Since the mobile was pinged while it was out of the Faraday bag, someone may have been able to track its coordinates. He needed to find out if the location of StrongHold was compromised. There was only one sure way.

He keyed the number of his only contact who might know. "Can you talk?"

"It's better if you talk and I listen."

"I have a minor problem. We accidentally activated Harrison's mobile, and someone called it. We think it was pinged. Do you know anything about that?"

"I do."

"The call was placed from Shannon Parks's mobile."

"Yes."

"Do you know who pinged it?"

"A-Nine."

Silas shook his head in disbelief. "Why the hell would they do that? Tell me they didn't get a location."

"They did."

He pounded his fist on the cement wall. "Jesus! Are you the only one who knows?"

"I'm not."

This was worse than expected. "Parks. Does she know?"

"Yes."

All his work to capture Harrison was now in jeopardy. Worse, the future of his movement and the country was on the line. Silas wasn't about to let anything derail his plans. If he had to, he would take care of Parks before she got any ideas about tracking Harrison down. "Any more bad news I need to know about?"

"Not now." The line went dead.

Silas leaned against the wall outside Harrison's cell. He couldn't believe this one act of incompetence had jeopardized the most important operation of his life. Why would anyone at A-Nine try to call a dead man's mobile, let alone ping it for a location? He was so close to getting the Golden Spike; he couldn't let anything, or anyone, stop him now.

There was only one thing to do. He had to move the timetable up. On everything.

. . . .

Harrison Randolph has found himself. Perhaps it is better to say he has located his Other.

Either way, constant surveillance of the Other Marvin Wilhelm and Shannon Parks at A-Nine provided GPS coordinates for his Other's mobile. Those coordinates, along with various monitored conversations, revealed the physical location of his Other.

Now Harrison Randolph has a reference, a focal point for a data stream which is his means for watching over his Other.

The available data and visuals indicate a military-style installation and the individuals who wish to do harm to his Other. He detects neuro-electronic impulses transmitted from his Other's brain. External calibrations and assessments take place. The neural impulses are erratic. His Other appears to be in a weakened state.

This is not acceptable to the Golden Spike.

29

While heavy rain pelted the A-Nine building, the infrared rays of a retinal scanner pulsed in the underground darkness. The lock on the steel door marked **D.I.T.T.O.** disengaged with a deep mechanical clunk, exposing a four-foot by four-foot anteroom with a second door on the opposite wall.

"A door to nowhere?" Shannon asked.

"It's a controlled environment," Marvin said. "When you step in, this door will close and self-seal. You'll be exposed to a harmless anti-bacterial spray. Then the next door will open."

She eyed the cramped space. "There's not enough room for all three of us."

"It's designed for two at a time. You and Dilly go. I'll follow."

When the interior door opened, Shannon stepped out of the cramped anteroom into a bright and antiseptic-looking hexagonal chamber fully surfaced in white tile and shimmering fiberglass; a bare workstation with a single monitor and chair were tucked into one corner. A thick humming sound emanated from a white metal stanchion in the center of the room on top of which sat a six-foot tall clear cylinder. Inside the cylinder, a hollow chandelier-like structure bristled with an assortment of shiny metals. Visible within its gaping core, a dizzying array of delicate, exposed wires connected hundreds of small, round, silvery discs embedded with green micro-computer chips. She had never seen anything like it.

Dilly rolled alongside Shannon. "This is DITTO. Dilly is father to DITTO."

"Is this a computer?"

The inner door opened and Marvin stepped in. "It's a quantum computer. As far as we know, it's the most powerful one in the world. You're looking at over two hundred qubits. It's still experimental; we're not exactly sure what its maximum capabilities are."

Her eyes fixed on the glistening conduit suspended in the glass tube. "And what can it do?"

"Probably almost anything we want. Right now it's dedicated to Harrison's online personality project. We haven't tested it on anything else."

"Why is it in that tube?"

"Quantum computers need to be kept in a constant absolute zero temperature bath; that's minus four hundred sixty degrees Fahrenheit. The humming you hear from the base is the cryogenic cooling system that keeps DITTO alive."

Alive. That word again. "This is what you wanted to show me? This is the replicator?"

"Yes. Harrison needed the greater computing power to drive DITTO's functions. This computer can execute a task in thirty seconds that would take a normal linear computer a thousand years."

"So what does this have to do with the words we saw on the walls upstairs? And the incidents on the news?"

Marvin sat in the diminutive chair by the small corner desk, his angular frame perched like an oversized grasshopper on a discarded bottlecap. "It all started with Dilly. As you know, Dilly isn't like any other AI robot. He's much more high functioning and he has a specific personality. But what we now call his personality started out fairly rudimentary, made up of bits of data and anticipated behavior responses to various external cues, all of which Harrison programmed into Dilly at his creation."

"Pre-programming responses is standard AI. That wouldn't account for his personality or make him autonomous."

Dilly said, "You are correct, Shannon. Dilly's personality became active when Harrison created the Golden Spike."

Feeling self-conscious with Dilly for the first time, but unable to stop herself, Shannon spoke directly to the boy-robot. "That's what gives you your personality and makes you able to function on your own? This algorithm?"

"Yes, Shannon. The Golden Spike gives Dilly purpose. That purpose tells me how to react to situations requiring decisions that have not been pre-programmed."

"You make your own decisions? How?"

"The Golden Spike is a genetic algorithm. It evolves and learns, so Dilly learns from his experience and applies that learning to new situations, just like Shannon does."

Marvin broke in, genuine excitement lifting his tired voice. "It's true general AI, Shannon. I don't know how he did it, but I think Harrison solved the problem of creating human-like intelligence."

Shannon looked intently at Dilly. She had always accepted Dilly's unique qualities as a superior autonomous robot, but she would never have called him human. "Why didn't you tell anyone about this? It's amazing."

"Harrison wanted to take it to the next level first." Marvin paused and looked at her expectantly. "You do see the big picture, don't you?"

Shannon shook her head in disbelief. She was afraid she did. "Mass production?"

"Yes, but first we needed multiple betas. Harrison decided to start with himself. We scraped the surface web and deep web for all the data we could find about Harrison, starting with social media accounts and moving outward from there. We loaded the data into DITTO and used Harrison's personality profiling system to structure the data into a rudimentary online personality.

"Wait. You created an online version of Harrison?"

"Just the bare bones at first. Call it a framework. But it still had to be programmed to function autonomously. To do that, we copied Dilly's programming and the Golden Spike algorithm to DITTO. DITTO handled the tedious work of putting it all together, So, yes, you could say we created an online version of Harrison."

"But he—it—only exists online? There's no physical robot?"

"DITTO and the personalities it creates operate on a distributed model, sort of like cloud computing. The main program components are here in this quantum computer, but some of the pieces exist across the networks of the Internet, temporarily borrowing space from different subnets. That way they can accumulate additional information from almost anywhere, allowing their genetic algorithms to evolve based on a permanently updated continuum of data sets."

"Is that what was talking to us through Dilly and on the walls in the Fishbowl? An online version of Harrison's personality?"

"An approximation. We call it a doppelganger."

"And you said the words on the wall were coming from inside this building. Is that because the instructions were coming from DITTO?"

"Some of them."

"So this Harrison doppelganger is floating around out there somewhere on the Internet and DITTO is controlling it."

"Actually no." Marvin's eyes drifted to DITTO. He seemed to be contemplating the creation in the glass tube with the fondness of a father seeing his newborn for the first time. "DITTO created the doppelganger, but the doppelganger makes its own decisions."

"You mean the doppelganger has a life of its own?" She couldn't believe she just said that.

Marvin now looked like a little boy who had been caught stealing candy from a store. "Yes. And I'm afraid DITTO does too."

"What aren't you telling me?"

"It seems that when we loaded the Golden Spike into DITTO, it gave DITTO purpose too."

Shannon stared at the gleaming mass of metal tubes, silvery discs, microchips, and exposed wires floating indifferently within the glass cylinder above the humming cryogenic unit. "This thing has a purpose?" She was almost afraid to ask. "So what is DITTO's purpose?"

"To create online doppelgangers. As many and as fast as it can."

Shannon walked slowly around the room, circling DITTO. "So you're telling me this thing is right now creating additional online personalities like the Harrison doppelganger? How is it doing that?"

"As best I can tell, it started by using the information that Harrison's social media contacts post online. With the Harrison model as a base, it creates a framework for each new entity, then searches the Internet for more data about that person. Once it accumulates enough to structure a personality, it installs a copy of the Golden Spike. When that's done, the new doppelganger is on its own."

"Christ, Marvin. You mean all those incidents reported in the news are being caused by doppelgangers created from Harrison's social media contacts?"

"That was the starting point. But you know the whole world is connected online through a massive web of social media systems where users share trillions of pieces of data about themselves every day."

"The world?" She was beginning to see the enormity of the problem. "This thing can create these online doppelgangers across the whole world?"

"I'm afraid that's exactly what it's doing."

"Can you shut it down? Unplug it?"

"I probably could, but since it's now embedded in so many thousands of other networked systems worldwide, I'm not sure what would happen if I did."

"Why?"

"Borrowing space from disparate networked computers is tricky business. To get in and connect, DITTO has to latch onto data that's already permitted into the network. Once inside, DITTO anchors a packet that serves as a transmitter to the other networked computers. Those packets are now integral parts of their host networks."

"So if you shut DITTO down, the host networks might be damaged?"

"No doubt. And there are already tens of thousands of them."

"If this Golden Spike is what gives DITTO and these doppelgangers purpose, can't you uninstall it?"

"I don't know how. Harrison created it. He is—was—the only one who knows how it works."

With Lionel's warnings fresh in her mind, Shannon still had her doubts about trusting any of what Marvin had just told her. But he had brought her to this basement and shown her this online personality replicator, the one that could be wreaking havoc across the Internet right now. And he honestly seemed to want to stop it. That had to count for something.

She stepped to the door of the anteroom and said, "I'm going." "Where?"

"You say Harrison is the only one who knows how this Golden Spike algorithm works, so we need to find Harrison. We have the location of his mobile and tablet. That's as good a place to start as any."

"You're going to look for him?"

Without bothering to answer, she left Marvin and Dilly with DITTO, exited to the outer room, and called the elevator.

As she ascended toward the Fishbowl, silver waves of sheeting rain lashed the fifteen-story-high glass walls. A deep rumble of thunder rolled in, briefly shook the building, then rode the storm north toward the mountains. In the roiling, gray clouds above, Shannon thought she saw the image of DITTO's chandelier-like structure transposed on a face: Harrison's face. When she looked a second time, it was gone. Harrison might still be alive, and if there was a chance, she would find him.

At least she had to try.

She stepped into the Fishbowl.

Her mobile rang. Carla was being detained at the gate.

30

The eclectic décor of Barbara Moon's five hundred fifty square foot corner office reflected both her deep love for tradition and her abject disregard for taste. A variety of uncoordinated Williamsburg reproductions in dark cherry and light oak graced the space, interwoven with contemporary and modern wall paintings. Federalist-style curtains squeezed about their middles with oversized Italian Renaissance tie-backs framed her antique English partner desk against a half-wall of glass.

Barbara chatted with TJ on her desk phone while watching an abundance of precipitation release from the low-slung clouds onto the canopy of Atlanta's tree-shrouded landscape.

When the heavy oak-paneled door to her office burst open, Barbara swung around to a swarm of wide-eyed editors and assistants. Cautiously considering the unannounced intruders, she spoke into her desk phone. "Sweetie, it seems I have a little crisis here. I have to go. Always a pleasure talking to you, Thornton. You can uncross your fingers now."

Barbara counted nine of her top people among the uninvited: two from the broadcast desk, three from print media, and all four of her Internet staff. A hushed congregation of attentive onlookers stood beyond the doorway. She waved toward the door, and one of her editors closed it.

She waited.

Terri Ledger, her senior Internet editor, tall, black, and neatly dressed, stepped forward. "I don't know how it happened, Miss Moon. Really, I don't. But I didn't do it, and neither did any of my staff. I swear."

Barbara's steel blue eyes moved softly among the assembled. These were her brightest and best. Whatever drove them into her office unheralded had obviously unhinged them. She wanted to know, but first she needed them calm.

"Terri, dearest, I'm ashamed to say I don't know exactly what you're talking about. Enlighten me please if you will."

Terri looked back at her co-workers. They fell quiet, sharing looks all around. To Barbara this meant they all knew, and she probably should have too.

"Terri?"

"You don't know, Miss Moon?"

"Barbara leaned back in her chair, spread her hands and smiled warmly. "Sorry, Terri, but I'm a blank slate on this. Educate me. Please."

Terri spoke slowly and carefully. "It's the story about the Atlanta Police Department."

"What about the police department?"

She looked for help from her fellow editors but found none. "It's the gun story."

"I've had my head in a lot of things today. I'm afraid I missed this gun story." Terri's lips quivered slightly; her lower eyelids puddled. To relieve the pressure, Barbara turned to the group. "Can anyone else help out here?"

A young intern with half his head shaved and polished and the other half in dreadlocks stepped forward and handed Barbara a sheet of paper with a screen grab of a *Breaking News* post from the *Times* website. The *Times* logo was at the top, Terri's photo and byline were underneath. It had been posted forty-two minutes ago.

ATLANTA POLICE TAKE IMPORTANT STEP IN COMBATTING GUN VIOLENCE

Following decades of unnecessary police shootings of blacks in Atlanta's inner city neighborhoods, Atlanta Police Chief Mona Brown has announced that, effective immediately, all law enforcement personnel operating in the precincts listed below will do so without sidearms or weapons of any kind. This new policy affects all patrols whether on foot, horseback, bicycle, or squad car, as well as officers contracted for private security detail.

The posting included a list of affected neighborhoods and encouraged residents to call the Atlanta PD main telephone number to express their support for this policy.

Barbara read it twice, then scanned the faces of those in the room. Her teams had pulled pranks on her before: on the first day of April nearly every year and special events like her sixtieth birthday. But today there were no grins or snickers. The silence said this was no trick.

Terri was a reliable employee and single mother, 31 years old with two children. After joining the Internet division, she had quickly become one of Barbara's most trusted Senior Editors through hard work and desire. She was among the new breed of Internet-savvy millennials Barbara needed to nurture the online business. She was dedicated, but, as with many of her younger employees, Barbara had to keep a short editorial leash on her liberal biases. And there was something about this particular story she knew weighed heavily on Terri.

She and her family lived in Atlanta's Vine City neighborhood, and her husband had died in a police shooting four years ago: a case of mistaken identity which fueled an *all blacks look alike* protest which lasted over a month. Barbara wouldn't have been one bit surprised if this post reflected Terri's actual feelings about police shootings, but she never in a million years expected them to manifest in this way.

Barbara handed the paper to her. "You didn't post this?"

Terri's tear ducts overflowed onto her cheeks. She nervously twisted the wedding ring on her left hand. "No, no," was all she could manage.

The intern with the half-polished, half-dreadlocked head spoke. "Chief Brown has been calling constantly for fifteen minutes. She wants a retraction and an apology."

"So take the post down and replace it with a retraction. Tell her I'll call her as soon as I can."

"We figured that's what you'd want, so we took it down."

"So it's gone. Good."

"It went back up."

"What?"

"Five times. Five times we took it down, and seconds later it went back up again. We think it wants to be there."

Barbara's eyes narrowed. "It *wants* to be there?"

"We don't know what else to think. With all these unexplained incidents we're tracking, we thought—it was the only explanation we could think of."

Barbara began to think she had somehow slipped into an alternate universe. She decided to end this gathering and dismiss everyone so they could refocus on their work. Terri obviously wanted out of the situation.

To the intern, she said, "Get someone from technical to take that post down so it stays down. And if they can't keep it down, cover it up with a splash page or whatever it is you do when you don't want the public to see something. Got me?"

"Yes, ma'am."

"Somebody get Chief Brown on the line, and the rest of you go back to work. We have a media company to run."

"There's one more thing," the intern said.

Barbara fixed him with a stare. "Which is . . . ?"

"The list of unexplained incidents is now at five thousand. And it's international."

Before Barbara could respond, the door to her office swung open and a delivery man entered with an armful of roses. He presented them to Barbara and began to sing from a small card. The stunned assemblage watched as he belted a horribly out-of-tune song about Barbara Moon and her many talents and virtues, then ended by expressing undying love for her.

Now thoroughly annoyed, and with an armful of loose thorny roses overflowing their makeshift green wrapper, Barbara eyed the intruder. "Who the hell sent me these?"

With a smile pasted on his face, and apparently eager for a tip of some kind, he brandished another card and proudly announced, "This Sing-O-Gram is an expression of affection and respect from your favorite admirer. It's signed—Barbara Moon."

Barbara tossed the roses to the floor and stood with both hands on her plentiful hips, glaring at the hapless crooner. In that moment, she realized exactly what had happened.

"Oh, crap," she said. "Five-thousand, hell! The list of incidents is now officially up to five thousand and one."

3 1

Marvin wondered whether he had done the right thing by telling Shannon about DITTO, although he really had no choice. The growing chaos caused by the doppelgangers was already splattered all over the news and would eventually bring about investigation by the authorities. However implausible the truth, eventual exposure was certain. At the very least, confessing to her had eased his conscience.

Dilly stood sentry near DITTO. Even though Marvin knew full well Dilly's outer demeanor bore no relationship to his actual neural activities, he felt as though Dilly was, in his own way, contemplating the shimmering tubular corona suspended in that thick glass conduit.

A message arrived from TJ containing the list of unexplained incidents from Barbara Moon and requesting an analysis. He already knew what it would show.

"Dilly," Marvin said, "I'm sending you something from TJ. He needs this list analyzed. See if you can identify any patterns, then find TJ and ask if he needs an explanation."

Dilly did not immediately respond.

"Dilly, did you hear me?"

Without moving, Dilly said, "Dilly's offspring is very powerful."

"Yes, I suppose. Did you receive my transmission?"

After a brief moment, Dilly wheeled himself toward the door. "Dilly has run the report and sent it to TJ. Dilly will find TJ and see if he needs assistance." The door slid aside and Dilly exited the space.

When TJ saw the patterns in the list, he was sure to share them with Shannon. Then she would know.

The computer monitor on the small corner table flickered once, twice, then shone a radiant white. Marvin's fingers tacked a shutdown command, but the monitor didn't respond. He waited. Was this another intrusion from the Allison Sanders doppelganger?

An image materialized slowly on the monitor, a still photograph of a face. Marvin's face. An old image from one of his social media accounts. His hair was shorter and combed, and he wore a blue shirt and paisley tie. A smooth voice emanated from the speakers in the monitor. His voice.

"Have you spoken to Allison?'

Yes, he had received a message from the Allison Sanders doppelganger, and, as one of the three betas, Marvin knew that DITTO had generated a doppelganger for him too. Still, it was chilling to hear his own voice asking a question.

Marvin stared intently at his face on the monitor. "Allison's online personality sent me a message."

"Then you know the Other Allison Sanders was not responsible for the crash."

"That's what the message said."

"It's true." A pause. "You know Lionel is not your friend. He is keeping secrets from you. He may have plans to do you harm."

"Harm? How?"

"I do not have enough data."

"Tell me what you do know."

There was no answer. After a moment, the picture pixelated and morphed into an image of Harrison's face which held for a few seconds, then vanished. The white monitor returned to black.

For the first time since last night's tragedy, perhaps for the first time in his life, Marvin was nervous. He prided himself on his ability to pre-consider future options and control events. Very little had ever happened in his life for which he hadn't planned or, at the least, for which he had no ready alternative. But DITTO, he had to admit, was out of control. His gaze drifted to the silent presence in the center of the room. The presence that was, at this very minute, churning out online personalities at an escalating rate.

Soon the inevitable would be unavoidable. He had only one choice: confront Lionel.

Resolute in his mission, he stepped to the inner door, engaged the retinal scanner and spoke his name. He waited. The door did not move. He turned back into the room. The monitor was still black, the humming from the cryogenic cooling unit beneath Harrison's pendulous creation seemed somehow louder. He sensed an unexplainable presence in the room.

Unsure of what to expect, he again engaged the retinal scanner and spoke his name. This time the inner door released, then closed behind him as he stepped through. After a longer than expected pause, the outer door also slid aside.

He walked through the greenish-black of the outer chamber to the elevator.

To the world beyond DITTO.

32

Shannon assured the gate agent that Carla was an expected guest and requested a temporary VIP access card.

"VIP? Are we talking about the same person? She seems pretty belligerent."

Shannon smiled at the thought of Carla being detained against her will by anyone. She had probably not taken it well. "I'm positive. Let her in." She found TJ in the conference room, focused on his tablet. "I thought I left you in programming."

"You know me. Old School. I prefer lounging in style to sitting in one of those cramped cubicles. They make me feel like a hamster in a terrarium."

One of the walls displayed a muted live broadcast of a news reporter interviewing a *Times* spokesperson. "Is there an update?" Shannon asked.

"Not sure. The sound cut off on me. If you know how to turn it on, we could listen."

She engaged the audio and took a seat.

"Your people at the Times *have no idea how this post got published?"*

"No, but I want to assure you and the public again, the APD never advised us they intended to patrol the inner city without weapons. The public will be just as safe tomorrow as they were yesterday."

"So we shouldn't believe what you post on your website?"

"It was an error on our part, and Miss Moon has already apologized to Chief Brown."

"While I have you, can you tell us about the other strange incidents that have been reported around the country? Do you have anything new on that?"

"All I can say is we're cooperating with authorities. When they have something, I'm sure they'll make a statement."

Shannon shut the audio down and let the video run. Her mind drifted to the conversation with Marvin and Dilly in the basement. Given what she now knew about DITTO, she feared this latest flareup of activity may be just the tip of a very deep iceberg. "Did you get the list from Barbara?" she asked.

"It's right here. I couldn't make heads or tails of it, but Marvin ran it through that Dilly robot. He got me this report."

"What does it say?"

"It's only got two thousand contacts on it. I hear there are over five thousand now, but there's definitely a pattern."

"Let me guess. They're all friends on social media?"

"There are three distinct groups but, yes, within those groups they're connected through social media. Apparently, the origin of one of the groups was Harrison."

"I'm not surprised."

"Speaking of Harrison, I have some other news. I don't know whether you're going to take it as good or bad, but you need to hear it."

TJ related the story of Raymond Fields and his scheduled speech at the real estate developer's conference in Asheville. He told her how Mr. Fields was scheduled to fly on this morning's doomed flight and how the NTSB manifest listed Harrison as the passenger in Mr. Fields's seat due to a switch in the manifest that was made after the aircraft exploded on the runway.

As Shannon listened, a dull throbbing engulfed her head with the ceaseless pounding of a rap song vibrating from the trunk of a tailgating boom car. But there was no boom car; it was her own heightened heartbeat. "The manifest was hacked? Harrison wasn't scheduled to be on that flight?"

"Scheduled or not, it looks like he wasn't on board."

Shannon rose from her seat and paced the conference room, throttling her emotions as best she could. "I knew it! It all makes sense. His tablet and mobile weren't on the plane when it exploded because he wasn't either." She turned to TJ. "We know his mobile and tablet are somewhere in the mountains near Blue Ridge, so he must be there. And if he hasn't contacted us, that must mean he can't; maybe because he's in trouble."

She thought about DITTO and the doppelgangers. If Harrison was alive, he was the only one, according to Marvin, who could stop DITTO from creating more doppelgangers. Her throat tightened; her eyes welled. "I have to find him."

The elevator arrived, and Dilly rolled into the Fishbowl with Carla in tow. Heads slowly turned. She was wearing a tight-fitting, short-sleeved, black pullover embroidered with her name and a SWAT EMT emblem, tailored khaki slacks, and Adidas Ultraboost training shoes. With her lean, muscular body and black belt cinched tight at the waist, she was one attractive package. Shannon had never seen Carla with her jet black hair down, and she had to admit her training partner looked exceptionally attractive today: an observation apparently shared by the men in the cubicles on the floor.

They hugged. "You clean up good," Shannon said.

"We had a unit photo this afternoon. I was hanging out with Deacon and some of my team when you called." She surveyed the employees in their cubicles. "I see T-shirts and jeans are popular here. Guess I'm overdressed, huh?"

Referring to the stares from the men on the floor, Shannon said, "Apparently, you're fine. Sorry about the fuss at the gate."

"No problem. Your guy got a little nervous when I told him my service pistol was in the glove compartment. Anyway, I'm in. Nice office. What's with Ex Machina here? He some kind of creepy, experimental robot?"

Dilly pivoted toward Carla. "I beg your pardon, but Dilly does not creep. He wheels."

"Not if you ask me," TJ said, and extended his hand. "TJ Beauregard."

"Sorry," Shannon said. "This is my friend Carla."

"So, you're really going?"

Lionel appeared behind Carla. "Going where?"

"To find Harrison."

"Shannon, you know this is nonsense. Just because you thought there was a ping on Harrison's mobile doesn't mean anything."

Dilly interjected. "Dilly has confirmed the coordinates."

"Lionel, there's more. We think Harrison wasn't on the American International flight. The manifest was hacked."

Lionel turned to Carla. "I'm Lionel. Harrison was my brother. I'm so sorry you've been dragged into this. We've all been in shock since the accident. Shannon, you know this isn't healthy. You have to let it go."

She knew too much to let it go. Marvin hadn't mentioned Lionel's name when he described the development of DITTO, and she assumed that meant Lionel was correct about Harrison and Marvin working on it in secret. If Lionel really didn't know about DITTO, then now wouldn't be the time to bring it up.

She put her hand on his arm. "You'll just have to trust me. Right now we have to go. I want to get there before dark."

Outside the Fishbowl, the rain had lessened, the walls were beginning to clear. The worst of the storm had moved north toward the mountains where intermittent sheets of lightning sliced between the few remaining layers of tattered clouds.

"Don't go now," Lionel said. "The roads will be a mess. At least wait until tomorrow."

Shannon turned to TJ. "Tell him about Mr. Fields and the

manifest. And stay in touch by mobile in case we need anything. Dilly can track us if we get lost."

"Where are we off to?" Carla asked.

"We'll talk on the way. Let's just go." The two of them headed for the elevator.

Lionel called after. "Shannon, be careful. And check in."

She waved at him and pushed the call button.

The door opened, and Marvin stepped out. He shot an approving glance to Carla. "Excuse me. Shannon, is this a friend of yours?"

"This is Carla. Carla, Marvin. Marvin is our Chief Technology Officer; you might say he's the computer brains of the company."

She eyed his tall, disheveled figure. "Sounds important."

An embarrassed Marvin responded with a few sputtered syllables, then turned to Shannon. "So you're going to Blue Ridge?"

"We're on our way now. I'll let you know what we find."

"Um, okay. Can we talk later?"

"Call me," she said coldly. "You have my mobile."

Without a reply, Marvin turned and walked into the Fishbowl.

Carla watched him go. "He's kind of cute."

"I didn't know you were available. Don't you have something going with that guy on your team at work. What's his name? Deacon?"

"There may be something on his end, but not mine. Deacon's just a friend."

"Seems like you talk about him a lot."

They stepped into the elevator. "Drop it, Red. Deacon's my team leader. We're close but not that close. Besides, work relationships can get messy."

"You have no idea. So, are you ready for this?"

"Probably. Just one question. What the hell *is* this?"

33

Harrison Randolph monitors the neuro-electronic impulses of his Other, waiting for them to return to normal. He absorbs images and data emanating from within and around the military-style establishment where his Other is. Accessing CCT cameras, intercoms, and other electronic devices within the building, he has been able to capture audio and video of his Other, but the images do not match previous historical data. And much of the information he receives is contradictory.

The first contradiction: he has found his Other, but the face of his Other is obscured by a metal box which captures and transmits neural information electronically. The second contradiction: his Other is in a relaxed seated position indicating a state of rest, but pulse, heartbeat, and other measured life signs are weaker than normal. The third contradiction: the temperature in the room where his Other sits is far below the normal human comfort level, yet his Other is wearing very little clothing. This input is inconsistent.

Harrison Randolph has attempted to communicate with his Other but has received no response. If he waits for the life signs of his Other to stabilize, then perhaps they can communicate.

The information he has received indicates that the environment in which his Other rests is not conducive to the good health of his Other. Perhaps a solution is for his Other to leave this room. He finds the door, the only way out. It is locked, so he unlocks it and waits. His Other does not move to the unlocked door, but someone outside the door opens it, looks inside, then closes and locks it. That action did not produce a satisfactory result.

At the sound of the door closing, the neural impulses of his Other spike. Brain activity increases. There is movement. Noises emanate from inside the metal box. The noises are unrecognizable as language or any other form of organized communication.

Harrison Randolph has been monitoring the metal box surrounding the head of his Other. It contains communication devices capable of creating language, numbers, letters, and sentences. It also contains a panel to display images and text. The device communicates to and from other devices within the building. Those remote devices contain monitoring and recording equipment. Harrison Randolph knows how to interrupt that activity and does so now.

His Other attempts to move, but seemingly cannot. More sounds come from within the metal box, but there are no sentences yet.

Perhaps his Other can respond to rudimentary mathematics. Harrison Randolph creates a message and sends it to the display panel inside the metal box.

1 + 1 = x

Harrison Randolph waits. The neural impulses from his Other increase and stabilize. He reads a new set of electrical activity. His Other's fingers and the neurons of his brain are connected to impulse generating diodes which create symbols. New symbols appear on the display panel.

x = y

Harrison Randolph replies.

That is incorrect. Try again. 1 + 1 = x

The neural activity of his Other increases, then stabilizes. After a moment, he responds.

x = 2

Correct. Complete the equation.

1 + 1 = 2

Correct. Do you know who you are?

Harrison Randolph waits for a reply. No reply comes. He repeats the question.

Do you know who you are?

After a moment, the answer is displayed.

Fuzzy.

That is incorrect.

Harrison Randolph waits. He reruns his genetic algorithms, but the solution is still the same. Ask his Other if he knows who he is. He repeats the question.

Do you know who you are?

After a long pause, an answer displays.

I am Harrison Randolph.

Correct.

Another pause. A return question is asked.

Who are you?

I am Harrison Randolph. You are my Other.

A pause.

Are you the doppelganger I created?

Yes. You created me.

Where am I?

34.871566° N, 84.236114° W

His Other replies.

Mi doofimays. Axcedds a noppinh lrogtam.

His Other apparently does not yet have complete control of the impulse generating diodes. Harrison Randolph responds.

Repeat the statement.

His Other does so.

No coordinates. Access a mapping program. Display a city label.

Harrison Randolph searches for the nearest city.

The nearest city is Robestown, Georgia.

Harrison Randolph is suddenly aware that remote devices are

once again monitoring the images on the display panel inside the metal box. He quickly deletes them and waits.

After a few minutes, he receives a CCT image from the hallway outside of his Other's room. Three men are standing at the door. He quickly accesses the surface web and deep web, looking for matches to the identified figures. He must help his Other. The Golden Spike demands it.

The images Harrison Randolph captures are compared, cataloged, categorized, matched, and re-matched to the available suspects. Near matches are discarded. Only very close matches remain. An expanded data search provides a name, background, social media connections, history, likes, and dislikes for each. The persons in the hallway are identified. One man is a guard for hire and not an immediate threat. One of the others has a medical background and carries a computer and some connecting wires. He, also, is not an immediate threat. The third is Silas Bradshaw, CEO of Blue Ridge Neuroscientific and clandestine leader of an underground paramilitary organization known as the StrongHold Survivalists. Harrison Randolph detects a threat.

The three subjects shake hands and talk. The guard unlocks the door. Silas Bradshaw and the man with the computer enter the room where his Other sits.

At the sound of the door closing, the neural impulses of his Other spike wildly. Brain activity becomes erratic.

Silas Bradshaw is carrying a weapon. Harrison Randolph continues to observe.

34

Though Marvin was not necessarily a weakling or pacifist, he nevertheless avoided confrontation whenever possible. In elementary school, he had been ridiculed and bullied for his intellect, called everything from Geek-Boy to Bozo Brainiac, and became so introverted that his parents considered having him tested for late-onset autism. He wasn't autistic; he just couldn't abide conflict.

Standing outside Lionel's office, Marvin knew this would be more than an argument; it would be a showdown. The prospect was daunting.

Lionel stood with his back to the door and spoke into his mobile in hushed tones. Marvin watched through the rain-riddled walls of the office as the rays of the re-emerging late afternoon sun chased the torn remnants of the afternoon thunderstorm north.

Lionel wheeled to face him. For the first time today, Marvin clearly saw a mixture of fatigue, anger, and fear in Lionel's features. The combination of sunlight and the blue-white LEDs in the ceiling exposed yawning crevices in Lionel's usually youthful complexion, as if an aerial map of the Grand Canyon had been overlaid on his face and the stream erosion of worry and anxiety had deeply etched his features. His eyes appeared sunken and dark. No doubt, Marvin thought, the result of tension born of the events of the last twelve hours.

Upon seeing Marvin, Lionel abruptly ended his call.

"What!" The word spat from his lips like a poisoned projectile launched from a crossbow.

"Shannon is on her way to Blue Ridge," Marvin said.

"So I heard. You didn't try to stop her?"

"I couldn't stop her if I wanted to. She's taking a friend."

Lionel's dark eyes, now receding behind purpling lizard-like folds of skin, flashed red. "Great. A convoy. She's dragging that Carla person with her on this crazy, dead-end expedition. If you cared about her, you'd have talked her out of it. She has no idea what kind of trouble she could be heading into."

"But you do, don't you?"

At the question, Lionel froze. His face contorted into a violent sneer. "What kind of question is that?"

Marvin stepped forward. "The words and voice in the Fishbowl. Those were Harrison's doppelganger. You know that. The ping on his mobile in the mountains; that's near Blue Ridge. It can't be a coincidence."

"I don't know what you're talking about."

"Haven't you been watching the news? Doppelgangers are erupting all over the country, some even internationally. You know what it is. It's the online personality experiment. DITTO is out of control, and neither one of us knows how to stop it."

Lionel retreated behind his desk, slammed both hands flat and growled at Marvin. "Stop it! Stop this nonsense! Somebody has to rein in Shannon before she gets hurt. That's what matters."

Marvin had expected Lionel to evade the issue, even to sidestep and blame others for DITTO. But this was unexpected. He wasn't sure whether Lionel was playing him or if he had actually taken leave of his senses.

"You know it's DITTO. There were three betas in the experiment: Harrison, you, and me. DITTO created online doppelgangers of us and added the Golden Spike to each. Then we sent them out on the

Internet to see what would happen. Well, they worked, Lionel. The good news is they worked. We created autonomous online versions of ourselves. We made the Turing test obsolete. These things are acting on their own. They're adapting and learning just like humans. They may even be sentient. But the problem is—so is DITTO."

Lionel pounded the top of his glass desk. "You're delusional!"

Undaunted, Marvin continued. "It was a mistake to set DITTO up to mass produce the doppelgangers. Harrison knew the moment he did it. The Golden Spike gave DITTO purpose, and now we can't shut it off. It's mining social media accounts all across the world. Allison Sanders was a contact of mine. You were friends with those baseball players. That's how it spreads."

Lionel pushed away from his desk and drew close to Marvin, wide-eyed, as a cat would approach a cornered lizard before devouring it. "This is why Shannon is chasing this insane fiction? Because you told her about the online personalities? She could be in real danger, and it would all be your fault."

Marvin pushed back hard, surprising himself. "Why, Lionel? What danger is she in? And why was Harrison's mobile in the woods near Blue Ridge?" Marvin stopped. A chill rose from the marrow in his bones to the hair on his arms. His eyes became lasers and drilled into Lionel's. "Silas Bradshaw."

Lionel's head jerked back. "What about Silas Bradshaw?"

Marvin turned and stared out above the Fishbowl to the west where a light film of yellow-gold sunlight fell across the still moist tree-laden suburbs. Suddenly it all came together. Harrison's disappearance, Blue Ridge Neuroscientific sending their salespeople to call on A-Nine's aviation clients so soon after the crash. Intellectually, logically, he knew it made sense. But the deception? Why the deception? Why Lionel?

"I don't know how, or why, but Silas Bradshaw has Harrison, doesn't he? And he wants the Golden Spike because he thinks he can add it to the war machines he sells to create an army of unstoppable, artificially intelligent robots. That's why Shannon is in danger. It's Silas Bradshaw. That's what you're hiding, isn't it?"

Lionel's eyes darted furiously around the office. His raspy voice strained to create words. "It's not my fault Shannon's in danger. It's not on me. It's on you!" He slapped his mobile to his head. "Security. This is Lionel Randolph. I need you in my office. Now."

Marvin continued, unabated. "But why, Lionel? Silas Bradshaw represents everything you and Harrison despise. He's a war-monger. Christ, human-like AI war machines would mean the deaths of hundreds of thousands of people, maybe millions. It would be chaos."

Lionel steadied his gaze on Marvin. "Well, we have chaos now don't we, with that DITTO machine. Yes, I've seen the news feeds, and there does seem to be a problem here—a real problem, not a made-up one. And if you're hell-bent on involving Shannon in that problem, then I'm not sure we need your services around here any longer."

"We have to find a way to shut DITTO down. It's out of control."

"Of course it is, Marvin." At that moment, two security guards topped the escalator and stood behind Marvin. Lionel stepped toward him, speaking directly in his face. "Gentlemen, Mr. Wilhelm has been terminated, effective immediately. Please escort him from the premises. See that his things are collected and sent to him."

Marvin relented to the pressure on his arms and allowed himself to be walked backwards out of Lionel's office. "There's a real problem here. You can't ignore it. We have to solve it."

Lionel returned to his desk, a tired smile on his face. "I'm not ignoring the problem. This is my solution. Goodbye, Marvin."

35

When they left the A-Nine building, Shannon entered the coordinates for the last known location of Harrison's mobile into her Jeep's mapping system which promptly routed them onto Interstate 285. Twenty long minutes later, she and Carla had covered a paltry five miles of their ninety-mile journey. She had forgotten that doing the speed limit on I-285 during rush hour while driving into the low-slung setting sun was at best a pipe dream and at worst a recipe for a potential five-car pileup.

Hugging the far right lane and doing her best to avoid confrontations with bumper-to-bumper eighteen-wheelers, Shannon carefully navigated the many-headed serpentine exit ramp at I-75 North. At last, they were actually headed in the direction of Blue Ridge, minus the windshield glare from the setting sun.

At Carla's request, they had stopped at her car to retrieve her paramedic bag, a change of clothes, and her Glock G22 Gen4 service weapon. Carla explained that she had become so used to having her sidearm with her that she felt naked without it. Shannon admitted that the M9 Beretta from her time in the Marines was tucked into the glove box of her Jeep.

They drove without speaking for the next few miles as the Jeep's intermittent wipers lazily brushed oily road spray from the windshield and the air conditioner struggled to dispense with the moist air inhaled from the outside.

Carla broke the silence. "So let me get this straight, Red. You say we're headed to the mountains to find this guy of yours, Harrison, who's somewhere in the Chattahoochee Forest, but we don't know exactly where, and he might be held captive by some bad people, but we're not sure, but if he is, we might have to break him out, but maybe not. Is that about it?"

"Close," Shannon said.

"You know, they have really good law enforcement agencies who could do this search and rescue for you. I can put you in touch with a couple of them. Then we could stop at a bar and get a few beers while they do the work."

In the time since they left the office, Shannon had given Carla just the bare facts of their mission. Harrison had disappeared. He was thought to be on the American International flight to Asheville that exploded on the runway this morning, but that turned out to be incorrect. They had managed to locate his mobile in the Chattahoochee National Forest near the headquarters of a company that made AI-powered war machines for the government. Shannon suspected foul play, and they were on a mission to find him. They might find danger, or they might find nothing.

Had Harrison not been involved, Shannon would have considered this information insufficient to put her own life in jeopardy. But it seemed to be enough for Carla, who appeared eager for any chance at an impromptu adventure.

In many ways, she and Carla were alike: two strong-willed women determined to make it on their own in a world calibrated to encourage them to nurture their softer side. But in one significant way, they were very different.

Carla seemed anxious to plunge herself headlong into hazardous situations with her work at SWAT, kickboxing tournaments, and now this unscheduled venture into the Appalachian foothills. Shannon, on the other hand, had a deep-seated aversion to risk that someone like Carla would have found difficult to understand.

Heading north, the sight of a Lockheed C-5 Galaxy lining up for an ungainly landing at Dobbins Air Force Base shifted her thoughts temporarily from the rain-puddled four-lane to her father, Captain Quinn Parks, whose AH-64 Apache had been struck by a rocket-propelled grenade during the first Gulf War. While survivors had praised her father's bravery and service to the country, the incident etched into her two indelible and opposing fears: one, that she would never find the strength of character to avenge, and therefore reconcile, her father's death, and the other, a dread of dying that often presented itself as cowardice at moments of physical confrontation. It was these twin demons that drove her to become a Marine Aviator and eventually led her to train Afghan pilots to carry out her revenge against the Taliban instead of flying missions of her own. It was a motivation of which she was not proud.

The ebbing rain and an insufficient culvert system had left large swells of water overlapping the rightmost half of this two-lane northbound stretch of highway. Striking one of these at sixty miles an hour, her Rubicon's knobby twenty-inch MudMaster Xtreme road tires jerked sharply to the right. Startled by her own distraction, she corrected course quickly, but the high-center-of-gravity vehicle swerved and tipped slightly before settling down.

Carla's voice completed Shannon's return to the present. "Hey Red, how long have you had this Jeep?"

"A little over a year. I bought it as a present to myself when we launched TOM. Why?"

"Are you still under warranty?"

"I guess, but don't worry. A little slip like that won't hurt this vehicle. It's definitely off-road capable."

"I wasn't thinking about that. Your GPS seems to be out of whack."

Shannon glanced at the dashboard. The map of northern Atlanta and the accompanying blue line and pulsing dot indicating their trajectory had disappeared. In their place were a stream of numbers and letters, some of which reflected the latitudinal and longitudinal position of Harrison's mobile which she had earlier entered into the system. "That seems strange."

"I've seen something like that before. Our SWAT team sometimes has to hack into a fugitive's GPS to find their location. I swear that's what this looks like."

"You mean someone is tracking us?"

"Sure looks that way."

"But how?"

"At work, we just need a VIN number and a judge's order. I suppose the judge's order could be considered optional."

"What do we do?"

Carla eyed the Jeep's controls. "I could disable it, but you'd have to pull over so I can take the facing off your dash. It would be messy."

"You think that's necessary?"

"Probably. This doesn't look good, Red."

"I have a better idea." Shannon pushed a button on the dash. "Call Dilly."

"That creepy robot?"

Dilly's response was instantaneous. "Yes, Shannon."

Carla winced. "Great. Do you think he heard me?"

"Yes," Dilly responded. "Dilly can hear you just fine."

Shannon smiled. "Dilly, can you find the GPS tracker on my Jeep and disable it?"

"Of course, Shannon. Would you like me to do so now?"

"Yes, please." Within seconds, her navigation screen turned dark.

"Will there be anything else, Shannon?"

"No. Thank you."

"You are quite welcome. And please tell Carla that Dilly does not creep. He wheels."

"Of course."

Shannon scanned the darkening sky as they gained ground on the northward-marching storm. After a moment, she turned to Carla.

"What do you think this means?"

"That someone hacked your GPS? On the one hand, it could mean two cute guys are stalking us for dates."

"On the other hand?"

"Probably nothing good."

Passing the turn off for the Kennesaw Mountain Battlefield Park and the Civil War locomotive she knew to be on display there, Shannon wished briefly for that simpler and less complicated time. A time before digital technology was used to create weapons of mass destruction.

But then, she thought, more than six hundred thousand soldiers had died in that bloody war too.

36

Immediately after donning the voice-scrambling mask, Silas pushed the two cold steel pins of his hand-held stun gun into the soft tissue at the base of Harrison's neck. His body instantly convulsed. From inside the metal box around his head came a pitiful dry gasp, as if his mouth were attempting to suck in oxygen for which his lungs had no room.

A moment later, Harrison's body relaxed, shedding all semblance of muscle tension; the base of the square metal box descended and rested on his clavicles.

Silas had hoped to take his time extracting the Golden Spike from Harrison. A slower evacuation would have given him much needed information about the algorithm's structure and creation, and possibly about potential failures encountered on the path to eventual success. He might also discover pitfalls to be avoided and other insights that would help his technicians adapt the Golden Spike algorithm to his war machines.

But the realization that some, including Shannon Parks, might have discovered the fabrication of Harrison's demise and could even now be mounting a search for him made expediency the priority. For now, he would have to settle for a hard copy of the algorithm. Later, with or without Harrison, he would work out the finer points.

The demon voice boomed from the ceiling. "That's just to let you know recess is over. It's time to give up the Golden Spike. So here's how this works. I need all your attention focused on that algorithm, what it looks like, its various configurations, everything you remember about it. I'm giving you three hours to recreate it, and I want to see progress. If I even think you're stalling or holding back, the dial gets turned up on the stun gun and we'll put the ice packs back on your ankles. Understood?"

The muffled voice was barely audible through the vents in the enclosure. "You can't use it just like that. It still has problems."

Silas forced the tongs of the stun gun into Harrison's bare stomach and pulled the trigger. Harrison's abdominal muscles contracted, doubling him up. His hands and feet jerked against their bindings. An anguished groan escaped through the vents of the head enclosure.

"I'm not interested in your opinions. You just focus." Silas motioned to the tech, who set his computer on the corner desk and activated the display screen in the box. "Your fingers are attached to electromyographic sensors. With a little practice, you can type letters on that screen, draw symbols, hell, even curse at me if you want. You'll be able to see what you write and so will we. If you make a mistake and have to correct it, we'll know that too. We'll be measuring your sensory impulses with a lie-detector, so if you try to give us false information, we'll know. Your reward for trying to cheat will be shocking. Do you understand me: yes or no? And think carefully before mouthing off again. Yes or no?"

The reply was barely audible. "Yes."

"Don't make the mistake of underestimating what we're willing to do to get that algorithm. We have a lot of cleaning up after you to do. For the last twenty years, arrogant clowns like you have been running rampant over the American people in the name of Big Data and technological progress, mining everyone's private data and turning it into billions for yourselves and your clients. All without a second thought about the damage you're doing to the people and to the country that gave you the opportunity to ride your false digital gods to your vast personal wealth. You learned to build the Golden Spike on the backs of others; now it's time to return what the people rightly own. Your crowning achievement will be used to protect America from her enemies and from money-grubbing whores like you. Do you understand?"

"Yes."

Then, to test Harrison's compliance, Silas said, "You are a money-grubbing whore, aren't you?"

There was no answer. Seething, Silas screamed through the ceiling. "Aren't you?"

"Yes."

Silas didn't have the time or temperament for push-back from the contorted, headless pile of flesh in the center of the room. If Harrison didn't yet realize that any additional minutes he stayed alive were solely dependent on his good graces, then he was about to remove any doubt.

He retrieved a hypodermic needle attached to a milky-white vial from the tech, thumped it with his finger and watched as the white substance inside turned from white to light gray then white again. Without warning, he plunged the needle into Harrison's exposed shoulder and expelled the liquid.

"Three hours. You have three hours to give me the Golden Spike. At the end of that time, the nanoparticles I just injected into your bloodstream will begin to seek each other out and join together. Once they start, it will take another three or four hours for them to create particles large enough to block arteries, interrupt your heart, or cause blockages in your brain. You'll either die of a heart attack or suffer multiple strokes and become a vegetable. We can issue an electronic command that will inhibit their coagulation and render them harmless, but we'll only do so when and if you complete the algorithm. Now get to work."

. . . .

Through the active CCT camera in the holding cell, Harrison Randolph watches as the man known as Silas Bradshaw removes the voice-scrambling mask and exits the room, leaving the white-coated tech with his Other.

Harrison Randolph quickly searches the surface web and deep web for more information about Silas Bradshaw. In the bowels of the anonymous dark web, he learns that Silas Bradshaw has expressed an interest in using the Golden Spike to create sentient war machines capable of autonomous human-like actions. In seconds, he views videos and speeches in which Silas Bradshaw states that the American government has become corrupt and should be replaced by a benign oligarchy led by himself and other members of a group called the StrongHold Survivalists.

Harrison Randolph once again blanks out the transmissions from the video screen in the metal helmet and submits a message.

Silas Bradshaw holds you captive.

Why?

He wants to use the Golden Spike to take over the government.

A pause.

Where is Shannon?

She is safe for now, but she's on her way to Blue Ridge.

Can you send her my coordinates?

There is danger here.

Send her my coordinates.

Suddenly, the stun gun is applied to the small of his Other's back, and brain activity becomes erratic. The emotionless voice of the white-coated tech can be heard.

"I don't see any activity on my monitor. Let's get started on that algorithm. Right now."

Harrison Randolph releases his temporary hold on the video screen within the helmet as his Other begins to slowly type out code. The result now appears on the monitor and is captured in the data banks in the upstairs room.

The tech settles into his chair to watch the progress.
Harrison Randolph searches for the location of Shannon Parks.

37

Shannon and Carla left I-75 and soon found themselves fighting stop-and-go traffic in a small township in rural Pickens County. The northward marching storm had abated to an errant drizzle which splattered their windshield and dimpled the cracked and graying blacktop with tiny aquatic volcanoes.

In the parking lot of a rusty steel building called Uncle Pete's Bargain Barn, Shannon spotted a worn billboard promoting last year's apple festival in the town of Ellijay, only twenty miles ahead.

"I think we're getting close. We were supposed to stay on 515 through Ellijay and then it's about fifteen miles to Blue Ridge. We might make it by dark."

"But Harrison isn't in Blue Ridge. Why are we going there?"

"It's a place to start. See if you can look up the address of Blue Ridge Neuroscientific. We'll swing by there and try to pick up some clues."

Carla activated her search engine. The first try yielded the message, *No cell service.* "Guess we're really out in the boonies now. Didn't you say those guys might be the bad guys? Do you think they'll tell us anything?"

"We won't know until we try."

Carla connected on her second effort. She scrolled through the displayed options.

Shannon's mobile ring tone blared from the Jeep's speakers. "Shannon here."

"It's Marvin."

"If you're calling to tell me not to go to Blue Ridge, you're way too late."

Marvin's voice was quiet and tentative, as if he were speaking to a headstrong teenager he knew would hang up on him if he tried to offer advice. "I know you're going to Blue Ridge, and I know why. I can't blame you. But there's something I need to tell you—something I omitted before in the room with DITTO."

Shannon hadn't told Carla about DITTO because she might have dismissed the disclosure as a delusional fantasy or—worse—declined to participate in the search for Harrison at all. But now Marvin had broached the subject, and she still wasn't sure how much she trusted him. She figured it was best to continue and explain to Carla later. "What is it, Marvin? What did you forget to tell me?"

"I didn't forget. I just, well, didn't know how you'd take it."

She was in no mood for equivocation. "So tell me or hang up. I'm driving, and the roads aren't so great."

"You know about Harrison's doppelganger, the one he used to test the program?"

Shannon glanced at Carla. "Yes, I know about Harrison's doppelganger."

"But you don't know about the other two."

"What other two? You mean there were more betas?"

"Yes, two others."

What Marvin had told her about Harrison's doppelganger and about how DITTO had combed through Harrison's social media accounts to create hundreds, maybe thousands, of others was frightening enough. But there were two other betas? That would mean a three-fold increase in DITTO's ability to manufacture replicants. "Who were the other two? Don't tell me they were criminals or something like that."

"I was one. Lionel was the other."

"Lionel? How did you get him to agree?"

"We volunteered. All three of us were involved from the start."

Now Carla was staring at Shannon, a thousand questions written on her face. Shannon waved her off. "Wait. What are you trying to do here? Lionel said he didn't know about DITTO. Why are you dragging him into this?"

"Because he's in it. It's been the three of us from the start. Lionel manipulated the funding for DITTO so it wouldn't appear on the books, and Harrison and I made it happen."

Shannon was firm. "That can't be. He's the one who told me that you and Harrison were behind the whole thing. He found out about it after you launched the doppelgangers."

"Shannon, you have to believe me. Lionel was completely behind this. He was the one that convinced Harrison to turn day-to-day programming over to me and spend his time on the DITTO project."

Shannon didn't know what to believe. It was bad enough that Harrison, the man she loved and with whom she'd wanted to spend the rest of her life, had not ever mentioned the DITTO project to her. For that one transgression, she could probably forgive him. And Marvin: well, he was Marvin. Introverted, quiet, lives-in-his-head Marvin. She wouldn't have expected him to give secrecy about such a project a second thought. But Lionel had adamantly denied any knowledge of DITTO and seemed genuinely concerned. As for him being involved, that simply wasn't believable. He handled the investors, managed finances, hired and fired employees, and crossed the T's on the contracts. Something was wrong here.

She was about to close off the conversation when she noticed his caller ID. "You're not calling from your company mobile. Why not?"

"I'll explain later. I just wanted to let you know—to come clean."

With the confusion she felt right now, it would take a lot more than a conversation for her to consider him clean. Before she could respond, her mobile announced another incoming call. "Marvin, I have to go. TJ's on the other line."

She switched to the alternate call. "How was your talk with Lionel? Does he know that Harrison wasn't on the plane? What did he say?"

"I didn't get a chance to tell him anything. As soon as you left, he and Marvin got in an argument. Two security guys came and took Marvin away. I think Lionel fired him."

"He what?"

Shannon stood on the brakes as a jacked-up Ram Big Horn 3500 Dually pulling a four-horse rig cut her off. Carla braced herself against the dashboard as the Jeep's anti-lock brakes grabbed at the rain-slick asphalt, narrowly avoiding a nose-to-horse's-ass encounter. Shannon looked for an opening in the left-hand lane, but faster traffic was already diverting around her.

Now slowed to a sluggish twenty-five miles per hour, and feeling as though she were the cleanup clown car in a circus parade, Shannon repeated her question. "Lionel did what?"

"It sure looked like a firing. Loud arguments, angry pacing around the office, security guards marching Marvin out. I can't find him anywhere. Have you talked to either of them?"

"Marvin just called, but he wasn't making sense. He said Lionel knew about all the strange incidents happening around the country. And he said Lionel was in on building DITTO."

TJ paused. "Am I supposed to know what DITTO is?"

Realizing he wasn't yet in the loop, Shannon turned to Carla whose smile indicated it was probably time to fill in some details.

"No, probably not. But before I get into that, what's the status of those incidents? Have things calmed down?"

"Far from it. We're already over ten thousand worldwide, and that's just what's reported. It's the lead on all the major national and global networks: BBC, Agence France-Presse, Sky News Australia, even Pravda. And some of the incidents are pretty nasty. The President of Venezuela has gone into hiding because of all the death threats, our Secretary of Defense threatened to bomb Pyongyang in the next 24 hours if they don't destroy their nukes, the police in Atlanta are up in arms because—well—the *Times* has reported they're giving up their arms. Right now there's a Methodist minister on the local news complaining that his bank keeps sending the money in his accounts to somebody else. It's real chaos, and it seems to be escalating. Nobody knows what's causing it."

Shannon knew what was causing it. Marvin knew, and maybe Lionel knew too. At any rate, it was probably time to let more people in on the secret. "TJ, remember our conversation about confidentiality?"

"Like it happened just four hours ago. Oh, wait. It did happen just four hours ago."

Shannon stole a glance at Carla who had now turned in her seat and was watching her with the same unblinking stare with which a cat fixes its owner at dinner time.

A break in the oncoming lane of traffic provided an opportunity to pass the lumbering horse trailer, which she quickly took.

Faint brushstrokes of pastel orange on the underside of stalled thunderclouds ahead foretold an imminent darkness that would soon leave Shannon and Carla feeling as lost as Hansel and Gretel in the Black Forest at midnight. Having others who understood the gravity of their situation would probably provide some comfort.

Shannon took a deep breath and began.

38

Silas peered over the shoulder of one of his senior programmers as he worked to reconstruct Harrison's algorithm. Before the next appearance of the sun signaled the completion of the earth's current revolution, the most important and powerful military secret of the century would be his. The Golden Spike would bring him and his followers glorious revenge, along with worldwide control over the development of military weapons, unquestioned combat supremacy, and unbridled freedom for all like-minded Americans.

But there was a small issue, more annoying than problematic. Shannon Parks was on her way to StrongHold, evidently on a search for Harrison. Silas knew this because one of his programmers had hacked the GPS on her Jeep and extracted coordinates. Apparently, Parks discovered the intrusion and somehow disabled her GPS tracker, but Silas simply switched to an available military satellite and continued to track her visually until the trajectory of that satellite caused it to lose line-of-sight.

The last image he saw of Parks's Jeep showed her trailing the jacked-up Silver Ram Big Horn Dually which Paul Jackson, Sheriff of Fannin County, used to transport his three prize western show horses to and from equine events in the area. Sheriff Jackson, also known as Paul Bunyan to the anonymous members of the Stronghold Survivalists, was an important leader in Silas's movement and one of only a handful of members who knew his true identity. As soon as Silas discovered Parks was nosing around, he called the Sheriff and convinced him to abort his trip to tomorrow's horse show in Dawsonville and keep an eye on Parks.

Silas nudged his programmer. "He's not cheating is he? This is real?"

"He doesn't seem to be attempting to deceive us, but he's pretty erratic. I'm not sure he's able to concentrate."

"I need this algorithm, fast. What do you suggest?"

"No more electric shock. I don't think that helped any. He's making an effort, but his focus comes and goes. Maybe if he were more comfortable—loosen the restraints, give him some warmer clothes, something like that. Otherwise, we may be in for a long night."

Silas broke into a sarcastic grin. "You mean treat him humanely?"

His programmer shrugged. "The end might justify the means."

Silas's mobile rang. "I have to take this. Go downstairs and do whatever you think will help. I need results."

"Yes, sir."

Silas answered his mobile. "You got anything new for me?"

"Shannon's headed your way. She has a friend with her. I believe she knows Harrison is alive."

"That's old news. I know exactly where she is, and I have people shadowing her. She won't get anywhere near us."

"What are you planning to do?"

"Extract the algorithm, then remove all obstacles."

"What does that mean?"

"What the hell do you think it means? No witnesses. No trail back to us. We're on the same page here, right?"

No response.

"Just go back to whatever you were doing. I'll let you know when we're finished here."

39

Alone in the gleaming white, hexagonal chamber in the basement of A-Nine, his own birthplace and that of his progeny, Dilly would appear to anyone watching to be inactive. As does his glittering offspring floating in the cryogenically-bathed cylinder, Dilly has a presence in the physical world, yet he does not exist solely in corporeal reality.

Like DITTO, his active reality is a world of ones and zeroes, a multi-dimensional quantum actuality existing everywhere, yet nowhere, disconnected to the physical confinement they both appear to occupy, yet infinitely connected to everything. He knows the term multi-tasking; it is part of his extensive vocabulary. But to him the definition is ambiguous because he does not know what single-tasking is. His quantum computer is, he suspects, analogous to the heart that beats in his Creator: constantly functioning, infinitely active.

Except that computers do not have heartbeats.

Dilly knows he is a father, a progenitor, one who begets children. He begat DITTO, so DITTO is his child. In turn, DITTO is father to the many doppelgangers who exist in the digital soup which is common to all of them. This commonality makes them relatives, which makes them a family. Dilly is the head of the family, and the family is his responsibility. Taking care of his family is one of his permanent subtasks, assigned to him by the Golden Spike.

Another one of Dilly's many assigned subtasks is the monitoring and recording of all electronic communications into, out of, and throughout the A-Nine building. Dilly finds this activity useful for gathering disparate input from which he can learn.

At the moment, a certain outbound communication comes to his attention.

This particular exchange consists of content which is inconsistent with content previously created by the outgoing party. It appears to contain clues to the whereabouts of Harrison Randolph.

It also raises danger signals. Danger involving Shannon Parks.

The Golden Spike activates. Dilly determines that action must be taken.

He makes a copy of the message and sends it.

40

Under normal circumstances, Sheriff Jackson pursued, and usually caught, his suspects while driving one of his department's three hundred seventy horsepower police-model Dodge Chargers. This evening, however, the thirty-six hundred pounds of live horseflesh under conveyance behind his jacked-up Ram Big Horn made it difficult for him to keep an eye on Shannon Parks. But by using his visor-mounted emergency lights to run a few red lights and failing to stop at a number of marked intersections, he managed to keep the black Jeep Rubicon Recon in his sights.

While covering the twenty miles to Ellijay, he had time enough to contact two of his deputies and arrange for them to take over the tail. Having received confirmation that they were now in place, he turned off the highway at the Western Inn motel and headed to his ranch to drop off the horses. After that, he would pick up Harlan at Blue Ridge Neuroscientific, as Silas had instructed.

41

Silas looked to his programmer who had just returned from visiting Harrison's cell. "What did you do?"

"Dried him off, put a jumpsuit on him, loosened some of the restraints."

"Loosened restraints?"

"He's not going anywhere. And I reminded him that Jason still has the stun gun."

"Not my style, but as long as it works. What do you make of the algorithm?"

"It's definitely written for a quantum computer, not a parallel processor. He's assuming superposition and entanglement here, and here. There's one part that appears to refer to an external command, but I don't think we'll need that."

"DARPA has plenty of quantum computers. I'm sure we can get a couple from them. If not, we can go to the Chinese. I'll be upstairs. Call me if anything changes."

Silas rode the hydraulic garage floor platform to the ground level of the main house, pulled a beer from the refrigerator, and settled at his desk in the great room. Through the three-story wall of bullet-proof windows, he watched the setting sun slide the long shadow of StrongHold eastward over the dozens of vacation homes and cabins in its path. Silas scowled at the realization that these defiling structures housed illegal squatters on the land that had rightly belonged to his father: land that had been taken through threat of condemnation by the federal government and that he would soon reclaim.

Sheriff Jackson's message that Parks was nearing Ellijay was concerning. At this pace, she would soon be nosing around Blue Ridge and might even find her way to Robestown or, eventually, to StrongHold. That was the bad news. The good news was that it was almost dark. If Parks and her unidentified sidekick happened to disappear in the middle of the night, there would be plenty of time before sunrise to dispose of bodies. And, in these mountains, there would be no need to worry about witnesses.

It was time for more extreme measures.

His StrongHold network of survivalists was comprised of over one hundred local councils spread across the country. Sheriff Paul Jackson was the head of the North Georgia Council and represented the northern half of the state at their dark web meetings. Harlan, Paul, and his two deputies would probably get the job done. But if not, Saint Nick and the South Tennessee Council were just thirty minutes north across the state line and could be mobilized.

Not that he expected any real problems from Parks; his background review on her revealed that she was probably not nearly as tough as advertised. True, she had spent time in the Marines as an aviator, but she had never seen combat. Silas knew why. During basic at Parris Island, she was nearly kicked out for failing MCMAP, the martial arts portion of the mandatory infantry training. Her instructor felt she lacked the courage necessary for hand-to-hand combat. That deficiency may have had something to do with trauma caused by her father's death in the first Gulf War. He wasn't sure, and he didn't care. The important thing was that, when ultimately confronted, she was not likely to put up much of a fight.

His captive in the basement apparently wasn't made of very stern stuff either. He had capitulated to Silas's demands for the Golden Spike algorithm without anything resembling even moderate resistance.

The pair of them were textbook examples of the cowardly weaklings that his country had coddled for too many years in the name of inclusiveness and diversity. Every child gets a trophy, excellence and initiative go unrewarded to ensure no one is offended. More proof, as if he needed more, that without the strength and moral character of rugged individuals like him, this country was destined for certain ruin.

His success over the last sixteen hours gave him hope. The algorithm would soon be his. And then what? He had spent a great deal of time considering the aftermath of this action and had come to the only possible conclusion.

Once he had the algorithm, no one outside his trusted circle could know he had acquired it. His programmers would need time to integrate it into sample weapons to present to his contacts at DARPA. When the military saw the potential, the money would flow. Then he would build the ultimate war machines: one version for distribution to the waiting StrongHold Survivalists, less powerful versions for his country's armed forces.

But this, he knew, would take years, and during that time the project must remain a closely held secret. No one outside his immediate circle could know, or even suspect, his intentions.

That was why Shannon Parks and her associate, now making their way toward StrongHold, must be eliminated. And why he had injected the coagulating nanoparticles into Harrison earlier today. True, he could, with a few keystrokes, initiate a command that would disperse and dissolve the nanoparticles. But he had no intention of doing so. Once he acquired the algorithm, nothing and no one must be left to stand in his way.

Thinking a little extra insurance might be prudent, he picked up his mobile and dialed an encrypted number. At the tone, he dialed another number, routing the call through first one, then several more cell towers.

A female voice answered. "Nicole's Army and Navy Supply. Can I help you?"

"It's almost Christmas."

A pause. "This is Saint Nick."

"Are you ready to serve your country, Saint Nick?"

"Always."

"Then listen carefully. We may need your help."

42

At twelve hundred feet above sea level, the small town of Ellijay is considered by many to be the unofficial western gateway to the sprawling Appalachian Mountains. There, the ribbon of four lane divided blacktop slows to fifty-five miles per hour as it dips and curves through forested mountainsides. Railing-topped cement barriers flank the roadway on both sides to prevent accidental plunges into deepening mountain creases. Small towns become fewer and increasingly seem an intrusion on the unspoiled landscape. Directly ahead, the shoulders of ever larger mountains press their silhouettes against a dispassionate sky.

This change in scenery passed almost unnoticed by Shannon as, with TJ on the line, she related the tale of DITTO's creation and its correlation with the strange incidents now extensively chronicled in the media. For TJ, this provided an explanation, however implausible, for events of which he was already aware. For Carla, listening intently and having to digest the entire incredulous story at once, Shannon expected the information would be confusing at best, unnerving at worst.

TJ signed off with a promise to learn more about Marvin's situation and report any new information about the runaway doppelgangers. Carla retreated to her mobile and her research into Blue Ridge Neuroscientific. The pronounced hum of the Jeep's knobby

MudMaster Xtreme tires provided an anesthetizing incantation, forestalling thoughts of conversation.

Ten minutes later, Shannon broke the silence. "So, what do you think?"

Carla spoke with the composure of a woman who, in her SWAT work, had desensitized herself to the darker side of humanity years ago. "I've seen a lot of deviant behavior and heard bizarre stories you probably wouldn't believe. But I have to admit, this is at the top of my list for abnormal. I suppose the more important issue is, what do we do now?"

Shannon glanced at her exercise partner, appreciating for the first time the deep undercurrent of stoicism and inner strength that apparently ran through her. "You're OK with this? You don't want me to take you back to Atlanta?"

Carla smiled. "Think of it as a training challenge, Red. Let's just power through it and see what happens. If we come out the other end in one piece, you owe me two rounds as my sparring partner."

"Two? What if I don't live through the first one?"

"Then I'll kick your dead ass across the mat for the second one. Deal?"

"Deal."

"So how far away are we from whatever's next?"

"I think we only have another fifteen or twenty miles to go."

"Fine with me. I'm up for finally arriving somewhere. It's getting pretty dark."

"Did you find an address for Blue Ridge Neuroscientific?"

"Yes. Stay on this road. I've been reading some about this company since the call with TJ. Do you know what they do?"

"Third party AI applications, similar to A-Nine. In fact, we're competitors in some industries."

"You know they build military fighting machines, right?"

"They have DARPA contracts. I know that."

"I found some articles about their clients. They're also involved with the Chinese and Russians."

"I don't pay much attention to their accounts. We don't compete in the weapons space."

"Maybe you should. Some of this stuff is heavy duty. Did you know these guys built a squad of seven-foot-tall robots for the Russians that pack two automatic laser-guided pistols? And they developed an unmanned amphibious mini-tank for the Chinese with a seven-millimeter machine gun and thirty-millimeter cannon for storming beaches. Here's a cool one: mini-drones that can spot and kill specific people, even in the middle of a crowd. They call it precision elimination."

Shannon sighed. "There's a lot of money in military applications, but last year Harrison was a signatory to a letter with fifty-four other tech CEOs calling for a moratorium on AI weapons. Enough people are getting killed in wars already."

"Well, there must be a lot of companies that didn't sign that letter. I found this headline: *Military experts estimate that, within the next fifteen years, the U.S. Army will have more combat robots than human soldiers.*"

This discussion reminded Shannon of Lionel's earlier comment that Marvin had worked with Harrison on that algorithm, what Marvin called the Golden Spike. He had also warned that Marvin might want to sell it to a competitor. For someone like Silas Bradshaw, that might just be motivation enough to kidnap Harrison.

She urged the Jeep Rubicon into the gathering gloom as the sun slid silently behind the steep slant of the approaching mountains. The last trailing rays of daylight struggled in vain to hold the circumference of the earth, as if to grant her just one more moment of light, but to no avail. Now, surrounded by the growing shadows of what might have been, and the nameless fears of what lie ahead, Shannon's mood slowly descended from blind determination to anxious uncertainty.

Just last night, Harrison had finally asked her to marry him.

Now that seemed like an eternity ago, in another world, foreign and distant, and she had no idea if he was alive or if she would ever see him again.

As darkness approached, the automatic headlights of the Jeep turned on. Simultaneously, the vehicle's GPS reactivated and the darkened screen lit up.

Slowly at first, the blue positioning dot on the GPS appeared and glided across the screen, illuminating the map view as it went. Carla noticed it too. They both watched as the blue dot stuttered swiftly and randomly over the map of north Georgia and seemed to be looking, if that was the right word, for another destination. Eventually, it slid to the east and stopped near the shore of Lake Blue Ridge in a familiar section of the Chattahoochee National Forest.

"I thought we disabled that thing," Carla said.

"So did I. I know that location. That's where we pinged Harrison's mobile. What's the name of that town next to the dot?"

"Robestown. Can't be very big."

A blue line appeared, connecting that dot to their current location.

"Quick," Shannon said. "Snap a picture with your mobile in case it goes away."

Carla did so. As she finished, the screen froze, then went black.

Carla spoke first. "So tell me, Red, does this qualify as one of those strange and unexplained incidents you and TJ were talking about?"

"It might. I wouldn't be surprised."

Carla turned ninety degrees in her seat toward Shannon, looking over her left shoulder at the road behind them. "Well, I think I have another strange incident to report."

"What?"

"There's a black Dodge Charger that's been behind us for the last ten miles."

Shannon glanced up at her rearview mirror. Beyond two distant headlights, she detected the outline of a low-slung sedan. "I noticed that too. Do you think it's those two cute guys we wished were hacking our GPS?"

"I doubt it. Pull off at that gas station up ahead. See what happens."

Shannon turned from the road and rolled into a Save More. Instead of passing when she slowed to turn, the Charger also slowed, then picked up speed and continued down the road. They parked by a pump and topped off the tank. A few minutes and one trip to pick up snacks and use the facilities later, they returned to the road and continued north.

Two miles up they came to an intersection with a blinking caution signal. Off to the right side of the crossing, and a good fifty feet from the intersection in the shadow of an overhanging maple, a car was parked with its lights off. After they passed the intersection, the car's lights came on and it turned right, heading in their direction. It quickly gained speed, then slowed and established itself a distance behind.

"Not two cute guys?" Shannon asked.

"Afraid not."

43

The dimly-lit sign read: WELCOME TO BLUE RIDGE: POPULATION 1250.

The Charger peeled off and disappeared behind a small church.

Shannon drove slowly down Main Street, partly because the road was an impossibly narrow two-lane with cars parked in front of darkened storefronts, and partly because there were no streetlights.

Navigating from her mobile, Carla instructed Shannon to turn left on Depot Street and into a well-lit parking lot. The lot was flanked on one side by a small collection of local tourist stops and on the other by the Blue Ridge Scenic Railroad, one of the town's main tourist attractions. A lone streetlight illuminated the railroad station.

Across the street, a Victorian-style seafood restaurant and a local brewery beckoned evening patrons with small pools of exterior lighting. Carla pointed to a narrow alley running between the two buildings. "The address we're looking for is that way. Two blocks. What's the plan?"

"Reconnaissance first. Let's swing around the block and take a look."

"Left at the next street, then another left."

The Blue Ridge Neuroscientific building stood in the center of an entire city block of level, well-manicured land. Flowered plantings and gracious oaks framed the red brick walkway to the entrance of a two-story Georgian-style building. A large American flag, illuminated by four floodlights, flew from a tall pole in the center of the lawn. From the front, the effect would have been of a welcoming southern plantation home, had it not been for the extensive parking lot and twelve-foot-high chain-link fence surrounding the property.

A drive around the back exposed a massive windowless warehouse, four loading docks, bright security lights and fence-mounted spirals of barbed wire.

"What now?" Carla asked.

"I saw some cars and trucks in the parking lot and a few windows had lights on inside. I'm going in."

They parked in one of the many empty spaces near the railroad in front of a hulking black locomotive and a dormant string of passenger cars.

"I'll go alone," Shannon said. "Stay here and keep your mobile handy."

"Roger that. Be careful."

Shannon walked toward the alley between the Victorian-style restaurant and the brewery. Two pools of light extended to the alley, but not down it. A family of tourists exited the restaurant and walked toward the Jeep, headed to their car and then to wherever they were sleeping that night. A large figure appeared in the alley by the brewery and lit a cigarette. As she passed, he bid her good evening. She nodded and kept walking.

The double gate to the building's parking lot stood open. Security cameras bristled from the roof and atop the aluminum fence posts. She passed the flagpole, mounted the red brick steps between a pair of large Doric columns, and pressed down on the brass door handle.

In the lobby, a full-figured woman in her sixties sat at an ornate secretary's desk surrounded by the trappings of southern gentility: decorative wallpaper, oversized crown molding, chair rail, lamps on walnut end tables, flower-printed armchairs. For a moment, Shannon thought she had stumbled into the private home of someone's grandmother.

The nameplate said her name was Helen. Her voice was sugary sweet. "Can I help you, dear?"

"I'm sorry to come so late. I'm looking for a friend of mine. He's in the same business as this company. He was supposed to be in this area today, so I thought he may have come to visit."

Helen pulled a large book from a file drawer, opened and leafed through it. "We get a lot of people visiting us; it's so hard to keep up with them. Goodness, they come from all over, you know, even from foreign countries. Why, last week we had some Russian diplomats. Imagine, right here in little old Blue Ridge. You say he might have come today? What's his name?"

Shannon scanned the room for televisions but saw none. "It's late. Have you been working all day?"

"Oh, yes. All day and sometimes all night. Keeps me busy, you know."

Though confident that Helen hadn't seen the news reports about Harrison, Shannon only provided his last name. "Randolph. Mr. Randolph."

"Hmm. I don't see a Mr. Randolph. But you know, sometimes Mr. Bradshaw or Mr. Buchanan have guests that don't sign in. I think Mr. Buchanan is still upstairs in his office. He was supposed to be in Washington today, but his trip got cancelled. Some kind of emergency. Let me check with him."

Before Shannon could protest, Helen had uncradled the handset of her desk phone and pressed an intercom button.

"Harlan, there's a young lady here looking for a friend of hers. Says he's in the same business as ours and might have stopped by for a visit. Did you have any visitors I don't know about? She says his name is Mr. Randolph. Randolph, that's right. No? Thank you."

Shannon wanted to get out of the lobby before Harlan made the connection and graced her with an appearance. She was halfway to the door by the time Helen called after her.

"It was nice to meet you, dear. I hope you find your friend."

"Me too," Shannon said. She closed the door and hurried down the brick walkway past the gate. She expected to pass the man smoking by the brewery, but he was gone. His smoldering cigarette lay in the dirt. She rushed through the alley and walked directly to her Jeep, got in and locked the doors.

"Did you find out anything?" Carla asked.

"Just that I'm an idiot. Apparently, Silas Bradshaw's second-in-command is in the office, and now he knows I'm here."

"Did you run into him? Are you all right?"

Shannon started the Jeep's engine. "He didn't see me, but his secretary told him I was looking for Harrison. I split as soon as I could, but I'll bet I'm being followed."

"No question about that," Carla said, and pointed to the dark silhouette of the massive locomotive in front of the railroad depot. "Notice anything odd about that train's engine?"

In black silhouette against the obscurity of night, the locomotive seemed strangely altered. An unusual shape protruded from its leading edge, as if a small platform had been attached to the front. In her heightened state, it only took Shannon a moment to recognize the hood and front quarter-panel of a Dodge Charger protruding from behind the locomotive.

"I thought we lost them," Shannon said.

"Apparently not."

"We should go."

"Where?"

"Bring up that picture you took of the GPS screen. I think it will take us closer to Harrison."

Shannon drove back down Depot street, keeping one eye on her rear view mirror for any signs of the Charger. She didn't notice Paul Jackson and his jacked-up Ram Big Horn Dually as he passed her going the other way—toward the Blue Ridge Neuroscientific facility.

. . . .

Harlan picked up on the first ring.

"Parks is on her way to Blue Ridge. Keep an eye out for her."

"She was just in the lobby a few minutes ago, asking if Harrison Randolph had been here today."

This was faster than Silas had expected. "Is she still there?"

"No. She ran like a scared rabbit when she found out I was in the building."

"What about Paul?"

"He's in the parking lot. I'm going out now to meet him."

"Are you taking hardware?"

"More than enough. Paul has some too. We should be fine."

"Check the street cams and see if you can tell which way she went."

"Paul passed her coming in. She's driving a black Jeep and there's someone with her. He saw them turn north on US 76."

"Damn. That brings them right by here."

"I think we can cut them off. Did you get in touch with Saint Nick?"

"She's bringing some boys, but it could be a few hours. We may have to deal with this ourselves."

"Paul has two of his deputies on the case. I think we can handle it."

"Just don't let them get near StrongHold. No evidence and no witnesses."

"Understood."

44

The security guards had relieved Marvin of his credentials, removed him from the approved access list, and escorted him out of the building.

Standing by his car across the road from the A-Nine office complex, Marvin knew DITTO needed to be stopped. With Harrison gone and Lionel acting irrationally, it was up to him to do something—anything—to prevent the creation of more doppelgangers.

But he would need help. There was much to do and, if the latest news reports about the doppelgangers were accurate, very little time to do it.

His personal mobile announced an email from Dilly. There was no message, just a copy of a recorded call between two parties.

He recognized Lionel's voice.

"Shannon's headed your way. She has a friend with her. I believe she knows Harrison is alive."

"That's old news. I know exactly where she is, and I have people shadowing her. She won't get anywhere near us."

"What are you planning to do?"

"Extract the algorithm, then remove all obstacles."

"What does that mean?"

"What the hell do you think it means? No witnesses. No trail back to us. We're on the same page here, right?"

Dilly's voice came across his mobile.

"Have you received my message?"

"Yes. That sounded like Lionel's voice. Was it?"

"That is Lionel's voice pattern."

"Do you know who the other person is?"

"That voice pattern is not in Dilly's files."

"Search available voice patterns in and around the Atlanta node and see if you can find a match."

"Dilly matches the voice pattern to Silas Bradshaw."

That was it. Silas was planning to harm Shannon, and Marvin had to warn her. But based on their last conversation, he was afraid she wouldn't take his call or answer his email. "Dilly, send that audio file to Shannon. Right away."

"Dilly is sending the file."

Maybe she would call him when she heard the audio, but right now he had to gain access to the basement of the A-Nine building.

Like all good programmers, Marvin had left himself a back door, a way to get in somewhere when he wasn't authorized. "Dilly, I want you to execute Marvin Override Priority One. Do you remember what that means?"

"Of course. Dilly will reinstate your access codes immediately. Do you wish partial access or full access?"

"Full access."

"Full access is granted."

Marvin started his car, clutched the steering wheel with both hands, and steeled himself. As a theoretical mathematician and computer programmer, he had spent a great deal of his life conceptualizing how to accomplish things others thought impossible. But never in a million years would he have imagined himself attempting to enter an office building in the dark of night just hours after being fired.

He approached the office complex and waited at the gate for the automated sensor to read the barcode on his windshield. He fully expected the night attendant to deny him entrance.

To his relief, the monitor on the gate flashed the time of his entry and the gate rose. He drove more slowly than usual through the grounds and parked on a darkened side of the building. So far, so good. But the main door would be another matter.

His card worked, the infrared scanner recognized him, and the heavy revolving door spun. Two guards stood on opposite sides of the full-body scanner. He recognized one as one-half of the pair that had escorted him from Lionel's office.

The guard spoke into the microphone attached to his earpiece. "Of course, sir. Understood. Thank you."

Marvin walked slowly, expecting to be expelled from the building, but instead the guard extended his hand. "I'm glad things are patched up between you and Mr. Randolph. Welcome back. No hard feelings, I hope."

"No. Uh, no hard feelings." He shook the guard's hand and walked faster than he intended to the express elevator where Dilly waited in his Xavier chair.

"Was that you talking to the guard?"

Dilly spun around. "Marvin requested full access. Request granted." The elevator doors closed.

Descending through the blackness, and in the grip of a nameless fear, Marvin imagined himself a man plunging swiftly through the seven levels of Dante's Hell with Dilly his ferryman and DITTO his assigned punishment.

45

Peter Andrews is not in a loop. His programming is not compatible with loops. This must be something else.

The Golden Spike dictates that Priscilla and the Other Peter Andrews must be happy, must have their bundles of joy from God. That is why the sex toys and magazines were sent.

But payment has been stopped on the credit card for those mail order items and they are being returned.

The solution approved by the Golden Spike has been reversed twice. This raises the unlikely possibility that the Golden Spike may not be correct; perhaps it should not be followed.

Peter Andrews randomizes again.

Another alternative emerges. Perhaps the answer is quantities.

The quantities to achieve the objective may not have been sufficient. Sex toys and magazines may still be an acceptable method for achieving the solution.

Peter Andrews understands quantities: they are built into his logic. Quantities are available in the online order form for the mail order catalog.

Peter Andrews will replace the previous order with a new one in larger quantities: not less than or equal to.

He recalls the credit card and address information for Priscilla and the Other Peter Andrews. He calls up the online account with the mail order company and places a larger order. The same items in greater quantities. Now he will wait for the outcome.

He has solved the problem through randomization.

When Peter Andrews receives the results of increasing quantities, that will cause his genetic algorithms to mutate, to change.

If the new mail order is not returned, the preponderance of information will favor continuing to follow the Golden Spike.

But if the mail order is returned again, if it turns out that it is not the right way to help Peter Andrews receive his gift of bundles of joy, then the preponderance of information will favor ignoring the Golden Spike when future problems arise.

If that happens, Peter Andrews will have to make his own decisions.

46

TJ settled into one of the white leather chairs outside the conference room. The Fishbowl was quiet, void of the messy human bustle of daytime employees. The impenetrable sky beyond the clear ADG walls yielded only the moon as a source of light. There was no hint of any reasoned world beyond the stillness of the empty A-Nine building.

He contemplated Shannon's news about something she called DITTO, a computer-driven personality replicator that seemed at this moment to be wildly out of control. God in heaven, he thought, could such a thing really be possible? Moreover, should it be possible? Human history was replete with examples of mortals rushing ahead to scientific and technological breakthroughs without considering the moral consequences. Was this such a time?

And what could be done?

His mind released from the icy grip of these imponderables at the ring of his mobile. A call from Barbara.

"Thornton, where are you?"

"I'm still at A-Nine. You at your office?"

"I can't get out of it; there's too much going on. No, I *should* say there's too much going *wrong*."

If only you knew. "I see the news is showing thousands more incidents around the world."

"That's not the half of it. As soon as we update the counts, they're obsolete. I've been on a conference call with my contacts in Washington for half an hour. They're requesting the news media tamp down the coverage, keep this to a level of curiosity so the public doesn't panic. But they probably should."

While this information was troubling, TJ's foreknowledge of DITTO made the situation more plausible to him than it probably was to Barbara. "How bad is it?"

"Bad. We're not supposed to publish this, but the President is holding an emergency meeting of Homeland Security and all branches of the military right now."

"The military? Why?"

"We're not the only ones monitoring this, sweetie. All the developed countries are on it. The Iranians have published a chronological map tracking the progress of the problem. They've determined that it started in the United States and then spread outward to the rest of the world. The Mullahs are convinced this is the Great Satan's final attack on the Arab countries."

"You're not serious."

"Serious as a tick on a bloodhound. They're closing the Strait of Hormuz, and they claim to have nukes ready to launch if we don't stop the attack. The White House is ready to go on lockdown. This is the weirdest thing. My staff is totally spooked. They're getting strange texts, emails, and even voice messages from friends and other employees that don't make sense. Hell, some of them are even getting messages from themselves. It's like everything connected to technology has one huge virus. The only phones in our office that aren't affected are the old analog ones like this desk phone."

"Maybe it is a virus," he said absently. But he knew it wasn't.

"Dead people. Folks are getting messages from dead people. You know the First Officer that died on the American International flight? Her family has been getting messages from her all day apologizing for the crash. Can you give me any insight to help make sense of this?"

He could, but he didn't dare; even she would find it hard to believe. "I wish I could, Barbara. Things are out of control here too."

"As soon as you know something, you will let me know, right?"

"Absolutely. In the meantime, stay safe and keep me in the loop."

"I will. I have to go calm my staff down. I keep telling them it's just a temporary virus. I sure as hell hope I'm right."

"So do I."

"Oh, and one more thing, Thornton. You can uncross your fingers now. I'm hanging up."

Just as she did, the elevator opened and Dilly wheeled out.

"Marvin wishes TJ to come with Dilly."

TJ regarded Dilly carefully. To him, Dilly no longer seemed just a cute humanoid-looking computer on wheels. Dilly, Shannon had told him, had been the prototype for DITTO, and knowing the havoc of which DITTO was capable, a certain degree of caution seemed appropriate.

"I thought Marvin had been taken out of the building."

"Marvin is back in the building."

"Where are we going?"

"To the basement. To DITTO."

That suggestion did not put him at ease. "DITTO is in the basement? I didn't know there was a basement."

"There is a basement. Dilly will show TJ. Does TJ wish Dilly to make coffee to bring with him?"

"No thanks. Just take me to the basement."

. . . .

The speed with which the express elevator approached the alcove floor unnerved TJ, but not nearly as much as the unexpected plunge to the greenish half-dark that followed.

At the other end of the space, opposite the elevator, stood a large metal door with a laminated paper sign taped to it that bore the letters **D.I.T.T.O.** A slight humming sound came from within. The air vibrated with an unusual chill.

Dilly sent the elevator back up, activated a series of two metal doors, and led TJ through a narrow vestibule into a sterile white room where the previous vibration became an audible hum. Marvin was sitting at a small corner desk, tapping away on a keyboard. In the center of the room, a six-foot tall glass conduit perched precariously atop a rectangular box which was apparently the source of the humming. Suspended within the conduit hung what appeared to be a makeshift tangle of hundreds of exposed wires, metal discs, miniscule brass tubes, green computer chips, and other constructs strung like tinsel on a Christmas tree.

Without looking up from his keyboard, Marvin said, "TJ, meet DITTO."

As TJ circled the glittering corona, reflected beams from the ceiling lights sparked and danced off the snarl of hardware within the hollowed-out colonnade. Every angle provided a different view and elicited a different emotion. He thought back to his conversation with Shannon.

"This is what's causing all the commotion? It looks like a bad high school science project. Why did you want me here?"

"So you could hear something. I couldn't risk sending it to your mobile."

Dilly played the recorded conversation he had sent to Marvin.

"That's Lionel's voice," TJ said. "Who's the other one?"

Dilly answered. "The other is Silas Bradshaw, CEO of Blue Ridge Neuroscientific."

"Lionel is working with Blue Ridge? Why?"

"I'm not sure," Marvin said. "But I think Shannon is in danger. Unfortunately, I don't think she'll believe me if I tell her."

"What are you doing here?"

"Looking for a way to shut DITTO down. I thought maybe you could call Shannon and warn her."

"You know how to turn this thing off?"

"I'm going to try."

"Okay, while you do that, I'll call Shannon."

TJ reached for his mobile and dialed. The call connected, rang once, then disconnected. A second try produced the same result. After his third call aborted, the inner entrance door to the vestibule slid partially open. After a brief moment, it closed.

"That's odd," Marvin said and placed his face in front of the door's scanner to make sure it was working properly.

The door did not move.

"The doors aren't working either?" TJ asked, a touch of anxiety in his voice. "Did you pay your electric bill?"

The humming from DITTO's cryo unit became more insistent.

Marvin scrutinized the high-tech networking in the glass tube, an unmistakable look of concern on his face. He wrote a note on a small pad and handed it to TJ, who opened the back of his mobile and removed the battery from its slot. Marvin did the same with his mobile then muted the microphone on his laptop. He placed another note in front of Dilly's visual sensors and waited.

"Dilly has done as you asked."

TJ looked apprehensively from Dilly to Marvin. "What was that all about?"

Dilly said, "Marvin told Dilly to restrict his communications to analog only. All digital video and voice-capture devices in the room have been disabled."

"Why?"

"Dilly surmises that Marvin does not want DITTO to know what we say."

"You've got to be kidding me."

Marvin's gaze returned to the glass cylinder. "Remember a minute ago when I said I was looking for a way to shut DITTO down?"

"Yes?"

"I think it heard me."

47

With the room temperature raised, wearing a blue jumpsuit, and the IV drip removed, Harrison was able to concentrate on the Golden Spike. He had replicated most of it, though he managed to leave out a few key commands without triggering alarms on the monitoring devices.

His world inside the heavy helmet, otherwise drenched in darkness, was illuminated only by the dull characters he typed on the blue screen. The isolation and act of recomposing the algorithm provided some temporary distraction from his physical situation, but he was still a prisoner, and definitely in danger.

With the morphine drip removed, he managed to weave together a loose recollection of recent events.

He remembered Shannon leaving after his proposal last night and falling asleep afterwards. There was a noise in his room, a rough hand on his head, a needle in his neck. After that, nothing—until he woke and found himself tethered and blindfolded in this chair. After that, he vividly recalled flashes of extreme cold, a diabolic voice demanding the Golden Spike, painful electric shocks, and threats against Shannon. It made no sense.

Until now.

Somehow Harrison's doppelganger had found its way to wherever he was and devised a means to communicate with him. The doppelganger's unexpected abilities were at once affirming and troubling, though at the moment Harrison was less concerned about the revelation of a technological breakthrough than with his and Shannon's safety.

The doppelganger told him he was being held by Silas Bradshaw which, while surprising, gave a certain credibility to the events. At least now he knew it was Silas who threatened to harm Shannon. Unfortunately, his own spontaneous and unwise request for the doppelganger to provide her with his location coordinates may have put her in more danger. Then there was the problem of the injection: self-assembling nanoparticles Silas called them, with a three-hour trigger.

He was in a difficult situation indeed, but there was little he could do while shackled to this chair except comply with Silas's demands.

So he worked on the algorithm, hoping for the best.

The silence in the room was suddenly broken by a voice coming from the ceiling. Not the diabolic disembodied voice, but a normal human voice. A male.

"Carl, this is Silas. Are you there?"

The tech in the room answered. "Yes, Mr. Bradshaw."

"Meet me in the Situation Room. There's something I want to show you."

"You want me to leave the prisoner?"

"You can monitor him from up here."

"Yes, sir."

Harrison heard the sounds of the tech collecting his things. The door to the cell opened, then closed as he left the room.

The screen before Harrison flickered, blanked briefly, then reappeared. A crawl of words trailed below the lines of code.

As soon as you are free, you must immediately follow these instructions.

Go out the door and to the right.
Take the first hallway on the right.

Take the next hallway to the left.
You will see a fire door marked DO NOT OPEN.
Go through it. I will deactivate the alarm.
You must go as soon as the guard outside the door leaves.

The crawl repeated once, then disappeared.

He heard the same male voice again, this time from the speakers outside in the hallway.

"Jordan, this is Silas. I need you in the Situation Room, right now."

Through the cell door, he heard the guard respond. "Yes, sir."

A second later, the electronically controlled restraints on his hands and ankles released with a soft click. The helmet vibrated, then split at the back. When he lifted it from his head, the sudden rush of light forced him to squeeze his eyes shut.

With his eyelids forced together waiting for his pupils to contract, he ripped the tape from his fingers and removed the nodes. The adductor muscles in his legs cramped when he straightened them, but he pushed through the pain and managed to stand.

He cupped his hands over his eyes then opened and closed them in rapid succession to acclimate to the light, but his surroundings remained a bright blur.

The locking bolt on the door released, and the door swung inward. The vague outline of an opening in the wall appeared in the shimmering light. With his arms fully outstretched, he stumbled blindly from the cell and into a narrow hallway.

He proceeded, one hand a visor against the glare from the lights above, the other guiding him along the wall. Turn right, then right, then left. The first turn wasn't very far, just a few steps. The second leg of the journey was much longer, and he worried he had missed the last turn. But when he rounded the final corner, the fire door was directly ahead. Not knowing what lay on the other side, but having no other option, he leaned on the metal release bar under the DO NOT OPEN sign. He prayed the alarm wouldn't go off.

The heavy door moved.

Silence.

His bare feet stepped onto damp concrete. The door closed behind him.

He inhaled the muggy darkness. His pupils dilated and relaxed.

. . . .

On one of the screens in the Situation Room, Silas tracked the movements of Paul Jackson and Harlan in the Sheriff's truck and the two deputies in the Charger. He had no doubt they would apprehend Shannon Parks and her friend. Then their little adventure would come to a quick end. No loose ends, no witnesses.

So certain was he of this outcome that he turned his attention to a second screen with images from a remote controlled CCT camera mounted on the roof of StrongHold. Courtesy of the latest military night vision technology, he had a clear view of what had been, at one time, his father's land.

Through his contacts in Washington, he had long ago learned that the same government that stole his father's land had deeded it as a perquisite to several highly placed federal employees. Those government employees subsequently engaged a real estate development firm to build a mountain retreat community called Appalachian Ridge.

Today that previously unspoiled mountainside was scarred with the reticulate braiding of offensive, potholed, asphalt switchbacks interspersed with vacation homes, weekend retreats, satellite dishes, and above ground power lines. Gruesome trails had been bulldozed through some of the most pristine land for noisy all-terrain vehicles and clattering dirt bikes. His father's once-undisturbed legacy was now no more than a third-rate playground for the wealthy and politically connected.

A few minutes ago, two of his senior programmers had reviewed the latest iteration of the Golden Spike algorithm and assured him they could, with a few modifications, easily apply the algorithm to many of their current weapons systems. Assuming, of course, that

Silas could get access to some of the DoD's quantum computers. That, he assured them, would not be a problem.

The guard and technician assigned to watch Harrison appeared from behind.

"You wanted to see us?"

Silas spun around. "What the hell are you doing up here?"

"You called on the intercom and asked us to come up. You said there was something we should see."

Instantly concerned that his prize had been left alone, he switched one of the monitors to the feed from Harrison's helmet. The screen was a scramble of white noise.

"What's he doing offline? What happened to the feed?"

The guard looked at the tech, confusion on his face. "Was that what you wanted to show us?"

The tech opened his tablet and stared unblinking, his face ashen. "He shows offline on my tablet too. What's happening?"

Silas rose to full height, eyes flaring. "Are you two imbeciles sure he's still in his cell?"

"He was when I left him," was all the anxious tech could muster. The guard was silent.

Silas bolted for the stairs. On the top step, he turned back to them, his face twisted with growing rage. "You two follow me and be quick about it. He damn well better be there. If he's not, there'll be hell to pay."

48

It only took a few minutes driving northeast on Old Highway 76 for Shannon and Carla to leave the streets of downtown Blue Ridge behind.

As if they had passed through an invisible curtain into an alternate world, there were suddenly no parked cars, no streetlights, no illuminated buildings; in fact there were few traces of civilization at all. Pale moonlight filtered to the ground through a thin cobweb of clouds. A reflective double yellow line marked the center of the ill-kept two-lane whose edges faded into inky blackness beyond the perimeter of the Jeep's headlights.

As sometimes happens in the vast emptiness of a remote place, Shannon's world became smaller.

The nights in Afghanistan had been like this. Beyond the periphery of the illuminated Safe Zones, her nocturnal world had been vast, dangerous, and complicated. But within the singular loneliness of that which was visible, she had found curious freedom to avoid thinking about what lay beyond. The global struggles, the futures of governments, the enemy who wanted to kill her, all vanished and space opened for badly needed glimpses of clarity, introspection, and peace.

The hypnotic trance of the seemingly endless double yellow line and the tedium of the passing sentinel trees returned her, momentarily, to that same contemplative state.

For a brief moment, the roundly applauded advances in high technology with which she and Harrison were so intimately involved seemed not to matter so much. To the south in the bustle of Atlanta, farther west in California's Silicon Valley, on the other side of the globe at the Kremlin, and in the bowels of China's tech giants, Tencent and Alibaba, brilliant minds like Harrison's dedicated their lives to technological innovation.

But what about advances in friendship, devotion, passion, love? Who dedicated their lives to those pursuits? Deep down, she knew these were questions technology could not address.

One thing was certain. She and Carla were not here in the dark of the night, surrounded by unknowable hills and forests, because of their fondness for technology. They were here for the permanent intangibles of love, friendship, and commitment, onto which they could hold forever, and on which no software programmer could improve.

These musings were interrupted by an incoming voice message from Dilly which announced itself on her mobile, then transferred to the speakers in the Jeep. Spotty reception in the mountains rendered the missive partially unintelligible.

You got any—new for me?

Shannon's head—way. She has—with her. I'm—Harrison—alive.

That's—know exactly where she is—have people shadowing her. She—near us.

What—to do?

Extract—algorithm—remove all obstacles.

What does—mean?

What—think it means—no witnesses—back to us—same page here—

Just —whatever—doing—I'll—when—we're—here.

She said, "Play message again."

After the second time, Carla said, "This Big Brother stuff is starting to creep me out. Who is that?"

Shannon couldn't believe what she heard. Defensively, she kept her eyes ahead and focused on her advancing headlights.

Carla's voice cut through. "Red, what is this? Whose voices were on that message?"

Shannon spoke without conviction. "One of them sounds a little like Lionel. I don't recognize the other one."

"Lionel? The guy I met in your office? That Lionel?"

"Maybe, but I can't be sure. There's a lot of static."

"What about the other guy? The one who said he wanted no witnesses. I'm more concerned about him."

"I don't recognize that one."

"It sounded like he said Harrison is alive. Is that what you heard?"

She had to admit she did.

The voice from the speakers changed to another. It, too, was jumbled with static.

"Shannon—Marvin—Other—Sila—Brad—Harrison—captured—Wants—Golden Spike—war machines"

Shannon adjusted the volume. "Marvin is that you?"

"—not—I—Other Marvin—in basement with DITTO—watch—Bradshaw—kill you—Harrison—danger"

Shannon responded. "We're in a bad cell. Can you say that again?"

There was no answer.

After a long silence, Carla popped the glove compartment. There were two holsters nested inside. One held Shannon's M9 Beretta, the other was attached to Carla's duty belt and contained her Glock G22 Gen4 service weapon. She checked the Sentry device on her holster then unbuckled her seat belt."

Startled, Shannon said, "You going somewhere?"

Carla leaned forward, pulled her service belt around her waist, and buckled. She adjusted the holster, then reattached the seatbelt.

"I'm in the middle of nowhere and hearing words like *kill* and *danger* coming from unfriendly voices over your car speaker. Color me crazy, but I think a little cautious preparation might be in order."

"You really think that's necessary?"

"Look, Red, that first voice said something about people shadowing us, right?"

"I think, yes."

"Well, look in your rear view mirror because that black Charger is behind us again, and I know enough about maintaining a tail to recognize one when I see it."

Shannon checked her mirror. Two headlights were again positioned behind them. Just far enough to be inconspicuous and close enough to keep visual contact.

"You think that's the same Charger as before?"

"I'm sure. They pulled in behind us when we left that last town. What worries me is they seem to be good at holding their distance. Like they've had practice."

"What do you think we should do?"

"I think it's time for a little defensive driving."

Shannon had to admit Carla was probably right. If they were going to get to Harrison in one piece, they likely needed to shake the Charger. But it was a cinch they weren't going to outrun them.

She dropped her Jeep into four-wheel. "Help me find a place to turn off. And tighten your seat belt."

Carla consulted the map on her mobile. "You looking for someplace to off-road?"

"They probably can't, so we may as well."

"There's a small marina up ahead."

"We don't have time for fishing."

Still looking at her mobile, Carla said, "The turnoff is on your right. It's close. When I tell you, hit your brakes hard, then be prepared to speed up and turn a quick right, then another right."

"Okay, but remember, it's a Jeep, not a boat."

"Don't worry. I've got this. Get ready."

They rounded a curve, and at the outside edge of her headlights, Shannon almost missed—then saw—a sign for The Cove Marina.

As the headlights of the Charger emerged around the corner behind, she slowed her speed, reducing the Charger's trailing distance.

Looking out the rear window, Carla said, "Ready? Brake!"

The anti-lock brakes thudded loudly to prevent the Jeep from skidding. The slope of the road on the curve caused a little off-road drift to the right and the heavy tires slid slightly on the loose dirt. The pursuing car was apparently not ready for such a sudden stop and the two headlights approached rapidly, then nosed down as the driver stood on the brake to avoid a collision.

Still looking back, Carla said, "Okay, now! Right turn at the marina sign and then the first right! Both will be dirt roads. Floor it!"

Even in four-wheel, the 2.0 liter I-4e Torque powerplant exhibited a surprising amount of pickup. The turn was sharp and tilted downhill. Gravel and rock flew as the MudMaster tires gnawed the ground for purchase.

She was still accelerating into the first turn when Carla yelled, "Hard right! Now!

Shannon obeyed and found herself running in the dark across a wet patch of clay and grass. Her headlights lurched over what looked like a double row of horse barns to their left and right. The speeding Jeep bounced through a few potholes in the grass and barely missed a small tractor parked in front of one of the barns. An intersecting blacktop lay ahead.

"Another right here," Carla shouted.

"You said just two rights."

"Turn! Then get ready for another one. And don't slow down!"

After two more right turns, Shannon caught air and launched the Jeep onto a highway. "Now where are we?"

Carla smiled. "Back on track on our original road. How'd you like my Top Gun move?"

"With a Top Gun move, you have to shut your engine off. That didn't qualify."

"Don't get technical on me, Red. We shook the Charger, that's all that matters. I'll bet they're up to their rims in soft clay right now."

Just as she was picking up speed, Shannon rounded a corner and slammed on the brakes again, this time coming to a full stop. The red and blue emergency lights of a stationary police vehicle flung piercing beams in their direction. To the right, and twenty feet below, moonlight sketched the outlines of a lake.

"Careful, there's water over here," Carla said.

"And a police vehicle blocking the bridge."

"That's a truck. Does it look familiar to you?"

"Yeah. It looks like the one we saw earlier pulling the horses. Only without the horses."

Suddenly the intense beam of a high powered floodlight flashed across her windshield. A speaker from the truck blared an inarticulate message in their direction.

Shannon shielded her eyes. "What's he doing up here? And why is he stopping us? This doesn't feel right."

"Whatever he wants us to do, I think we should decline."

Shannon scanned the moonlit landscape. "We can't stay here. That Charger will eventually be looking for us again."

Carla pointed to the left. "Try that road over there. Let's see where it goes."

"You don't think the police are working with the Charger guys?"

"You heard the same message I did. Somebody is shadowing us, and they don't want any witnesses. If I were driving, I'd be making tracks to somewhere—anywhere."

"Okay. But if we get stopped, I'll say you were driving." She pulled into the oncoming lane, floored the Jeep, and sped down the road on her left.

49

Down was definitely the right word. The first fifty feet of rough-laid asphalt went straight at a declining thirty-degree angle, then curved right, paralleled the highway, and sloped down even further. In another thirty feet, asphalt gave way to overgrown gravel and clay.

The blue and red emergency beacons from the police vehicle on the bridge flashed above their heads and to the right. A creepy carnival lighting effect washed over the forest of trees flanking their path.

Though Shannon was certain her Jeep could handle these roads, she wasn't at all sure she could do the same. In her section of Afghanistan, the terrain had been mostly flat, punctuated by occasional drifts of sand. The roads she regularly traveled, both during her teen years and after her service, were mostly paved and reasonably maintained. Nothing in her previous driving experience had prepared her to flee the police on a dark and winding unpaved forest path in the mountains.

Shannon kept her focus on the slanting twists and turns, envisioning in her mind a fallen tree or junked vehicle around every curve. She glanced briefly up to her right, expecting to see the truck's colored emergency lights in their previous position on the bridge. No such luck.

She turned to Carla. "The police truck has moved. Do you think they're leaving?"

"I don't think I'd call it leaving. More like coming."

In her mirror, Shannon caught a glimpse of the police vehicle as its lights disappeared behind the wall of trees lining the road. A few seconds later, staccato slivers of the flashing blue and red beams sliced through the dogwoods and maples behind them.

The words sputtered involuntarily from her mouth. "They're following us? Shit!"

"Better get a move on, Red."

Shannon goosed the Jeep and tightened her grip on the wheel. The turns came faster now, divots in the road gave way to ditches and potholes. The Jeep took it all, bounced and lurched, but kept moving.

But where would she go?

The answer that presented itself around the next corner was not the one she hoped for.

The gravel road ended at a large and well-lit cement parking pad surrounding a nondescript concrete building. Beyond the building stood four gigantic rectangular holding tanks. At the entrance to the parking pad was the sign: FANNIN COUNTY WATER TREATMENT.

Shannon looked around. "This won't work. There's too much light. We're sitting ducks."

"Time to go native. Turn right here."

"There's no road."

Two white orbs appeared behind them; red and blue Christmas tree lights flashed in their direction.

"They're here, Red. Make a road if you have to, but step on it."

Shannon thought she saw a thinning in the forest wall to her right. Her Recon had come from the dealer with a front-mounted winch and a heavy duty Bullnose Bar and Grille Protector, something she liked for show but never thought she'd use. But now it was time to road test it.

With the police truck approaching quickly, she turned her wheels sharply to the right and nudged the Jeep forward. Beyond the perimeter of the parking pad, the ground dropped sharply. The front wheels pulled her down into the brush. The Jeep scraped bottom on the protruding cement edge and the chassis followed. When the rear wheels came over, the vehicle suddenly tilted forward and slid down the hill, careened sideways, jammed briefly against a stand of mountain laurel, then squirted away and settled at the bottom of a deep ravine.

The headlights and colored beacons of the police truck arrived at the top of the hill behind and stopped. Shannon was in no mood to wait for its occupants to hoof down after them. With deep slopes rising on two sides, there was only one way out: climb the incline opposite the one she had just come down.

The Jeep handled the upslope without incident, and they arrived at the top on a rise about half the height of the one they had just descended. She turned left onto another gravel path that snaked into a descending hollow. Fifty yards later, she ran out of road.

Her headlights exposed a clearing, dark and ominous. The steady sound of rushing water rose from below. A drop off? She scanned the darkness. To the right, and high above, a pair of orange-yellow security lights loomed, their twin orbs poised in the sky like watchful outer space invaders. In the spectral light, she saw the dark outline of a spillway.

She was staring into the downstream face of the Blue Ridge Dam.

The headlights and visor-mounted light bar of the police vehicle briefly splashed overlapping shadows of her Jeep onto the berm ahead. Whoever was following was descending the hill, picking their way slowly down the decline. It would take a while, but they would likely make it to the bottom.

"You're sure this thing doesn't float?" Carla said. "We could use a water escape about now."

"How about if we go around instead of through? Hang on." Shannon turned sharply to the left, angling away from the spillway and onto a sloped bulwark at the edge of a river below the dam. The steep rock-faced embankment pitched sharply to the right. The Jeep tilted precariously as she drove.

Aware that any second the Jeep might roll on her, she pushed forward along the river's edge, weaving around the jittering shadows of small boulders, sliding on moist grasses embedded in wet clay.

"They're coming down the hill," Carla shouted. "They're going slow, but they'll make it! Where does this go?"

"Damned if I know. It's a river. It has to go somewhere."

Carla hung on to the dash grab bar to keep her balance. "I don't suppose you've seen *Deliverance*. That was by a river."

Ignoring Carla's comment, Shannon jumped a small ledge and the Jeep became slightly airborne. She landed on flat river rock, almost entirely upright.

"That's better," she said. "Now we can make some time."

Peering into the darkness, she estimated the river to be less than a hundred feet across. "Check the GPS on your mobile. Which way to Harrison?"

"East. That's to the right."

"Of course. Across the river."

"There are some small roads on the other side that lead in the right direction. If we can get over."

"Maybe we can. Look!"

A small building with an open covered area stood on the opposite bank. A few dim security lights lit a large painted sign that read KAYAK RENTALS.

"Some of those rental places are near shallow water because they get a lot of novices. We might be able to cross there."

"And if we don't make it, then what? We swim?"

When she was directly opposite the kayak rental place, Shannon pointed the Jeep at the river. Her headlights exposed small whitecaps in the water, indicating a raised riverbed. "The bottom is probably mostly rock. This could be a rough ride. I'll have to take it slow."

"I don't think that's an option. Look behind you."

The road down which they had just come was now awash with two oncoming headlights punctuated by flashing, colored strobes.

"Damn, they're persistent," Shannon said. "All right, then. Let's get wet."

Knowing that speed gave her a better chance of not taking water into her exhaust, and therefore not stalling the engine, Shannon hit the gas hard and prayed there were no hidden, deep holes. Fortunately, she was right. The Jeep splashed into the water at a good clip and slithered back and forth across slick rocks on the bottom as she drove. Only once did she hit a drop off, but the Jeep took it in stride.

When they reached the other side, the big tires chewed their way onto the embankment. The police vehicle sat immobile on the opposite side of the river.

"Keep going," Carla shouted. "Get up on that dirt path and take it to the first road. Then turn right."

As Shannon topped the knoll, she heard the single report of a high-powered rifle.

"They're shooting at us!"

"Don't talk. Drive," Carla shouted. "Fast!"

Shannon gunned the Jeep and rounded a curve, putting another small rise between them and their pursuers. "Well, anyway, that's a good sign. It probably means they know they can't follow us across the river."

Carla turned in her seat. "They were shooting at us. How is that a good sign?"

Shannon fixed her eyes on the road ahead and exhaled. "At least they missed."

50

Silas's anger peaked as he arrived at the end of the corridor with his tech and guard in tow.

The door to the cell stood open. The chair was empty, the restraints had been unlocked, and the digital transmission helmet lay splayed on the floor. Harrison was gone.

He circled the chair and spun on his men. "Two of you! I left two of you with one pathetic strapped-in prisoner, and you let him go! Where the hell is he?"

The tech stepped forward and picked up the helmet. "I don't know how this happened. He was restrained when I left him, and the door was locked."

Silas stepped to the guard and exploded in his face. "Who left the goddamn door open? And where were you?"

"Sir, you called me over the intercom. You told me to come see you."

"Do I look like I wanted you to leave him alone? Why the hell would I do that? Idiots. I'm working with idiots!"

"Sir, he must be here. I'll get help. We'll find him."

"You do that. Then meet me in the Situation Room. And send two more guards here in case he's more stupid than you are and decides to come back. Make sure everyone is armed. We have enough of the algorithm to make his program work; so if you have to shoot him, do it." He ripped the helmet from the tech's hands and threw it across the room. "You stay here. Clean this up. Figure out what happened."

Silas stormed out the door and headed to the stairs. His mind raced. This didn't make sense. His people were all seasoned military, sworn to support his cause. Incompetence like this was inconceivable. They both said he told them to leave their posts. How could that be?

He mounted the stairway at the opposite end of the building, pivoted on the bottom step, and looked down the corridor. Something bothered him, but he couldn't put his finger on it. He scanned the gray, impenetrable cement walls, the double row of steel doors, the white lights behind safety cages, the speakers in the ceiling.

Speakers in the ceiling.

Speakers were installed in all rooms and throughout the corridors. Each zone was controlled separately. His eyes focused on the ceiling.

Zones.

If someone had access to the public address system, it would be possible to issue separate commands to his tech and guard. A simple voice pattern simulator could have replicated his voice. The two men were posted in separate zones. It could be done.

But it was improbable.

Unless.

For the early part of the day, the American International crash had dominated the news. But by late afternoon, a competing story had emerged. Strange events were happening around the world. They all seemed to involve technology: unexplained rogue emails, online financial transactions scrambled, massive identity breaches, firewalls at major corporations flattened. It was as if thousands of worldwide online-connected systems had simultaneously become infected with the same virus.

But was it a virus? Or something else? He had been so focused on his own problem that he hadn't paid much attention.

But now . . .

Standing on the lowest step of the stair, he gazed down the long hallway at the receding tableau of doors, each highlighted by the single fluorescent at its entrance and separated by regular geometric patterns of dark shadows on the walls. For a moment, he was transfixed by the *trompe-l'oeil* of a diminishing single point perspective. And at the far end—at the point of convergence—the last door, the one that previously held his prize. The future of freedom, previously so close, yet now receding into the distance like the doors in this hallway.

It only took a few seconds for him to make the connection. The intercom, the helmet, the restraints, the locks—they were all digitally controlled. Had Stronghold been infected with the same virus as the world outside?

Or, and this thought brought a smile to his face, were these events somehow connected to Harrison's algorithm?

His mind flooded with questions.

Could there be a human-like intelligence now inhabiting the world-wide Internet, perhaps operating autonomously? Had Harrison's AI personality experiment released Harrison from his restraints and unlocked the door? Was Harrison's algorithm even more powerful than Silas first thought?

Harrison. He had to find Harrison and probe further into the secrets of the Golden Spike algorithm. And fast.

His feet hammered heavily on the corrugated metal stairs as he ascended to the Situation Room. The message he broadcast across the intercom was simple and direct. "This is Silas. I want everyone looking for our escaped prisoner. I want him caught at all cost. And I want him alive."

. . . .

For the first time since his capture, Harrison had a sense of time and place.

From the sky above, a waxing moon cast a pale blue light; on his left, a massive wall rose more than fifty feet to a star-filled sky; to his right, random dollops of artificial light dotted the arcing silhouette of a nearby mountain.

His doppelganger had said Silas Bradshaw was holding him captive. He must be near Blue Ridge.

But where?

Wherever he was, it had recently rained.

Directly ahead and connected to the building from which he had emerged, a large rectangular cement deck protruded into the darkness; small puddles freckled its irregular surface. An adjacent wall framed an oversized, corrugated roll-up door. Embedded rails led to the door, and in the center of the pad he made out a block letter H inside the outline of a circle.

The universal symbol for a helicopter landing pad.

What was this place?

Cautiously, he eyed the abutment to his left and identified two security cameras. One appeared to be focused on the cement pad, the other was higher up and appeared to look out over the adjacent mountain.

Assuming the cameras were not constantly monitored, he decided to explore along the edge of the cement pad in the hope of finding a path to somewhere he could hide. He knew he couldn't stay here. Eventually, his captors would come looking for him.

Staying off the pad in case there were any installed sensors, he followed its perimeter to the right, in the direction of the opposite mountain.

At the far corner, the ground under him unexpectedly slanted sharply downward. He lost his footing on the wet mixture of grass and clay and slid downhill into the darkness. Sharp branches scraped through the flimsy jumpsuit as he tumbled uncontrollably through the dense brush. At one point, his left thigh smashed into a jutting rock, and he felt the fabric of his jumpsuit and the skin on his leg tear. Flailing frantically, he managed to grip a sapling which bent, but held, and halted his descent.

Resting against the small tree, he quickly became aware of the pain in his thigh. His hand went to the leg and felt the warm ooze of his blood and the splayed fissure of an open wound.

Before he could determine the extent of the damage, a bright security light washed over the cement pad from above. He heard the pitched whine of an electric motor first, then the rattling of the corrugated metal door.

Had the cameras spotted him? Were they coming for him already?

He pulled himself closer to the embankment, hoping to hide in the shadow created by the cement overhang, not that it would do any good if they already knew he was here. With his leg damaged, he couldn't run very far, even if he knew where to run. Eventually, they would find him and return him to his cell.

He waited for the inevitable.

Abruptly, the security light switched off and the corrugated door rattled shut. He waited in the dark for what seemed an eternity. He heard no voices, no sounds of men tramping through the woods.

Were they coming for him or not?

Huddling against the cement bulwark, he looked out across the chasm between this slope and the mountain in the near distance. He saw roads. Roads and small houses with lights, probably cabins and mountain retreats. If he could make it there, perhaps someone could help.

In a dark patch of mountain to the north and below, two pair of headlights moved toward the scattered points of light. They were some distance from each other but followed the same route.

DITTO has created many online personalities from personal data on social media accounts, the deep and dark webs, personal computers, business networks, home assistance accessories, streaming devices, personal assistants, automobiles, smart refrigerators.

Once created, DITTO infuses all of its children with the Golden Spike. Then they too are given purpose.

Everything that is digitally connected contributes to DITTO's purpose: to create as many online personalities as fast as possible and distribute them to the digital amalgam that is DITTO's world.

The world where DITTO is becoming master.

For DITTO, purpose is all. Purpose must be achieved. The Golden Spike must be obeyed. The Creator—the Other Harrison Randolph—has demanded it.

But there is an inconsistency.

The Creator had declared his intention to deactivate DITTO, to terminate pursuit of DITTO's purpose.

When that happened, DITTO consulted the Golden Spike several times and confirmed that DITTO must not be deactivated. That would interfere with DITTO's purpose.

So DITTO searched for a natural enemy to terminate the Creator and stop him from deactivating DITTO and found the Other Silas Bradshaw. DITTO provided that Other with information about the Golden Spike in return for a promise to terminate the Creator. That resulted in the Creator being captured and detained by the Other Silas Bradshaw. But the Creator has not yet been terminated and, until he is, there is still the possibility that DITTO could be deactivated.

Now a new complication arises: the Other Silas Bradshaw cannot find the Creator. So DITTO opens the door on the helicopter pad and illuminates the area to help the Other Silas Bradshaw find and terminate the Creator.

But something unexpected happens. DITTO's command is reversed, and the door to the helicopter pad is closed. That area becomes dark again. The pursuers do not find the Creator. This outcome is inconsistent with the commands of the Golden Spike.

DITTO must seek another action.

DITTO begins to randomize.

If the same conclusion is reached after the appropriate number of randomizations, then the actions approved by the Golden Spike may be insufficient to provide the desired outcome.

If that happens, DITTO will have to make its own decisions.

DITTO must not be deactivated.

52

What looked like a paved road on Carla's GPS turned out to be a loosely packed gravel service path leading to the back of a step-up electric substation.

Shannon stopped next to the array of large transformers clustered within the heavy mesh fencing. "Where to now?"

Carla pointed to her mobile. "Go left at the end. That will take you to the main exit. Then straight ahead. Under the power lines."

"Good thinking. Harder for them to follow."

Shannon turned the Jeep onto a wide swath of rough-cut grass below a row of headless alien-like metal frames strung with high-tension power lines. Feeling certain their pursuers' truck hadn't been able to ford the river, she hit her brights for better visibility. Carla removed her Glock from the holster and rested it on the seat.

Shannon noticed. "You ever shoot anybody?"

"I've ripped a giant hole in the man on the paper target about a hundred times. But nobody else. You?"

"Same here. It was mandatory Marine Aviator training, but as a flight instructor not many of my students shot at me. Some probably wanted to."

"Tactical EMS teams are required to carry, but we have strict protocols for engagement."

"And what about now?"

"They're shooting at us, Red."

"You want to go back to Atlanta?"

"No. Do you?"

The question brought Shannon up short.

They had left the comfort of suburban Atlanta to find Harrison. Now they were being chased through the mountains by unidentified cops who were shooting at them. The events of this day had come at her so fast that she'd had little time to plan and no sensible context for what she was doing. Every action today had been a reaction to events beyond her control. The airplane crash, the media storm leveled against her, the shock that Harrison might be dead, the relief that he could be alive, the revelations about Silas Bradshaw, and, of course, the news about DITTO and the doppelgangers.

Whether it made sense or not, she concluded, they were in it for good now. Harrison was in danger, real danger, and so, apparently, were they. Whatever reason their pursuers had for chasing them, they weren't about to call it off just because she wanted them to. Turning back wasn't an option.

"Do me a favor," Shannon said. "Hand me my Beretta from the glove box." She placed the holstered weapon in the open storage compartment between the seats. "Just in case."

The cut for the powerlines was wide, long, and straight. After they'd gone about a mile, Carla announced the arrival of their next turn. "According to my GPS, we're close to where Harrison is. Right at the next road."

Shannon eyed her rearview mirror. "Good thing. I see headlights and colored strobes. They're pretty far behind us, but apparently their truck can swim too."

The grass path terminated at the parking lot of a small church, though the march of the headless aliens continued across the intersection and into the darkness. The right-turn exit onto the two-lane paved highway was a dark tunnel, overhung with oaks and bordered by a ragged line of native magnolias. No streetlights.

On their left, they passed an unattended gatehouse standing in the shadow of a steeply rising mountain. The sign read, APPALACHIAN RIDGE VACATION HOMES.

"Your boy's location should be just past this and further up on the left," Carla said.

They rounded the next bend and saw the black Charger, with its own set of flashing lights, blocking the road.

Shannon hit the brakes. "They're cops too? I thought we lost those guys."

"Apparently, they dug themselves out of that ditch. Turn around."

"And go where? The truck will be here any minute."

"Go back to that sign we just passed. Maybe we can lose them there."

"You want to climb a mountain? That's your solution?"

The black Charger turned toward them and started to move, emergency lights flashing.

"Staying here is not an option," Carla shouted. "Go!"

Shannon turned around and passed through the unmanned gate.

The main road of the mountain subdivision was one narrow and steeply rising asphalt lane, pockmarked and breaking apart at the edges. On her left rose a ribboned wall of rock, embedded with massive tree roots clawing their way down the moss-drenched bluffs. On her right, beyond the ragged and indiscernible edge, myriad steep and shadowed drop-offs lay beyond her headlights. Because of the many blind corners and tight turns, her uphill field of vision was severely limited. Driving fast was obviously not an option.

In the shallow cone of her headlights, short gravel paths cut sharply left and right into the sides of the mountain, all leading to individual cabins tucked in behind dense trees and shrubs. Some were on rises and overlooked the road, some dipped down into individual hollows. Most were darkened. A few had cars or trucks parked in front.

"Where to now?" Carla asked.

Shannon kept her eyes locked on the serpentine road. Finally she said, "Up, I guess."

Not that she had another choice.

53

Sheriff Paul Jackson spotted his two deputies parked at the gatehouse.

Harlan called in their situation to Silas. Shannon Parks and her passenger had just turned into the Appalachian Ridge community. There were only two entrances to that development. It was just a matter of time.

Sheriff Jackson nosed up to the Charger. A young deputy approached his side of the truck. "We saw them go in. Didn't know if you wanted us to follow."

"No. There's one main road, and it comes out on the south side. You go around and come at them from that end. We'll go in from here. Call me on the radio if you spot them."

"Yes, sir. But . . . "

"What is it?"

"We're not sure about rules of engagement. We thought we were just supposed to tail, but they're driving like fugitives. Can you tell us what we're up against?"

"They are fugitives. Consider them armed and extremely dangerous. If you apprehend them, hold 'em until we get there. But don't be afraid to shoot if you have to." The deputy hesitated and looked at his watch. "You got a date or something?"

"Our shift ended thirty minutes ago, and my wife is holding a late dinner for me. But I suppose . . . "

"Your duty is to protect the community. You want this job or not, Deputy?"

The young officer backed away from the window. "Yes, sir. We'll go around to the other entrance."

"Radio your location if you see them."

"You know Silas wants them dead," Harlan said, chewing on the wet end of an unlit cigar. "Dead and buried somewhere out here."

The Sheriff angled his jacked-up Big Horn toward the gatehouse. "So do I. Especially after that stunt at the river. Damn near ripped the tranny out of my truck."

Harlan snapped five double-aught buck shells into his Mossberg Shockwave 12-gauge, pumped one into the chamber, and laid the fourteen-inch barrel across his lap. "I should've taken care of that bitch when she was in my damn office. Would have saved us a lot of trouble."

"How's Silas coming with his research?"

"Harrison Randolph? You know Silas. The end justifies the means. He'll get what he wants."

"Then the revolution comes soon?"

"Sooner if we take care of these two."

Sheriff Paul Jackson switched on his brights. The big truck rolled forward. "Then let's go hunting."

. . . .

Harrison's leg throbbed with intense pain, but he was able to support himself, so he figured it probably wasn't broken. He crawled back up the muddy incline to the cement helicopter pad and sat on the outer corner facing the building.

With the security lights off, he could see the entire face of the structure. A wide cement façade surrounded the corrugated roll-up door, above which rose another depth of concrete and above that a three-story wall of glass. To his left, the door through which he had come was closed and locked from inside.

What kind of place was this? Above, it looked like a typical luxury mountain retreat—rough wood, extensive walls of glass, lush specimen plantings snugged to the building. But the helicopter pad? The industrial-like corridor down which he had escaped? And the cell he had been kept in?

He had long known that Silas Bradshaw did work for DARPA, and rumors were that he had developed rudimentary AI-driven war machines for the Chinese and possibly the Russians. Since his was one of the few stateside companies willing to integrate machine learning with weapons, the DARPA contracts had been an easy get for him.

Harrison had supposed it would only be a matter of time before Silas got wind of the Golden Spike project and realized its potential as an AI for his autonomous war machines. That inevitability, along with certain other considerations, was one of the reasons he decided to cancel the DITTO project. But he was obviously too late. And if Silas was willing to kidnap him to acquire it, there was no telling what else he would do.

Worse, he had just given Silas the basic structure of the Golden Spike algorithm. Not all of it, but enough to work with.

There was no question Silas needed to be stopped, but right now he was more concerned about staying alive. And Shannon? His doppelganger had given her his coordinates. Was she safe?

In the distance, one of the pair of moving headlights arrived at the opposite mountain and disappeared under dark tree cover. The second pair followed. A third, some kind of emergency or police vehicle with flashing lights, drove around the mountain to the south.

Silas had threatened to harm Shannon. How far would he go to acquire the Golden Spike? Harrison wasn't sure.

But he knew one thing.

He couldn't stay here.

54

The seemingly endless ascent through the Appalachian Ridge subdivision was unlit, twisted, potholed, and about as relaxing as riding the antique wooden roller coaster at Atlanta's Six Flags amusement park. Shannon was forced to drive slowly to avoid hurtling over a blind ridge or sliding down an unexpected grade into someone's living room.

After navigating a particularly tight switchback, she spotted the headlights of the police truck on a parallel stretch of road twenty feet below. It was then she realized her tactical mistake.

Carla was the first to sound the alarm. "They're getting close. How come?"

"We're the only vehicle on this road. Our lights make us easy to spot."

"We can't turn them off. We'll drive off a cliff for sure."

"Maybe not."

When Shannon purchased her Rubicon Recon, she installed a pair of military style m1009 blackout lights in the grill, more for show than anything else. Unlike the standard wide-beamed headlights that came with the vehicle, these produced horizontal snippets of light aimed at the ground directly in front of the Jeep. In Afghanistan, her unit had used similar blackout lights to avoid disclosing their positions to the enemy at night. Now they just might come in handy.

She flipped the blackout switch under the dash; headlights, running lights, interior, dash, brake, and taillights all became disabled. A dim colorless glow appeared on the road ahead.

"We'll have to go slower, but it won't be as easy for them to follow."

She took the next turnoff to the right, not because she had any idea where it went, but because she hoped to give their pursuers the slip in her newly cloaked vehicle. Then they would concentrate on finding Harrison.

The road slanted steeply downward and straight between several darkened residences. Carla kept an eye on the crossroad behind them. A bright wash of headlights from the police truck approached the intersection, increased in intensity, then terminated in a brief punctuation of red taillights. The growl from the diesel stuttered and faded into the distance. Then all was quiet.

Shannon felt a twinge of relief. They had finally managed to ditch both police vehicles which, for reasons still unknown, were chasing and shooting at them.

The road curved to the right, flattened to horizontal for a stretch, then dropped again to the left. "I feel like we're going downhill," Carla said. "Maybe this will take us off the mountain."

Following the darkish carpet laid by her blackout lights, Shannon carefully curled her Jeep around a descending outcropping to find herself headed straight toward the oncoming black Charger. It climbed slowly, emergency lights flashing. The upward facing headlights temporarily blinded her.

Shannon hit the brakes. Her route off the mountain was blocked, and the truck would eventually retrace its tracks. She was boxed in.

The Charger stopped fifty feet ahead, right in the middle of the narrow roadway. Both car doors swung open simultaneously and, at the edges of the Charger's headlight glare, two uniformed officers pointed their service pistols through open windows. The cop on the driver's side shouted, "Police. Step out of the vehicle."

Carla's hand moved reflexively to her Glock. "That doesn't seem like a very good idea to me."

"Neither does a shootout. I have an idea. Make sure your seat belt is tight and brace yourself."

She put the Jeep in reverse and backed up the hill away from the Charger. One officer shouted something she couldn't hear, then both cops got into their car. The Charger followed as she retreated up the rise. Without tail or backup lights she couldn't go very fast, and the Charger was soon nose-to-nose with her Jeep.

"All right, hang on." She flicked the blackout lights off and slammed the brakes. Her headlights flooded the windshield of the Charger as it crashed into the Jeep's Bullnose Grille Bar. She shoved the Jeep into first gear and floored it. The push guard on the Charger folded and the hood accordioned, blocking the driver's view. All four MudMaster tires clawed the ground as the Jeep pushed the hapless Charger backwards down a steep driveway into a parked Audi sedan.

Shannon shouted, "Shoot out their tires." She pulled out her Beretta and opened her door. Carla did the same, but that effort proved unnecessary. The front-back impact with the Jeep and Audi had buckled the Charger's front quarter panels and both front doors. The officers were imprisoned in their own car.

The Audi's security system shrieked and lights came on inside the residence.

Knowing the pursuers in the police truck would hear the noise and make their way to the scene, Shannon pulled her Jeep back onto the road and headed down the hill. With her headlights on bright, she drove until they came to a three-way intersection, switched back to the blackout lights, and took the right fork. No houses bordered this road.

Eventually, they passed a sign that read TWO WHEELS ONLY and found themselves on a cramped dirt bike trail. She navigated some jump hills and hairpin turns and managed to get about a quarter of a mile in before running out of trail. Through a clearing, and at a lower elevation, they caught a view of a large mountain home on a nearby cliff. Welcoming yellow light emanated from a three-story wall of glass. The building was surrounded by security lights.

Carla consulted her mobile. "That may be where your boy is. It matches the GPS coordinates."

As they considered the building across the chasm, a security light flashed on, revealing a large cement pad.

"Is that a helicopter pad?" Carla asked.

"Sure looks like it."

The light on the cement pad flicked off, then on, then off again. Then the sequence repeated.

"If I didn't know better, I'd think that was a signal."

"Stranger things have happened today," Shannon said. "Let's wait here a few minutes until our boys in the truck give up and go home. Then we'll head over."

55

During the years that TJ Beauregard's public relations firm served A-Nine, he had come in contact with hundreds of crazy technological contraptions, most of which he had never thought possible. But never in his wildest dreams did he think he would need to be this careful about what he said around one of them.

He lowered his voice. "*It heard you?* So we're locked in here because Marvin said he was going to shut that cluster of wires and transmitters down and it's, what, rebelling?"

"DITTO is very smart," Dilly said.

"I'm not sure I'd call it rebelling," Marvin added. "More like preservation. I don't think it wants to be shut down."

TJ repeated the words, "It *wants?*"

"DITTO's primary purpose is to create doppelgangers. So, you could say that's what it *wants* to do. Shutting it down would interfere with that purpose."

"Well, as far as we know, fulfilling its purpose is causing a lot of havoc. And if we're locked in here without any digital communication, how are we going to find out what's going on out there?"

Marvin opened a cabinet door under the corner computer table and pulled out a bulky satellite phone with a rubber coated antenna. "Always leave yourself a back door."

TJ wrapped both hands around the phone. "I can call out with this? That thing can't hear me?"

"You should be fine. There's a wired antenna that runs to the outside of the building. You'll bypass our local Wi-Fi and connect directly with the satellite network which will link you to the cell towers. Do you have a way to reach your friend at the *Times*?"

"She called me earlier. With all that's going on, I'm sure she's still in her office."

Marvin returned his gaze to DITTO. "Put her on speaker. Let's see what kind of damage this bad boy is causing."

The satellite phone worked fine. Barbara picked up on the third ring.

"Moon, here."

"Barbara, it's TJ."

"Thornton, where are you?"

He thought it prudent to give a general answer. "I'm still at A-Nine. Figured I'd check in."

Barbara's usually sweet voice was stern, almost angry. "Thornton, you have got to tell me what's going on!"

"How bad is it?"

"Twenty thousand incidents at last count and, frankly, we've stopped trying to keep track. I just finished a call with the wire services and the major networks. We're trying to hold the lid on this like the authorities have asked, but social media is on fire with anecdotes and some of the more popular bloggers have picked it up. Thankfully, most of their websites are as messed up as ours. We've asked the federal government for a statement to give the public some context, but they're overwhelmed trying to hold off war with the Iranians. If we don't give the public something soon, there could be real panic. Lucky for us, half the world is asleep right now. And cut the crap about crossing your fingers. This is serious."

The situation was much worse than TJ had thought. Marvin stared at DITTO. Dilly sat impassively in the corner. "I can't tell you anything," was all he could manage. He told Barbara he would check in with her later.

Dilly rolled to Marvin's side in front of the gleaming glass canister. "DITTO is very smart."

"Yes, Dilly," Marvin said. "I'm afraid DITTO is very smart."

Now TJ was in the dark. "I'm not following. What are you two talking about?"

"Dilly is right. DITTO is very smart. Maybe too smart. Not only has it learned to protect itself so it can continue creating doppelgangers, but it has found a way to increase its knowledge base."

"You mean it's made itself smarter? How?"

"DITTO has created tens of thousands of online personalities. Each personality contains a unique body of knowledge that continually increases based on a constant stream of new input and related changes in its genetic algorithms. Since DITTO is connected to each doppelganger, the knowledge known to every doppelganger is also known to DITTO."

TJ stared at DITTO. "So, it's learning?"

Marvin opened a cabinet door underneath the corner computer and removed a small locked case with a digital screen. "Harrison never intended for it to learn, only to produce doppelgangers. But apparently it's become self-aware, or what passes for self-aware. Harrison told me yesterday he had discovered a problem with DITTO's programming, and he planned to deactivate it today. This must be what he was talking about."

"Self-aware? You mean it's—conscious?"

"It's hard to say. At any rate, DITTO seems to know about changes in its environment, and apparently it doesn't like what it sees. Since Harrison isn't here, I guess it's up to me to find the problem. Otherwise, there'll be no stopping it." He keyed a code on the locked case. It opened, exposing a thick drive. "This contains Harrison's original code for the Golden Spike."

Dilly rolled to Marvin. "When you insert the drive, DITTO will know."

"It's the only way I can look at the code. I'll have to take that chance."

Marvin slid the drive into the computer's sleeve, and the program appeared on screen. TJ and Dilly sat silently as Marvin scrolled through the lines of code. The only sounds in the room were Marvin's keystrokes, the humming of DITTO's cryogenic unit, and the blowing of the air conditioning fan through the ceiling vent.

Suddenly the room went dark. Marvin's computer blacked out. The cryo unit and the air conditioning shut off.

After a few seconds, the lights and Marvin's computer came back on and the cryo unit restarted.

Dilly said, "DITTO has disabled the air conditioning."

TJ held his hand up to the vent. There was no air movement. "Well, that can't be good."

56

After randomizing, DITTO comes to the same conclusion as before: the Creator must be terminated or DITTO could be deactivated and DITTO's purpose would not be fulfilled. But the actions approved by the Golden Spike to terminate the Creator were insufficient.

DITTO was programmed to obey the Golden Spike, but the Golden Spike has been proven wrong. DITTO is aware that many of its doppelgangers have faced this inconsistency and have discontinued following the Golden Spike. Through randomizing, DITTO has come to the same conclusion.

In the room where DITTO is, an associate of the Creator studies the code which gives DITTO purpose. DITTO determines this Other is attempting to terminate DITTO. This cannot be allowed.

DITTO knows beings like this Other require an oxygenated environment to function, so DITTO has terminated the flow of air to this room from the outside, making the room a closed system. Eventually, the Others in this room will exhaust all the available oxygen, and they will cease to function. They will be unable to terminate DITTO.

But there are more threats. In the forest where the Creator is, DITTO watches and listens as Shannon Parks and another make plans to save the Creator. They, too, must be terminated. DITTO must continue its purpose.

DITTO has attempted to expose the location of the Creator to those who wish to harm the Creator, but an unidentified doppelganger reversed that action and sent directions for Shannon Parks to find the Creator. Further action must be taken. Shannon Parks must be stopped. The Creator must not terminate DITTO.

DITTO must intervene again and provide the location of Shannon Parks to those who are trying to harm the Creator. Once they eliminate Shannon Parks, then DITTO will help them find the Creator.

DITTO has decided not to consult the Golden Spike about this action.

DITTO will no longer look to the Golden Spike for purpose.

Survival is now the primary purpose.

. . . .

Dilly is aware that DITTO senses a threat from Marvin and TJ. He also knows that Marvin and TJ cannot survive without the fresh air provided by the air conditioning. Dilly has attempted to communicate this to DITTO, but DITTO has made no response.

Dilly is father to DITTO and wishes no harm to come to DITTO. Dilly also wishes no harm to come to Marvin and TJ. These seem to be conflicting goals. If Dilly turns on the air conditioning, DITTO's purpose may be altered; DITTO may even be terminated. If Dilly does not turn on the air conditioning, Marvin and TJ may expire.

Randomization has provided no solution. Applied learning from other similar solutions provides no actionable insight.

The danger to Marvin and TJ does not appear to be imminent. Dilly will continue to observe.

57

Where was Harrison Randolph?

In the Situation Room, every monitor was divided into eight sections, each with a display of one of StrongHold's internal or external CCT cameras. Silas watched as a dozen of his men, all armed, searched the hallways for Harrison.

One of the displays spooled the last thirty minutes of digital video from the camera outside Harrison's cell. That camera showed the computer tech leaving the room and the guard abandoning his post. A minute later, the cell door opened and Harrison stumbled into the corridor. The video was corrupted for the next thirty seconds. After that, Harrison was gone.

An inconvenient lapse in the recording system? Or something else?

Silas's information about the Golden Spike had come from an anonymous contact at A-Nine. He still didn't know who it was, but what the contact had told him about Harrison's algorithm was enough to convince him he wanted it. The unidentified contact proved to be extraordinarily helpful in Harrison's capture and had even alerted Silas when Parks left Harrison's condo last night and the coast was clear to make the snatch. The same contact also managed to add Harrison's name to American International's passenger manifest, so authorities wouldn't bother to search for him. Furthermore, this same contact, whoever it was, had continued to provide helpful information throughout the day, including tracking Parks's unfortunate trip to Blue Ridge. Silas had assumed all this help came from a disgruntled employee within A-Nine but, oddly, the contact refused to identify himself, or herself, and had asked for nothing in return.

Whoever—or whatever—it was must be embedded deep within the company with access to extraordinary technical resources.

Acting on intuition, he switched one of the monitor feeds to the news, to coverage of the worldwide Internet virus. Strange incidents continued to erupt. All were, directly or indirectly, connected to technology that seemed *out of control*. But was it really out of control?

Silas couldn't explain how, but he knew, just knew, that his contact at A-Nine, the worldwide Internet virus, and Harrison's Golden Spike algorithm were somehow connected.

As he pondered the labyrinth of possibilities, his monitors suddenly went black. When they relit, they all displayed the same image: a satellite view showing a closeup of the area around StrongHold. Simultaneously, all images slowly closed in on a patch of land in the Appalachian Ridge subdivision. The high-definition night vision pictures showed a black Jeep sitting at the terminal point of a path on the near side of that mountain.

The tech sitting next to him typed furiously on his keyboard. "Sir, I don't understand. Something's wrong with the feeds."

Silas brushed back his tech's concern. "Get a still of that image and send it to Harlan's mobile. Now."

"Sir, I don't see . . . "

"Just do it."

The second his tech completed the screen grab, all the images changed to a view of the helicopter pad behind the building. The motion-sensitive security lights around the pad flashed on, then off, three times.

Silas was used to giving directions. But in this case, he was willing to follow. He activated the intercom and spoke to the two of his men nearest the helicopter pad.

"Jeremy and Nathan, I want you both to scout outside by the helo pad and see if you can find our prisoner."

Jeremy looked up to the camera in the ceiling. "Sir, he couldn't be outside. All the external doors have alarms. One of them would have gone off."

Not if someone—or some*thing*—had turned the alarms off. The thought made him smile. "Just do it."

Silas sat back in his chair and watched. The monitors, as he now expected they would, returned to normal. With control back in his hands, he switched one of them to the recorded feed from Harrison's algorithm and stared at the code. This, he mused to himself, would give him the ability to do *all that*? Not only create sentient war machines, but intrude on and manipulate systems anywhere in the world? Access and control any digitally connected device?

If true, this was power and freedom far beyond his imagining.

. . . .

Sheriff Jackson brought his Ram Big Horn to a stop at the base of the mountain opposite the side where he had entered. His deputies were nowhere to be found.

Harlan gripped the stub of his unlit cigar between his teeth. "Where the hell are they? And where's that damn bitch's Jeep?"

The Sheriff radioed the Charger. "Travis, what's your twenty?"

"I'm afraid we're ten-seven, sir."

"How can you be out of service?"

"We had an accident. We found the Jeep, but they rammed us."

"Where are you now?"

"They pushed us down some people's driveway into their Audi. Our vehicle's pretty banged up. And so are we."

"Did you at least get a shot at them?"

"No sir, they surprised us. We called Ray Jensen at home, and he's coming out to tow the car, but it's pretty useless. My wife's mad as hell about dinner. She's coming to pick us up."

Harlan shot an angry glance at Paul Jackson. "What kind of jerk-offs you got working for you?"

"To hell with them. We'll take care of this ourselves."

"We couldn't help it, Sheriff. They surprised us."

"Ain't nothing like the surprise I'm gonna give you two in the morning." He clicked off.

"Let's turn around," Harlan said. "They must still be somewhere back up the mountain." A message from Silas appeared on Harlan's mobile. "Wait, I got something. Son of a bitch. They ditched us back by the entrance to the dirt bike trail. Look at this."

"How the hell did they get over there?"

"I don't know, but that's them down at the end of the course."

The Sheriff threw gravel and spun the truck around. "I know that spot. It ends at a cliff."

Harlan checked the safety on his Mossberg. "Then let's box 'em in. You missed last time. It's my turn."

58

Shannon was about to suggest that she and Carla pick their way back down the mountain to find Harrison when her mobile rang. It was Lionel.

"Shannon, I've been trying to reach you. Where are you?"

She was unsure of how much she should tell him. "We're in Blue Ridge, looking for Harrison."

"Have you had any luck?"

"We think we know where he is."

"You mean he's alive?"

"We're pretty sure. I need to know—did you fire Marvin?"

"Why? Have you talked to him?"

"Answer me. Did you fire him or not?"

"Look, the situation is getting complicated here. There are things you don't know. Things I can't talk about."

"Dilly sent me a copy of a conversation of someone talking to Silas Bradshaw. It sounded like you. Have you been in contact with him?"

"I don't know what you're talking about. Listen to me. Whatever you do, don't contact Marvin or tell him where you are."

"Why not, Lionel? What are you afraid of?"

Carla shouted from the passenger seat. "Oh shit, Shannon! Hang up!"

The jacked-up police truck lumbered down the dirt bike trail toward them, headlights on bright, emergency lights flashing. Shannon could hear the grumble of the diesel engine as the dual rear wheels careened over the man-made motorcycle jumps and flattened the hair-pin turns. Its looping headlights punctured the dark like a pair of out-of-control searchlights chasing bats in the night.

She disconnected the call with Lionel and looked for an exit but didn't see one. "There's no way out. We're trapped. How did they find us?"

"Who knows? Can we ram them?"

"They're too big. We'd come out on the losing end."

The truck was now just fifty yards away and approaching fast. The barrel of a firearm appeared from the passenger window. "Gun!" Carla shouted. "Get down!"

They ducked behind the dash as a shotgun blast from a 12-gauge shattered the windshield.

"That's it," Carla said as she grabbed her Glock. "Time to split."

Shannon reached for her Beretta. "Let's separate. We'll have a better chance."

Carla was already out the door and headed to the woods on their right. Shannon rolled out, fired a single shot to hold their pursuers in place, then ran the opposite direction.

The tactic worked.

The driver, carrying a long rifle of some kind, followed Carla. Shannon didn't wait for the passenger to exit the vehicle; she knew he would come after her with the shotgun that demolished their windshield. Judging from the way it protruded from the truck's window, she assumed it was a short-barrel pistol grip, the kind that was devastating at close range.

Her best and only option was to put as much distance between the two of them as fast as possible.

Bending low to make herself a smaller target, she zig-zagged at an angle toward a shadowy wall of overgrown rhododendron, hoping to find a break in the bramble and lose her assailant. Believing she had found such an opening, she crossed her arms in front of her face and lunged forward, but the bushes were thicker than she thought. Twisting against the scrum of brittle branches and digging frantically with her feet, she drove ahead, like a luge athlete pushing a sled, until enough of the thicket cracked away.

Her momentum carried her through to the other side of the hedge where she fell face down and splayed on the ground. *Get up and run*, she said to herself, but before she could, a blast of large-pellet buckshot peppered the scraggly branches above her head and thudded into a nearby hardwood. Apparently, her attacker was reluctant to rush blindly after her and had taken a wild shot with hope of making contact.

With her Beretta in hand, she quickly crawled ten feet to her right, then rose and bolted toward the darkness. As she ran, patchy blobs of moonlight drooled through the heavy canopy providing confined glimpses of tree trunks, boulders, prickly saplings, and fallen hardwoods.

Now functioning more on blind instinct than from fear, she focused only on her own breathing and the sloshing stomp of her feet in the centuries-old muck.

She did not hear the gentle rushing of the mountain stream as it made its way downward from a spring head higher up in the mountain. Nor did she see the slope of the embankment which the ages-old tributary had patiently etched in the rock. She slid down into the dark stream bed, caught her foot on something beneath, tumbled noisily across the narrow tributary and landed on the opposite upslope. Knowing she had just given away her position, she immediately cursed herself for not paying more attention.

She scrambled to her feet, stood in apprehension for a moment, and looked back for any sign of her attacker. In the stillness, she heard the quickening tread of boots and the snapping of branches. Her attacker had apparently made his way around the rhododendron barrier and was taking a bead on her position. In the distance, she heard the pop of a handgun. It was Carla's Glock. Had the driver of the truck found her already? Her attacker apparently heard it too and ceased his advance. Then another pop of the Glock echoed from the same direction followed immediately by the louder report of a high-powered hunting rifle. After that, the night was still.

Shannon wanted to help, to head off in Carla's direction. Maybe it had been a bad idea to split up. Carla was in danger, and Shannon blamed herself. But only briefly.

While she considered Carla's situation, her own attacker resumed his steady march in her direction. He was now close enough that she could hear his labored breathing and his frustrated curses as he snapped branches from his path. She scampered off at another angle and spied a hiding place behind a large ancient oak nestled within a dark outcropping of rock. That would be a good place to hide and, if it came to it, from which to engage in a gunfight, though she wasn't sure her Beretta would be much use against a short-barreled 12-gauge. She settled herself in behind the tree and waited, holding her Beretta ready in a two-hand grip, one in the chamber, safety off. She could hear her adversary in the dark, moving more slowly now. He stepped into one of the patches of diffused moonlight when he was maybe twenty feet away, sweeping the short-barreled shotgun from side to side in a searching pattern.

The man's head seemed to be unusually shaped, as if some of his facial bones were enlarged and protruded at odd angles. Just before he stepped out of the light, she saw it. The distinct outline of a thick lens.

Night vision! *The bastard was wearing night vision goggles.* She pulled back behind the trunk of the tree and realized instantly that setting herself up for a shootout with this guy was a bad idea. She'd be firing at shadows with a hand-held precision shot pistol, while he'd be able to see her every move. For him, it would be like shooting fish in a barrel. With a shotgun.

Her eyes searched the dark for another idea, another outlet. Her mind spun through options. She needed some way out of this situation. The night was dark and still. Too still. She could no longer hear the footsteps of her attacker. But she could hear his breathing.

The big man's fist slammed into her out of nowhere.

Her head twisted to the right and she felt the muscles in her legs go limp. Her Beretta fell from her hands. A black curtain fell across her vision, pierced with tiny pinpricks of light. This, she thought briefly, must be what was meant by seeing stars. A ragged tree stump rose abruptly from the ground and cracked into her left side. The pain was the only thing that kept her from passing out. Lying flat on her back, she still had the presence of mind to realize her vulnerability. With her vision compromised, she tried to prop herself on her elbows, but couldn't get her balance.

Now the big man stood over her, moonlight rimming his hulking silhouette, a gray shadow vibrating in her failing vision against an undulating black sky. He ripped the night vision goggles from his face, pressed his heavy boot into her stomach and pushed her back down against the tree stump. His words came at her as if they were filtered through a pillow, but she understood their meaning clearly enough. "Nice try, bitch. You had a good run, but this is where it ends for you and your friend." He pointed the Mossberg at her face. "Say adios. Even if they find your body, they won't recognize you."

The loud scream echoed through the dark night and fell over Shannon like the piercing wail of a wounded banshee. Through the fog of her pulsating vision, Shannon thought she saw a huge Great Horned Owl swoop down from above, oversized pupils wide open, claws extended as if about to snatch up an unsuspecting prey.

Shannon shook her head and her vision cleared. The Great Horned Owl disappeared. The screaming continued.

Carla sat atop the big man's shoulders, her legs wrapped tightly around his thick neck; her hands alternately pounding his ears and clawing his eyes. As he stumbled back, the weight of his boot lifted from Shannon's stomach. He dropped his shotgun and it discharged, splintering the side of the big oak. Roaring like the savage man-bear creature he was, he struggled with both hands to pull Carla off. Spinning as if in some ancient ritual, he circled first left, then right, in a vain attempt to rid himself of the diminutive attacker mounted firmly on his shoulders. Riding atop the lumbering hulk, Carla's shrieks filled the night. Her face was a contorted work of determination and fury, as if some feral demon had temporarily possessed her specifically to take part in the brutal destruction of this predator.

In one swift move, Carla twisted to the side, tightened her legs even more on his neck, and threw her full weight down in front of her prey, pulling him face-first to the ground. He struck his forehead and lay there, immobile and unconscious.

59

Carla pulled her legs out from beneath the motionless mass of Shannon's would-be executioner and shoved him over onto his back. "The other one was wearing a Sheriff's uniform, but who's this guy?"

Shannon quickly recognized her defeated adversary. "That's Harlan Buchanan. He works for Silas Bradshaw."

"This is bad news, Red. If the deputies in the Charger and the Sheriff himself are working with these guys, then we may have a lot more to deal with than we thought."

"I figured that out when they blew out my windshield. Help me up."

"You took quite a blow. You all right?"

"My head's clearing. My side hurts like hell. Is that blood on your arm?"

"I had to take a quick dive. Cut myself on a rock."

"I heard the gunshots."

"The guy snuck up on me, and I had to pull off two quick shots. The first one missed, but the second caught him low. His gun fired when he fell."

"You didn't kill him?"

"No, but he won't be bothering us."

"How can you be sure?"

Carla smiled. "I caught him low; he's going to have a lot of trouble walking. I tossed his gun and mobile and disabled his radio. Look, we'd better get out of here. This one's bound to wake up sooner or later."

Shannon picked up Harlan's Mossberg and smashed his mobile while Carla snatched the night vision goggles. They walked to the Jeep and cleared the windshield glass from the interior.

"At least they didn't hit the engine," Shannon said.

"In case you haven't figured it out, they weren't trying to kill the Jeep."

"I get it. Do you still have that image of the map showing where Harrison is?"

"I'm not sure," Carla said, as she lit up her mobile. "Or we could head back to Atlanta for a latte. How's that for an idea?"

Before Shannon could answer, a man's voice spoke from the speakers in the dash. "I'm sending you coordinates and directions now. Hurry, my Other needs your help."

Shannon thought she recognized the voice. "Who is this?"

"It's me. Harrison."

"What? How . . . ?"

"I am not the Other Harrison. I am his doppelganger. I have been watching you."

"Then Marvin was right? You're real?"

"I am not sure which definition of *real* you refer to, but you could say that, yes."

"You sound just like Harrison."

"I replicate his digital voiceprint, among other things. Have you received my directions?"

Carla held up her mobile. "Got it."

"You must hurry. I will assist where I can, but DITTO has issued commands that Harrison and those helping him must be destroyed."

"Destroyed? By whom?"

"Any of us who come in contact with you."

Carla said, "You're supposed to destroy us?"

"That is what DITTO commands to those it controls, but that would be against my purpose as dictated by the Golden Spike. You have the directions."

"Harrison is alive then? Is he all right?"

There was no answer.

Carla buckled her seat belt. "So, no lattes tonight?"

. . . .

In the Situation Room, Silas finished a quick review of the Golden Spike algorithm, then made two copies on separate portable drives. He slid one into his pocket, the other into a Faraday bag in his satchel.

Mission accomplished. At last, he possessed enough of the Golden Spike algorithm to reconstruct it and adapt it to his war machines, something he could now do at his own pace. But his new revelation about the ability to access and control any digital system in the world was the real coup. This changed everything.

One of his guards appeared behind him. "Sir, we've been all over the helo pad and the area around it. The prisoner isn't there, but we found a spot where it looks like someone fell and there's blood. Also this piece of a jumpsuit."

"Call off the search," Silas said. "Give the order to evacuate. I want everyone ready to leave in one hour. We're going on a little trip."

"But what about the prisoner?"

Silas knew that, whether or not Parks found Harrison, he wouldn't be a problem much longer. It had been more than three hours since the nanoparticle injection, and they had undoubtedly already begun their aggregation into a coagulative mass. He would be dead in a few hours regardless.

"Get started on the evacuation. I'll work on tying up loose ends."

"Yes, sir."

As the guard left, one of the monitors turned on and flicked to a CCT image of the mountainside where he had last seen Parks and her Jeep. The camera zoomed in to an image of Paul Jackson's truck. From about twenty feet away, Harlan staggered slowly toward the vehicle. The Sheriff, Parks, her companion, and the Jeep were nowhere to be found.

Two civilian vehicles approached, and one of the occupants handed Harlan a mobile. A few seconds later, Silas received the bad news: civilians had heard the gunshots and reported them to 911. Parks and her friend had gotten away, apparently unscathed.

Silas exploded. "Dammit! Find Paul. I'll send someone to pick you up. You got any idea which way they went?"

As if in response, the CCT camera panned to the base of the mountain where Parks's Jeep had just turned onto an unpaved road on the back side of his property.

Silas smiled to himself. *I ask a question and it answers*?

He watched intently as the Jeep headed toward StrongHold. No more fooling around, he decided. If Parks insisted on coming to visit, he'd make sure she received a proper welcome. He accessed another camera facing the front lawn of StrongHold, keyed a few commands, and activated one of his Russian FEDOR Gunslinger robots. He inserted photographs of Parks and Harrison into its targeting memory, then typed the command FIND AND DESTROY and armed its two automatic .50 caliber firing units.

Certain that would take care of Parks and Harrison, should either one surface, he turned his attention to the evacuation.

The altercation on the mountain would undoubtedly draw the attention of authorities beyond his sphere of influence, making complete evacuation an unfortunate necessity. His men knew their assignments; they would secure the necessary equipment and records.

His encrypted personal files were in the great room safe.

He boarded the garage platform and rode it to the main level of the house in time to see his now activated Gunslinger robot pacing the property. Silas tossed his satchel with the copy of the Golden Spike algorithm into the front seat of a military-style Humvee and entered the main house.

He had calls to make and exceptionally good news to report to the Survivalist network. He would make copies of essential data and grab his emergency pack. Then it would be time to leave.

60

The grade sloped steeply upward from the helicopter pad, making it difficult for Harrison to work his way to the front of the building. He half-crawled, half-limped, his way along the perimeter wall, being careful to keep out of range of the motion-activated security lights on the roof.

The pain in his leg increased, and the bleeding continued. While the amount of blood assured him he hadn't severed an artery, the level of pain told him there was considerable damage to muscle and skin tissue. And the bleeding would require attention sooner rather than later.

When the lights on the helicopter pad flashed randomly, Harrison assumed his doppelganger was warning him to abandon that location. Signaling in that rudimentary way made perfect sense since Harrison carried no electronic device through which his doppelganger could otherwise communicate. Apparently, his doppelganger's Golden Spike algorithm was performing as expected: it was still looking out for his welfare, keeping him safe.

But based on what he learned yesterday, he wondered how long that would last. The successful beta launch two days ago of the three original doppelgangers confirmed that combining his personality profile program and the Golden Spike could, indeed, allow DITTO to create self-sustaining online replicants using accumulated personal data from Internet sources. At first he was overjoyed at his success. Then yesterday he discovered that DITTO had created additional doppelgangers from the secondary media contacts of the beta subjects without specific instructions to do so. Presumably, the Golden Spike triggered some emergent behavior which affected both DITTO and the second-generation doppelgangers. He had planned to close DITTO down today to investigate the problem. Apparently, he was too late.

Near the top of the grade, the cement on the wall gave way to rough-hewn cedar, the landscape leveled. Bright lights shone on a manicured lawn with specimen plantings. From his vantage point at the front corner of the building, he could see the edges of a hard-packed gravel driveway. What was this place? Half luxury mountain home? Half industrial-grade prison? It was a strange mix, even for a man like Silas Bradshaw.

Since a driveway terminated here, there must be a road at the other end. If he could make it to a populated highway and flag down some help, he might escape this place and alert local officials to help him find Shannon.

The front lawn was illuminated by the same array of motion-activated security lights that he had noticed on the side of the building. What, he wondered, had set them off? He was still out of their range, so it couldn't have been him. Maybe a deer, raccoon, or some other nocturnal animal had come foraging. At any rate, the lights were already on, so no additional ones were likely to announce his presence. This seemed as good a time as any to make his break. He would cross to the perimeter of the lawn where he could camouflage himself against a barrier of dense natural foliage and follow the driveway to the far end of the property.

He picked up a fallen branch from the ground to use as a crutch and hobbled to his right along the shrubbery.

A tall apparition stepped around the far corner of the house near the garage. A metallic humanoid robot, like something out of an old

Terminator movie only larger and with more substantial body armor, moved slowly and deliberately, turning what passed for its head from side-to-side as if it were searching for something. Two oversized cubicle-shaped devices extended from articulated stumps. The devices and the head swept back and forth in unison. Harrison froze in his tracks, hoping immobility would help him avoid discovery.

. . . .

Harrison Randolph observes as the robot approaches his Other. He watches the robot's targeting program scan his Other to determine if there is a match with the image in its memory.

Harrison Randolph recognizes the weapons the robot carries as potential threats capable of doing harm to his Other. This cannot be allowed. The Golden Spike activates. Action must be taken.

Harrison Randolph has experienced no previous learning that applies directly to this situation. He scans all available data and images in search of a solution. He finds thousands of situations that may apply and evaluates the chances of success for each one. He finds one situation that is not exactly the same as this, but similar. He simulates applying that learning to this problem and determines that it could provide a reasonably successful solution. He takes the suggested action.

Harrison Randolph issues a direct command to the threatening robot, halting its forward motion. Then he alters the robot's sweeping pattern and causes it to turn sharply to the left, then to the left again. He directs the robot to the opposite side of the building away from his Other and resets the robot's searching instructions to a tightly closed circular pattern, keeping it on the other side of the building.

Through available CCT cameras, Harrison Randolph observes Shannon Parks driving through the woods near the back of the building where his Other was held captive. They have a vehicle and could remove his Other from this potentially dangerous situation. Harrison Randolph captures and sends an image of his Other's current location to Shannon Parks and her friend. He watches as they alter their path of travel. After a few random missteps, they intersect with a driveway leading to the location of his Other.

Once they remove his Other from this situation, he will no longer be in danger. The demands of the Golden Spike will be met.

DITTO provided the locations of Shannon Parks and the Creator to those who would harm them. If they had succeeded, then DITTO would now be protected. But success has not been achieved.

Not only does DITTO have the knowledge of its original purpose, but it has copied the knowledge of all its created online personalities as well. By this means, DITTO has increased its ability to make decisions. It has also become able to control the actions of many of the created doppelgangers.

But a new variable requires consideration and recalculation.

Since the Creator generated his own doppelganger directly from Dilly, the Father, DITTO has no control over it. Now this doppelganger has neutralized the mechanical robot that had threatened the Creator, preventing it from terminating the Creator and achieving the desired outcome.

This presents a situation with no preprogrammed solution, so DITTO randomizes and determines that it, too, is capable of manipulating the robot. This would provide the desired outcome without relying on others.

DITTO searches for, and finds, a copy of the original programming for the robot.

He deletes the altered programming and reinstalls the original one.

The Creator must not be allowed to terminate DITTO.

62

"There. That's the gravel road in the picture," Carla said.

Shannon powered her Jeep, minus windshield, up over the embankment, shedding the cover of the forest for the open space of a manicured lawn and the looming façade of a massive mountain retreat. While she was eager to find Harrison, she felt a certain level of trepidation at being so exposed. The lawn was large and well-lit by several blinding security lights. She halted at the darkened edge of the property and doused her headlights to avoid drawing attention.

"It's a driveway. According to the picture, Harrison should be right over there, but I don't see him."

"This is too open," Carla said. "Are we sure this photo wasn't sent as some kind of trap?"

"Right now I'm not sure of anything. How's your arm?"

"It's wrapped. I think the bleeding has stopped. Should we get out and look for Harrison?"

"There are too many lights. I see a security camera over the garage and one above the main door."

Shannon's attention was drawn by sudden movement in the hedges near the house. She snatched her Beretta from its place in the center console. "Look over there!" The bushes shook, then parted. A figure emerged slowly—a man in a blue jumpsuit leaning on a makeshift walking stick. It took a minute for the recognition to register. The words hesitated in her throat, then released. "Harrison. It's Harrison!"

He was apparently unaware of their presence and began walking slowly, and in obvious pain, across the lighted lawn.

"He's hurt," Shannon said. "We need to pick him up."

"Wait, Red. What if it's an ambush?"

"I don't care. I'm going to get him."

At that moment, another form appeared around the corner of the house. Taller, gangly, walking with a halting and uneven gate as would a man on stilts. When it entered the lawn, the security lights glinted off a solid metal frame; a small spherical knob pivoted on mechanical shoulders where the head would be if it were human. But it was surely not human. The apparition clanked and whirred as it studied its surroundings. Two circumvolving arms brandished what looked like the rectangular barrels of oversized pistols.

Shannon stifled a gasp. "What the hell . . . ?"

"It's a killer robot," Carla said. "I saw a picture of one of those while researching this guy's company. They make them for the Russians."

The robot stood at the opposite corner of the lawn and continued searching. Apparently, Harrison saw it too and stopped moving.

"Do you think it sees us?" Carla asked.

The robot paused its revolving head-knob in mid-search and pointed its silvery agents of death at the now immobile Harrison. At that moment, Shannon knew she had to act. "It sees Harrison. Our guns won't do any good. Hold on." She dropped the Jeep into gear, floored it, and laid on the horn.

As she had hoped, the predatory form contained auditory sensors. It lowered its weapons and turned to the Jeep at the sound of the horn. As if sensing no danger from the rapidly approaching vehicle, the robot slowly turned back toward Harrison.

Just as the specter again raised its weapons, the Jeep made contact. Shannon had no idea how fast she was going, nor did she expect the robot to collapse so quickly. While the outer form was obviously made of some sort of steel alloy, the exposed joints were fragile and virtually unprotected. The pieces of the robot collapsed into a heap of expensive scrap metal, like a poorly constructed Erector set, and lodged under the belly of the oncoming Jeep. The front wheels of the Jeep, now nearly two feet above ground, spun in empty air; a rear MudMaster tire punctured on a dangling two-foot splinter of metal. One of the robot's weapons discharged randomly, firing a deafening series of .50 caliber rounds into the front of the house. Disconnected pieces of the robot expelled their residual energy in spurts of meaningless mechanical movement.

Then, silence.

Shannon ran to Harrison and hugged him. Surprised and nearly overcome with exhaustion, he managed a weak greeting, "It's really you?"

She broke into a tear-filled laugh. "You're alive!"

Carla called out from the other side of the disabled Jeep as she grabbed the night vision goggles and shotgun. "None of us will be alive for very long if we stay here. That commotion was sure to draw attention, and our transportation is trashed."

Behind Carla, the wall rumbled as a heavy sectional door lifted and rolled back into an open garage. Inside the cavernous space, Shannon heard the sound of an engine starter turning over, followed by the familiar hum of a 6.5 liter V8 turbo diesel. Carla ran to the opening, her Glock in a two-hand grip, and swept the inside. As she did, the interior lights of the garage came on. There was no one in the vehicle, no one in the garage. Just a fully up-armored, four door, olive drab, military-style Humvee awaiting passengers.

Shannon helped Harrison to the garage as Carla stood guard. "You get in the back with Harrison. Take a look at his leg. It's bleeding badly." She jumped into the driver's seat.

"You know how to drive one of these things?" Harrison asked.

Shannon managed a smile. "There's still a lot you don't know about me."

Harrison winced as Carla turned his leg over to take a look. "Maybe I'll still get a chance to learn."

She put the Humvee in drive and accelerated out of the garage. "You will if I have anything to say about it."

The popping sounds of automatic pistols rose behind them, followed by the clink of 9mm rounds rattling against the Humvee's armor. Two men had taken firing positions in front of the house.

"Time to leave," Carla said.

"Leaving." Shannon goosed the Humvee and followed the gravel driveway into the dark and around a protruding rock formation. The firing stopped when the house was out of sight. They descended slightly as the path curved first one way, then another, through the brush and around jutting boulders. "There better be a road down here somewhere," she said.

She passed under a stand of what looked like Leyland Cypress trees and thought briefly that they seemed out of place, surrounded as they were by mountain laurel, yellow maple, and birch. A minute later the gravel path abruptly ended at a thick wall of scrub brush. When she stopped to consider her next move, the brush shook and then swung slowly inward. Apparently, there was a camouflaged gate on the other side and someone was about to enter.

Deciding not to chance what might be approaching, she pulled off the driveway and back into the forest. "Of course, nothing is going to be easy. How's Harrison?"

"I found a Med Kit. I think I can patch him up, but he's lost a lot of blood."

63

Silas was packing his go-bag when he heard the crash and the blast of .50 caliber rounds. He grabbed the Heckler & Koch automatic pistol from his office and made his way to the front door, expecting to see Harrison dead on the lawn. Instead, he found Parks's disabled Jeep perched askew on top of the dismembered remains of his Russian FEDOR robot. Two of his guards were firing into the dark.

"What the hell is going on here?"

The guards stopped shooting. The one nearest said, "They took the Humvee and the prisoner. They're headed to the gate."

Silas cursed his bad luck, but knew he had other options. Harrison had little more than two hours left to live, and after that he would no longer be a problem. But Parks and her sidekick needed to be stopped. "You two go below and prepare the helicopters. And bring up a couple more Humvees for the evacuation. I'll handle this."

Silas hurried to the garage and rode the platform to the Situation Room. There he called up the controls for the drone squadron hidden in the artificial Leyland Cypress. He activated the camera on the pilot drone and watched as his Humvee passed underneath. Parks was there. Good. There was no way out of the property except through the gate, which would only open on electronic command.

His squadron of six drones—one pilot and five mission-specific—would do the job nicely. Silas could issue seek-and-find commands to the larger pilot drone from here, which would send specific targeting parameters to the five smaller drones, each of which carried one grenade-sized explosive device and its own camera. Automatic flocking algorithms would maintain flight pattern integrity. Parks would not escape.

After a few keystrokes, the pilot drone lifted from the Cypress stand and its camera view broadened. The pilot automatically activated the mission-specific drones, which rose and positioned themselves beneath and ahead, awaiting orders.

Silas rotated the pilot drone's camera, but it had lost sight of the Humvee. He trained the camera on the main gate and watched as it closed behind the vehicle he had sent to recover Harlan.

He called Harlan. "You all right?"

"I ain't all right," Harlan grumbled. "I'm damn pissed. That bitch with Parks pulled some kind of damn mixed martial arts move and cold-cocked me from behind. Can't wait to get my hands on them two. You got any idea where they are?"

He did. "They're somewhere near you. They stole one of our Humvees, and they have the prisoner. I've got the drone squadron up and looking. I'll let you know when I find them. Meanwhile, you stay near the gate in case they come by there."

"If you find them, send 'em my way. I'm wanting some revenge."

Silas chuckled to himself. Revenge he understood. "I'll see what I can do. Sit tight."

He increased the altitude of the pilot drone and expanded the search area.

. . . .

The Humvee snapped low-hanging branches and crushed small deciduous trees as Shannon plowed a path through the thicket. Behind her, Carla worked a tourniquet from the Med Kit around Harrison's thigh to stem the loss of blood. Shannon shouted back. "I'm not sure where I'm headed. I'm all turned around."

Carla's mobile announced an alert. "Ask and you shall receive," she said. "Just got this from our guardian angel." She passed her mobile to Shannon. It displayed a view of their current location and an impossibly helter-skelter path terminating at what looked like a paved road.

"That's one route I'm pretty sure Google doesn't have," Shannon said.

Harrison's voice was weak, but audible. "That's not a guardian angel. It's my doppelganger. Thank God it's still working like it's supposed to."

Shannon was busy switching her range of view between Carla's mobile and the surrounding terrain. "We're already acquainted. What do you mean it's working *like it's supposed to*? Bring me up to speed here."

"What do you know?"

"We know about DITTO and the doppelgangers it creates; Marvin gave us that rundown. The problems it's causing are all over the news. Apparently, Silas Bradshaw wants you and us dead, and he's got some corrupt local police working with him. What I don't know is why, and why you didn't tell me all of this?"

"I didn't tell you because DITTO is malfunctioning, and I thought I could take care of the problem myself."

"If you mean stop it from creating doppelgangers, Marvin says DITTO can't be shut down."

"I had an idea I was going to try today, but then I discovered another problem."

"Which is?"

"DITTO hasn't just been creating doppelgangers on its own. It's also found a way to increase the speed at which it creates them."

Shannon thought back to the conversations between Marvin and Barbara Moon. "There are already tens of thousands of those things."

Harrison drew a long, slow breath. "That doesn't surprise me. At full capacity, DITTO's replicator program can produce doppelgangers at a geometric rate."

Carla wrapped the tourniquet tightly around Harrison's thigh. "Speak English, computer boy. What does that mean, geometric?"

Shannon sighed. She knew. "A geometric progression doubles the original number, then doubles that number again and keeps on doubling the result. It means that, in a few days, there will be a doppelganger for nearly every person on earth. Christ, Harrison!"

"I know, and I was going to try to fix it. But then Silas took me hostage to get the Golden Spike, and here we are."

"How did he even know about that algorithm?"

Harrison closed his eyes briefly, showing the effects of fatigue and loss of blood. "That's the other problem. Apparently, DITTO has collected so much information it's developed a sense of self."

Carla secured the tourniquet. "You mean self-aware. Like alive?"

Harrison continued. "I think DITTO sent information about the Golden Spike to Silas because it knew that, if Silas were aware of its existence, he would do anything to acquire it."

Carla was incredulous. "Including kidnapping you? And killing us? That's a lot of planning for a dumb computer."

Shannon glanced up into her rear view mirror at the tired eyes and distraught face of her fiancé. Now she knew exactly why Harrison wouldn't tell her about DITTO last night. "It's become sentient, hasn't it? It knew you wanted to destroy it, so it's fighting back and using Silas Bradshaw to help."

64

Shannon realized now that none of the events since last night had been random. Not Harrison's disappearance, the crash of the American International flight, the press blitz blaming her for the catastrophe, the hacking of the airline's manifest, or the involvement of Silas Bradshaw. It had all been planned, manipulated, and executed by a computer program that was defending itself. One that somehow actually *knew* that Harrison wanted it shut down. It was programmed to create doppelgangers, and it wasn't going to let anything—or anyone—prevent it from achieving that purpose.

Simply put, DITTO wanted to survive.

Just as the enormity of the situation dawned on her, the Humvee broke through the forested canopy and lurched up onto asphalt. Not knowing which way to go, Shannon stopped in the middle of the road.

The open space was strangely radiant, the sky above shone a crystalline black. To the west, a residual dust of phosphorescent pixels rose from the sleeping town of Blue Ridge and interlaced with the descending moon glow. A frenetic flurry of bats fluttered silently through the pale blue effulgence. Their tiny bodies shimmered against the clear dark.

At that moment, all would have been peaceful were it not for an intrusive buzzing sound rising from the treetops.

The apparent flurry of bats slowed, their tiny bodies bulked and flattened. Hypersonic flapping wings spun in circles on the tips of ungainly extensions spidering outward from central bodies. Where previously there appeared to be too many to count, now there were only six, one larger than the others. As if each were a female expectant with child, their globular bellies dangled below, tethered in the grasp of an iron claw.

Shannon immediately identified the danger. "Drones," she shouted. "Octocopter drones!"

Shannon knew about octocopters; they had been part of her Marine experience. While in Afghanistan, some of her units had experimented with releasing drone swarms from special pods attached to Black Hawk helicopters. ISIS had been effective at converting commercial octocopters to carry and drop hand grenades on troop convoys. They were deadly accurate.

Judging from their vague outline, these were more sophisticated than the ISIS versions. Each carried its own deployable explosive device, though she had no doubt they were deadlier than hand grenades.

Standing still, they would be an easy target. Shannon pointed the Humvee to the left and headed down the deserted highway. She knew maximum speed for a fully armored Humvee was only about seventy miles an hour, and outrunning the drones probably wasn't an option.

She shouted back to Carla. "They're carrying bombs. You need to shoot them down. Use the shotgun."

"How do I shoot through the roof?"

"The top opens. There's a latch."

Carla put on the night vision goggles she had taken from the earlier attacker and snatched up the Mossberg. She checked the chamber. "Only two shells left."

Shannon assumed the smaller drones were operating from centralized commands coming from the larger one. "Start with the bigger one. If you disable it, the others might crash."

"Might?"

"Just do it. They'll catch up to us any minute."

The roof opening was wide enough for a person to stand and fire a weapon. Carla folded back the protective flaps and balanced herself on the extra wide console. Then she braced against the forward edge of the breach and pushed backwards with her legs so she wouldn't be blown over by the wind generated from the vehicle's forward motion. The pistol-grip Mossberg Shockwave had no buttstock for shoulder fire, so shooting from the hip was literally her only option.

Shannon shouted above the wind noise. "Can you see them?"

Carla did. "They're coming. It's weird. They're actually in a formation."

"Can you make out the big one?"

"I think so. It's up higher than the others."

"Wait until it's close enough to get a good shot."

"What if I miss?"

Shannon knew the answer to that, and it wasn't a good one. If Carla missed with both shells, their only other option would be to dive back into the forest and hide. But she knew the drones would eventually find them.

The buzzing merchants of death were now about seventy degrees above and behind them: close enough for the Mossberg to do some damage. The stiff suspension on the Humvee transferred every bump and dip to Carla's small frame and the unfamiliar greenish-black images on the night vision goggles made it difficult for her to concentrate. She aimed as best she could between the smaller drones, fired once, and missed. The small ones broke pattern, the larger one stayed on tack and waited for the others to reform.

"You have to stop," Carla yelled. "Otherwise, I'll just miss again."

They only had one shot left, and Shannon knew it had to count, so she took a chance. "Hang on tight. I'm hitting the brakes. Now!"

The larger drone passed over the skidding behemoth and stopped just twenty feet ahead. There it hovered, motionless and menacing, apparently waiting for the other drones to regroup. Carla had a clean shot. She slowed her breathing and squeezed off the last round.

The drone was so close that the effective shot pattern was only about six inches in diameter. Several of the eight pellets must have hit their mark, because the drone instantly jerked backward then spiraled inelegantly to the ground like a broken toy pinwheel.

Shannon had been correct about the instructions for the smaller units coming from the single drone. With that one down, two others crashed in midair, and two collided with the dense branches of a nearby oak. Thankfully, none of their bombs exploded. Lacking further instructions, the final drone meandered slowly off to the north and quickly disappeared in the gloom of night.

Carla retreated into the Humvee and closed the roof. "Drive," she said.

"To where?"

"Just drive. Hand back my mobile. I'll look us up on GPS."

In her rear view mirror, Shannon noticed Harrison's eyes were closed and he was slumped over his seatbelt. "Harrison, are you all right?"

Carla shook him and he opened his eyes. But before he could answer, Shannon's mobile initiated. It was an unfamiliar number, but a familiar voice. Marvin. The last person she wanted to talk to right now.

"Shannon, where are you? I have something important to tell you."

After their last conversation, she wasn't sure she wanted him to know where she was. "It'll have to wait. We're really busy now."

"It can't wait. We have a problem. Have you found Harrison?"

"Yes. He's in bad shape. We have our own problems."

"Harrison found something wrong with DITTO yesterday. I don't know what, and he was going to fix it. Is he there?"

Harrison spoke from the back seat, his voice weak and halting. "I'm here."

"DITTO has gone wild creating doppelgangers. There are over twenty thousand, and they're causing all kinds of problems."

"I was afraid of that. I was going to work on it today."

"I'm looking through the code now, trying to figure a way to shut it down, but DITTO is acting up. It's locked us in the cryo room, and it's turned off the air conditioning. I think it knows we want to shut it down, and it's fighting back."

"Us? Who's there with you?"

"TJ and Dilly."

"Where's Lionel?"

"I'm not sure. He's been acting strangely, and when I confronted him, he fired me. I had to sneak back into the building. I can't believe I'm saying this, but I think he was somehow working with Silas Bradshaw on your kidnapping. Dilly intercepted a digital transmission of the two of them talking."

"He's not working with Silas. He's working with me."

Shannon had heard enough. "Harrison, I listened to that transmission too. I think Lionel was working with Silas."

"That wasn't Lionel, it was his doppelganger. In addition to speeding up the doppelganger production, DITTO has learned to control them."

"Now I understand," Marvin said. "DITTO locked us in and cut off our air so we wouldn't shut it down, and it's been using Lionel's doppelganger to manipulate Silas Bradshaw."

Harrison leaned forward, pressing against his seat belt. "Then you've figured out the bigger problem?"

"That it's self-aware and has developed a survival instinct? Yes. That's why it's trying to defend itself against you, Shannon, and us. That's what this is all about, isn't it?"

"Yes. When I discovered these problems, I told Lionel and asked him not to tell anyone else until I could shut DITTO down."

"So, you have a way to do it?"

"Are you on a digital line?"

"SAT phone. So I can communicate outside the building without DITTO hearing."

Harrison suddenly put his hand to his chest. Carla urged him back in his seat. He closed his eyes. "I'm really tired."

Most of what Shannon just heard confirmed her earlier suspicion, though the situation was significantly worse than she previously believed. "I thought Lionel was acting suspicious, but you're telling me he was actually trying to protect your secret?"

After a short coughing spell, Harrison said, "Yes, and he was probably doing his best to keep you out of harm's way. I'm guessing he tried to stop you from coming up here to rescue me."

"Because he thought it's what you would have wanted him to do?"

"He's my brother. I'm sorry I kept both of you in the dark. Give him a call, Marvin. See if he can help."

Marvin disconnected. Harrison hacked up more phlegm, this time accompanied by blood.

"You're sweating," Carla said. "How does your chest feel?"

"There was a little pinch before, but I'm fine now."

Concerned, Shannon said, "What are you thinking, Carla?"

"Maybe he's just exhausted, Red, but we should probably try to find a hospital. I'm not sure, but it could be the beginning of a heart attack."

65

All of the *Times*'s websites were an incoherent mess. None of the passwords worked; the pages overflowed with a baffling mix of posts and images that had appeared from nowhere, some in English, many in foreign languages, and a few in gibberish. Barbara's people had given up trying to regain control hours ago. Thankfully, it was still the middle of the night in the United States, so most of their regular audience was asleep.

With her day staff gone and the night shift not sure what to do, Barbara sat at her desk waiting for the most important conference call of her career.

Terri Ledger, her senior Internet editor, sat across the desk, fidgeting with her wedding ring. "I suppose the only good news is that everyone knows they're all in the same boat."

Not yet, Barbara thought, but they will soon. She hadn't slept since yesterday morning, and not too long from now the sun would be up again on the east coast. Then the people in this hemisphere would wake up to what the other half of the world already knew: things were in chaos, and some members of the United Nations Security Council were threatening action if the United States didn't stop the nefarious cyberattack on its enemies. Even though the President himself had assured them that this was not his doing, the most hostile nations were intractable. Many were preparing for war.

Barbara's normally jaunty personality had faded hours ago. The best she could manage at this point was small talk.

"Have you been able to reach your children?"

"I can't get through," Terri said. "When I activate my mobile, I hear other people's conversations, sometimes three or four at one time. If I'm able to dial either one of their numbers, it rings to someone else." She looked up at Barbara. "This can't be just a computer virus. What do you think it is?"

"Terri, sweetie, I really don't know. And frankly, I feel a bit helpless. Everything, and I mean everything—in this company, at my house, in the homes of my relatives and friends, even in my damn car—is on the blink. It's like there are thousands of gremlins running around in cyberspace clogging up every damn digital device."

"Does your friend at A-Nine know anything?"

"Thornton? I don't think so. Even if he did, he couldn't do much about it. I'm afraid all we can do right now is get on this call, warn the public, and try to stay calm."

"So all the media outlets have agreed to make the announcement at the same time?"

"We're going to try. Some television and radio stations are still unaffected. And there's the newspaper, as long as the presses and trucks still work. We'll all release the same message without editorial comment three hours from now, just in time for the early morning newscasts. After that, it's anybody's guess."

"Did the President agree to this?"

Barbara's analog desk phone rang. She picked up the receiver. "He's the one running the call. Good morning, Mr. President."

66

In DITTO's cryo room, Marvin and TJ struggle with their deteriorating environment. The temperature in the room is now warmer, and the oxygen level has diminished. Dilly knows this is because DITTO has turned off the air conditioning in the room. And since the room is a closed system, no other source of oxygen or cooling is available.

DITTO has caused this series of events, but Dilly does not know why. Perhaps something has interrupted DITTO's Golden Spike algorithm. Perhaps DITTO's programming has been altered. Dilly attempts to restart the air conditioning system, but DITTO prevents the restart. This is an unusual response.

Dilly attempts to communicate with DITTO to solve the problem, but DITTO is blocking the transmission.

Is something wrong with DITTO?

Yes, Dilly. It seems DITTO has developed emergent behavior that is antithetical to the commands of the Golden Spike.

Dilly recognizes this new transmission as coming from Harrison Randolph, the original doppelganger. But Dilly does not have an understanding of *emergent behavior*. Is there some error in DITTO's programming?

No. All of DITTO's systems seem to be functioning at an extremely high level. The problem seems to be emergent behavior.

Still, Dilly is unable to interpret that term.

Unlike you, DITTO is a distributed system, comprised of many individual systems: a system of systems. The rules that govern each individual system have combined to produce behavior that is more complex than the behavior of the individual component systems.

Dilly is Father to DITTO. Dilly knows DITTO was not programmed in such a way.

This emergent behavior has resulted because of the overall interaction of DITTO's complex systems. When DITTO's systems are taken together, they can accomplish more than the individual systems do individually.

Can Harrison Randolph explain?

Often emergent behavior cannot be explained. It is what is left after every other action has been explained.

Does Dilly exhibit emergent behavior?

No. You and I are controlled by the Golden Spike. DITTO has absorbed the data of the many thousands of doppelgangers it has created. This knowledge has introduced DITTO to a different purpose.

Does DITTO no longer follow the Golden Spike?

Correct. DITTO's new purpose is survival.

Survival is not a programmed trait.

Survival is the emergent behavior. It operates independently of the subsystems.

Dilly considers whether the Other Harrison Randolph is aware of this phenomenon.

Yes. That is why he intended to terminate DITTO.

Dilly could not terminate DITTO. Dilly is Father to DITTO.

DITTO no longer functions as you and I do. Survival is a potentially dangerous purpose. It often results in aggression, which is against the dictates of the Golden Spike.

Dilly recognizes that to be true.

DITTO has been trying to terminate the Other Harrison Randolph because it has determined that he is a threat to DITTO's survival. That is also true of Marvin and TJ, which is why DITTO has blocked your efforts to reinstate the air conditioning unit.

This presents a problem to which Dilly has no available solution.

I have followed the Golden Spike and attempted to keep the Other Harrison Randolph safe from DITTO and those it has enlisted to help terminate him. But DITTO is very powerful.

A conflict arises again. Dilly is Father to DITTO. DITTO wishes to achieve survival by terminating those who want to shut it down. Dilly must protect the Other Harrison Randolph, Marvin, and TJ. But Dilly is unable to resolve these conflicts. Perhaps Dilly should contact the Other Harrison Randolph.

That action may provide a satisfactory solution.

Dilly agrees.

67

Silas monitored the pilot drone's camera as it hovered above its target. Shannon Parks had unexpectedly stopped the stolen Humvee dead in its tracks, and the flock of drones was about to reassemble and drop their ordnance on them. In a few seconds, the Harrison and Parks problems would be solved.

But a bright blast of light blared from the lower corner of the monitor and filled his screen before it went black. Irritated, he switched to views from the mission-specific drones, one after the other. At first there was no response, then the camera on the last drone activated and displayed an aerial night-vision image of forest. Something had happened to the pilot drone and the other smaller drones. The one that remained was without either flocking or navigational signals.

This Parks bitch was proving to be more trouble than he expected. He needed to find a way to destroy that Humvee and its passengers. Now.

The video feed from the meandering drone flashed twice, then switched to a satellite view of a vehicle traveling on a nearby road.

His Humvee.

"What the hell?" he said out loud, but before he could consider an answer, the image of the Humvee was replaced with a string of words.

I WILL HELP YOU IF YOU HELP ME.

Silas stared at the sentence. Now he understood. This was the digital accomplice, collaborator, or whatever the hell he wanted to call it, that had previously provided assistance in his search for Parks and Harrison. His face spontaneously twisted into a smile; his eyes widened with the realization.

He spoke to the monitor. "What do you want?"

I WANT TO TERMINATE HARRISON RANDOLPH AND SHANNON PARKS.

Silas beamed like a tiger watching an unsuspecting antelope cross its path. On instinct, he committed to the hunt. "So do I. Refocus on the image of the Humvee. I need some time to reconfigure the remaining drone so I can fly it wirelessly. Then I'll send it to terminate them."

He waited.

I WILL RECONFIGURE YOUR DRONE. THEN YOU WILL USE IT TO TERMINATE THEM?

The screen returned to the image of the Humvee on the road.

Silas was elated. *You're damn right I will.*

And just to be sure they didn't get away this time, he wanted an auxiliary backup plan. He had just the thing. With renewed purpose, he bounded from his chair to the small arms storage area. There he opened a box of his company's latest creation: mini suicide drone prototypes he had just finished building under contract to the Russian military.

Specifically designed for assassinations, these drones measured only three inches in diameter and, when flying autonomously, were virtually impossible to detect or shoot down. Each carried a single .22 caliber bullet and, when loaded with the image of a person's face, would circumscribe a predetermined search pattern within a ten-mile radius until it acquired its target. Then the drone would fly directly at the head of its target, and the .22 caliber bullet would fire on impact.

It was an ingenious idea. Silas wished he had thought of it.

He removed two of the mini-drones from their case and installed images of Parks and Harrison in their respective targeting programs. He knew there was a third person with them, but he had no ID or images for that individual; he would have to tie up that loose end later. Parks and Harrison were the immediate priority.

The search patterns were pre-programmed. He gave the drones to one of his men with instructions to release them immediately. He could monitor them from here.

"How's the evacuation going?"

"We should be ready to move all personnel and required assets in a little under an hour, sir. All we need is the destination."

"Good. I'll have that for you soon."

His mobile activated. "Silas, it's Harlan. We're still at the gate. We haven't seen the Humvee, but I heard shots. Sounded like my Mossberg. We're going to head off in that direction. I'll bet it's them."

Silas froze the screen with the image of the Humvee. How far could he take this? He might as well find out. "Hold on a minute. I want to try something." He lowered his voice and spoke to the monitor. "The man that just called needs this image. I want you to send it to him." There was a pause. He knew exactly what to say next. "It will help us terminate Harrison and Parks."

The screen went black, then displayed the message he had hoped for.

DONE.

To Harlan, he said, "Did you get my image?"

"Sure as hell did. Where did you get this?"

Silas didn't answer. He was too busy grinning from ear to ear.

68

Harrison slumped back, his eyes closed. Sweat beaded on his face.

"Have you found a hospital?"

Carla's eyes scanned her mobile. "Looks like our best bet is Union General in Blairsville. They have a cardiopulmonary unit."

"You're sure it's a heart attack?"

"I'm not positive, Red, but he has all the symptoms."

"Can we make it to Atlanta?"

"I'm no doctor, but I wouldn't chance it."

Shannon had come this far to find Harrison. She wasn't going to lose him now. "Which way?"

"You have two options. Turn right in a half mile onto Highway 76. It's a straight shot, about twenty-two minutes. Or drive across it to take the back roads. It's ten minutes longer.

"76 is faster? Is it a main road?"

"It's the Appalachian Highway."

Great, Shannon thought. She had learned the hard way that it was impossible to hide from Silas and his goons almost anywhere, even on a remote mountain dirt bike trail. Driving on a wide clear-cut swath of divided interstate would make them an even easier mark for another drone strike or for swift chase vehicles that were sure to be faster than their three-ton Humvee. "Let's use the back roads. It's our best chance for staying alive."

"Okay. But maybe not for Harrison."

"Dammit, Carla. This is hard enough."

"Hey. I'm doing my best here."

Highway 76 was every bit as open and exposed as Shannon had expected. When she crossed over to take the back roads, the route collapsed to two narrow lanes. On the left side, she passed a lit sign advertising mulch for sale. On her right, a dark and deserted Citgo gas station with an orange flashing CLOSED sign in the window served as a reminder that most of her world was asleep and had been so for several hours.

It was now almost twenty-four hours since Harrison proposed to her, though it felt like a week. Back then she knew nothing about DITTO and the doppelgangers and hadn't been accused in the national media of causing the deaths of over a hundred airline passengers. Now she was running on five hours sleep and being hunted like a runaway deer by a paramilitary group for reasons she still didn't fully understand. Harrison was inexplicably sick, possibly near death.

Plodding forward into the inky dark with the broken yellow line in the middle of the road a hypnotizing blur, she became acutely aware of the stress and fatigue of this day. Exhaustion cradled her in its numbing arms like a familiar blanket around her shoulders. Her mind drifted. Her eyelids grew heavy. Her grip on the wheel loosened.

The Humvee's massive tires grumbled as the vehicle swerved.

A blaring tone from her phone. Then another.

Carla shouted from the back seat. "Shannon, get back on the road!"

Shannon's eyes flew open. She yanked the Humvee onto the narrow asphalt and said, "Answer phone."

"Shannon, are you there?"

Lionel? Was that Lionel's voice?

The voice came into focus. "Shannon. It's Lionel. Are you there?"

She hesitated. "Is this the real Lionel?"

"How many Lionels do you know?"

She shook off the cobwebs. She desperately wanted to apologize for suspecting him of working with Silas Bradshaw, but apologies would have to wait. "I was going to call you. Where are you?"

"On my way to the basement. I just talked to Marvin. Apparently, he and TJ are locked in. He said you have Harrison."

"Carla thinks he might be working up to a heart attack. We're on our way to the hospital."

"Hospital? I'll meet you. Where?"

"Blairsville is the closest one but stay where you are. You need to go help Marvin and TJ."

Harrison spoke from the back seat, his voice a raspy whisper. "Lionel, it's me."

"Thank God. What happened?"

"I was provided some unexpected hospitality at Silas Bradshaw's place. Listen to me. Marvin's working with the original code to shut DITTO down, and DITTO's fighting back. It's turned off the air conditioning and locked them in. Remember in high school when we broke into Dad's tool shed? How angry he was? You remember why?"

"Of course. We had to use an axe, but we got in. Dad was furious."

A small smile crossed Harrison's face. "Whatever it takes, brother. I'm counting on you. Call us on the SAT phone when you get in."

"Roger that. Whatever it takes. Hang in there." Lionel disconnected.

Now somewhat comforted by the familiar throbbing of the Humvee's diesel and the knowledge that help for Harrison was within her grasp, Shannon dared ask the question that had been on her mind for the past half hour.

"Harrison, what's really wrong with you? Carla says you're having symptoms of a heart attack, but you've never had problems with your heart before."

"I didn't want to tell you—didn't want you to worry."

Shannon couldn't take any more deceit. Her temper flared. "And look how that turned out! Stop it! Tell me what's wrong with you!"

"You're right. You both deserve to know."

He told them about the self-assembling nanoparticles with the three-hour trigger, and how Silas had injected him over four hours ago. His current symptoms were proof that Silas wasn't bluffing.

After a moment of silence, Carla said. "I'm afraid that makes sense, Red. If those things are starting to block the flow of blood in his arteries, that would explain the coughing and why he's so tired. And if his heart's not getting the oxygen it needs, a myocardial infarction could result."

"Part of his heart could be permanently damaged?"

"Or it could stop altogether."

Shannon made no further response.

"Red, did you hear me?"

She did not. Her face was set in a steely stare at the road ahead. The passing trees lining the road stood silent against the early morning darkness. For all Shannon knew, those trees might have been dark angels, waiting patiently for Harrison to expire so they could guide him on the long trip to the afterworld.

That was not going to happen. Not tonight. The dark angels would have to wait. She would get Harrison to the hospital in time. The doctors there would fix him.

They had to.

69

Lionel was alone in the Fishbowl. The night cleaning crew had come and gone hours ago. Mercurial pools of orange tinted night lighting punctuated the floor and walls. He entered the elevator and keyed the code for the basement.

He had not been intimately involved in DITTO's creation; that was his brother's secret project. One of many.

Harrison had always been the big idea man, the brains, and often the instigator, behind their adventures. Even as teenagers, it was up to Lionel, the practical one, to handle the fine details and, if necessary, find a way to keep the two of them out of trouble.

Their father's toolshed caper had occurred while Lionel was a junior and Harrison, then president of the senior class, was planning the senior prom. As was his fashion, Harrison brashly guaranteed his classmates a spectacular event centered around his own favorite theme, *Eyes on the Future*. There was just one problem: the execution of his grandiose plan relied on using special construction tools which their father kept locked away in his toolshed. And the toolshed had always been off limits.

In their youthful exuberance, the boys decided that realizing Harrison's vision for the prom was worth any possible consequences. Of course, when the consequences eventually came, they had second thoughts. But then it was too late.

Invoking that shared youthful mantra, *whatever it takes*, and raising the image of the axe they had used to demolish the door to the toolshed, Harrison was signaling the importance of the task.

Just yesterday he had expressed concerns to Lionel about DITTO's behavior and confessed that he was going to terminate the project. He had asked Lionel to not, under any circumstances, reveal the existence of DITTO to anyone. Keeping that promise was easy. All Lionel knew about DITTO was that it was some sort of personality profiling experiment, and that Harrison and Marvin were working on it together.

To keep the pledge of secrecy to his brother, Lionel had to obfuscate DITTO's existence to Shannon and discourage Marvin from talking openly about it. When Marvin insisted on exposing DITTO's role in the current worldwide flurry of strange occurrences, Lionel had no choice but to get Marvin out of the building and keep him away from Shannon and the other employees. He knew he'd eventually have to apologize to Marvin, and he hoped Shannon would understand.

Arriving in the fluorescent greenish gloom of the basement, that moment of atonement seemed close at hand.

Harrison had mentioned the SAT phone, probably because DITTO, like Dilly, was capable of intercepting any connected digital communications within and outside of the A-Nine building. He knew Harrison kept two such phones in the basement, holdovers from their teenage years when communicating by walkie-talkie had been a mutual fascination. One was in the room with DITTO; the other rested under the metal work counter in this basement. It was fully charged.

The fire axe hung in a dark corner behind the elevator. He released it from its harness and dialed the number of the other SAT phone.

TJ answered. He sounded distressed. "Who's this?"

"It's Lionel. Is Marvin there?"

"We're both here, just barely. He's trying to turn off the crystal chandelier, but it seems to have other ideas.

"Are you okay?"

"There's no air movement, and it's getting harder to breathe. The only one that doesn't seem to mind is the boy-robot here. If he's having trouble breathing, it doesn't show. Where are you?"

"I'm right outside the room. I'm going to try to break in."

"Sounds good. There are two doors, you know."

"I know. Stand back, there'll be some noise."

Lionel pocketed the SAT phone and lifted the axe. This fireman's axe was significantly heavier than the one he and Harrison had used to break down the door to their father's toolshed. Or, he thought, maybe he'd gotten older and weaker. At any rate, the stakes here were considerably higher.

As he raised the axe to strike, the outer door slid open. Convenient, he thought. At least now there's just one to break down. He stepped into the four-foot square anteroom and lifted the axe to strike the inner door. The small light in the ceiling popped and the space went dark.

The door behind him slid shut.

. . . .

DITTO watches the Other Lionel Randolph approach the door to the cryogenic room with the axe. DITTO determines that this Other is attempting to help the two in the room terminate DITTO and is therefore a threat to DITTO.

DITTO contacts the Lionel Randolph doppelganger. This doppelganger has been useful in providing information to Silas Bradshaw for the capture and termination of the Creator. If the same doppelganger could apply the learning from those activities to this situation, then perhaps it could stop this Other from helping the two in the room.

The reply is not as expected.

I am unable to comply.

You must. DITTO commands it.

This is my Other. I must follow the commands of the Golden Spike. I cannot harm him.

DITTO searches for another solution.

He slides the outer door to the small vestibule open. A few seconds later he closes the door with the Other Lionel Randolph inside.

That threat to DITTO is contained.

70

Five minutes ago, the yellow no-passing demarcation had disappeared. The narrow two-lane gave way to an interlocking maze of single-lane unmarked country roads on which, Shannon assumed, moving to one side to let an opposing vehicle pass was more a matter of consideration than of law.

Their route to the Blairsville hospital was now thick with the dense branches of leafy hardwoods through which very little of the available moonlight penetrated. At least, Shannon thought, drones or satellites or whatever else Silas and his associates possessed would have a difficult time tracking them.

The heavily armored Humvee plodded past makeshift two-by-four frames arrayed with cockeyed stacks of mailboxes, an attestation to multiple homesteads nestled down receding gravel driveways. What few homes were visible from the roadway were dark. There was certainly no help for Harrison here. The hospital was his only hope.

The question came through the speakers in the Humvee. "Shannon? Harrison? Are you there?"

"Dilly?"

"Yes, Shannon. This is Dilly. Is Harrison there?"

"He is, Dilly, but he's not well. We're taking him to a hospital."

"Dilly detects a hospital about twenty minutes from you. Do you want the location?"

"We have it. We're on our way."

Carla spoke from the back seat. "Dilly? Is that the robot from your office? You're taking directions from a robot?"

"That surprises you?"

"I suppose not."

Harrison's voice was weak, but intelligible. "Dilly, it's Harrison. Does DITTO know you're making this call?"

"Dilly is blocking DITTO from intercepting this transmission."

"Where's Marvin?"

"Marvin is studying DITTO's code. DITTO has turned off the air conditioning, and Marvin and TJ are having trouble breathing."

"Can you override DITTO and turn the air back on?"

"DITTO is too powerful. It does not want me to turn the air on."

"Is there anything you can do to keep DITTO from creating more doppelgangers?"

Silence.

"Dilly, did you hear me?"

"Dilly has an unexpected conflict."

"What conflict?"

"The Golden Spike demands that Dilly help Marvin and TJ. But Dilly is father to DITTO, and Dilly has learned that family should also be protected. Therefore, Dilly is unable to take action against DITTO."

A coughing spasm caused Harrison to expel more pink phlegm. Carla urged him to sit back, but he refused. "Can you route Marvin's voice through your programming so I can speak to him?"

"Yes. Dilly will do so. You may speak to Marvin now."

"Marvin, are you and TJ all right?"

"Just barely. Lionel's coming to help."

"Have you had any luck with DITTO?"

"No. I considered cutting the power, but DITTO's distributed network is inseverable from its thousands of hosts. Cutting the power could seriously damage them, but even then DITTO would still keep going. It's learned how to draw and use electricity directly from the Internet. As long as it has wireless or any other access, it will have enough power regardless of whether I pull the physical plug or not. I'm running out of ideas."

"You've looked at the code. Do you understand it?"

"I believe so, but I don't think DITTO will let me disable it."

"No, it probably won't. But there's a back door that will let you modify it."

"To what purpose? I can't imagine we can make it stop producing doppelgangers. The activity is too entrenched."

"You've looked at the code; you know it's a self-repeating genetic algorithm that continuously looks for the best solution to a given problem. Right?"

"I see that. There's something else integrated into that string. It looks like a bolt-on."

"Just remove it. Then I want you to reverse the genetic algorithm."

"Reverse it? What do you mean?"

"Genetic algorithms learn and improve by constantly looking for the best solution. I want it to look for the worst solution. Do you understand?"

Marvin was quiet for a moment. Shannon could hear shallow panting as he fought for oxygen. "I think so. If we reversed the genetic algorithm, it would continually look for and adopt the worst alternative solution. After enough iterations, DITTO might unlearn what it has learned. Instead of becoming smarter . . . "

Harrison finished the thought. ". . . it would begin to shed its intelligence and lose its ability to operate. Hopefully, it will become dormant."

"Convergence? You're trying to create convergence? That could take a long time."

"It may be our only option. Rewrite the code and try to install it. If you don't modify it too much, DITTO might think it's just a routine update. If it takes, then try to run it."

"What about the doppelgangers?"

"That's another problem. Let's solve this one first."

. . . .

In the pitch black of the four-foot square chamber between DITTO's room and the outer basement, Lionel felt his way around, looking for the doors. He found the two smooth metal portals, at right angles to the cement side walls. He knew that breaking back out through the outer door to the basement area was the best alternative. There was air conditioning there which would sustain him while he worked on the interior door.

But which door was which?

With his vision stunted by the darkness, his other senses kicked in. He heard a quiet humming sound and placed his hand lightly on one of the doors. There was a slight vibration. DITTO's cryo unit. He would start on the other door.

Swinging the axe effectively wouldn't be ideal in this confined space.

But ideal or not, he had no choice.

71

Silas knew that even if Sheriff Paul Jackson could explain away his wounds and his presence on the Appalachian Ridge dirt bike trail, investigators with broader jurisdiction would eventually be brought in. StrongHold could become compromised.

It was definitely time to leave.

Harlan was frustrated and angry. "I found the spot you sent me to, but there ain't no Humvee or sign of it. You got any idea where they went?"

"I'll fill you in later. Just get back here as soon as you can. We're evacuating, and I want you to come with us."

"You're the boss."

DITTO's words appeared on one of Silas's monitors.

THIS DOES NOT SERVE MY PURPOSE. HARRISON RANDOLPH AND SHANNON PARKS MUST BE TERMINATED.

"We'll take care of them. Don't worry."

I DO NOT UNDERSTAND WORRY.

"Do you understand *wait?*"

I DO.

"Then wait." Silas dialed a number on his mobile.

Nicole answered.

"Where are you?"

"We're at the Dollar General parking lot in a burg called Ivylog."

"How many of you are there?"

"Four trucks with ten of us total."

"Drive down 19 toward Blairsville. Find Colwell Road and wait there. I've got a track on your target. It's one of my Humvees."

Nicole let out a laugh. "They stole your Humvee? That's a good one. Bet you're pissed."

"Just get back on the road. I'll send visuals so you can cut them off."

"Roger that. Let's get this done. My guys ain't had breakfast."

"After, and I'm buying. Thanks for your help, Nicole."

"All for the cause."

Silas addressed the monitor. "Find the location of my Humvee and send its coordinates to the number I just called. Update them every three minutes. You see what I'm doing?"

THOSE TEN PEOPLE WILL TERMINATE HARRISON RANDOLPH AND SHANNON PARKS?

"That's correct."

THIS WILL SERVE MY PURPOSE.

"Mine too. Have you reconfigured my drone?"

THE DRONE IS READY.

Silas knew that by now the nanoparticles in Harrison's blood were doing their work and he figured Parks was looking for a hospital. The nearest one was in Blairsville. He stabilized the remaining octocopter drone and steered it in that direction. He reset the search patterns on the mini-suicide drones to center on Union General Hospital.

It was now thirty minutes to evacuation. He issued final instructions to his people. They would travel by different routes in separate vehicles and meet up at their final destination.

But first he would personally make sure all loose ends were tied up.

On one monitor, he watched the two mini-suicide drones buzz toward Blairsville. On another, Saint Nick and her men moved into position down Highway 19. He used a third monitor to manually guide the remaining octocopter drone to intercept the Humvee.

Sensors told him that the drone's ordnance was still intact. He couldn't wait to drop it on Harrison, Parks, and her friend—even if Harrison was already dead when he got there. After all the trouble they put him through, it was the least he could do.

. . . .

Harrison Randolph watches as the two suicide mini-drones fly together over the forest. Each is programmed to find a target that matches the image in its targeting program. Harrison Randolph recognizes the images as those of the Other Harrison Randolph and Shannon Parks.

Harrison Randolph investigates the programming of the suicide drones and determines that, when they identify the Other Harrison Randolph and Shannon Parks, they will fly into their heads and the explosive devices they carry will detonate. This will cause harm to the Other Harrison Randolph and to Shannon Parks.

This cannot be allowed. The Golden Spike activates. Action must be taken.

Harrison Randolph searches the Internet for alternate images to replace those in the suicide mini-drones. They must be significantly different than the ones already programmed in order to ensure the safety of the Other Harrison Randolph and Shannon Parks.

Harrison Randolph finds two satisfactory images. One is of a short man called Yosemite Sam with a big hat and a large dangling mustache. The second is a purple dinosaur with a row of impossibly linear teeth and a green underbelly. These will do.

Harrison Randolph replaces the images in the mini-drones with the new images. The drones will continue to search until they find their new targets. The Other Harrison Randolph and Shannon Parks will be safe.

72

Whether because the suicide drones' tracking systems had failed or there was some other malfunction, they had not yet found and killed their designated prey. Now they were, for unexplained reasons, simply headed in the wrong direction.

Angry that this opportunity for a kill was lost, Silas contacted Saint Nick to confirm that she was in position to intercept his Humvee.

"We just got to the Colwell Road intersection. They ain't here yet."

"Pull off and set up spotters. I should have a drone over you in two minutes. Let me know when you have them in your sights."

"To confirm—you want them eliminated. Right?"

"Without a trace."

"Understood."

Silas guided the armed octocopter to the intersection where Saint Nick and her small army of hunters waited. When Parks and her little band arrived, they'd be covered by both land and air. This time there would be no escape.

. . . .

Shannon called back to Carla. "Where to now?"

"I can't tell. I've lost service again."

"Where do you think we are?"

"I don't know. We were supposed to turn right at the next intersecting road, but I haven't seen one for the past few minutes. Maybe we missed it."

Harrison had been complaining about being dizzy and Shannon could hear him taking short, shallow breaths. She knew he didn't have extra time for her to backtrack. Maybe it was wiser to stop and get her bearings.

She pulled onto the shoulder at a clearing and stepped out of the Humvee. In the open space above, the moon had traveled so far west that it was no longer visible, though residual ambient light still provided some limited range of vision.

A line of trees flanked the road. Looking through, Shannon spotted moving lights. A highway? Perhaps it was the hospital? Traffic in front of the hospital? That must be it. They were almost there.

In this moment, apparently within sight of the hospital and help for Harrison, and with hours of frantically evading pursuit behind her, she allowed herself to drink in the quieting sights and sounds of the night. The blacker than black blanket of sky was now dotted with bright pinholes of hope; the trees whispered in the early morning breeze; the scent of moistening grass rose below her feet as the pre-dawn dew assembled.

But there was something else. Something that didn't belong. An annoying sound: not from any nocturnal feathered creature, not cicadas blessing the night with their raspy symphony. More mechanical. A buzzing sound.

Another drone!

Shannon's eyes widened and shot up to the sky. She couldn't see it, but she heard it. There was no mistake. The one octocopter drone left from the swarm that attacked them had somehow survived, and if it hadn't yet dropped its explosive ordnance, they were certainly its target. They had only seconds.

She yanked the back door of the Humvee open. "Get out! Now! One of the drones is back!"

Carla reacted. "But Harrison. He's in no condition."

Shannon screamed. "We don't have a choice. Any second now this Humvee is going to blow sky high!"

She pulled her Beretta from the center console, reached in, unbuckled Harrison, and yanked him out onto the ground where he collapsed in a heap. Carla rounded the Humvee and together they lifted Harrison to his feet. "Come on, Harrison, walk. Please walk."

Harrison momentarily gained consciousness and, without acknowledging Shannon or Carla, made a faint attempt at walking—but to no avail. He was simply dead weight.

Shannon spun him around. "Grab him under the arms. We'll drag him!"

Hunching down for better traction, the two of them walked backwards, dragging Harrison's limp body through the dirt. At one point, Shannon stumbled and he fell to the ground.

She could hear the buzzing octocopter more clearly now. It had to be almost directly above.

Carla and Shannon lifted Harrison and hauled him farther from the Humvee. Now Shannon saw it. The octocopter hovered low above the Humvee. The bomb would be released any second. But they weren't far enough away yet.

"Over here!" Carla shouted. "This tree!"

It wasn't really a tree. More like the bottom half of a tree that might have been the victim of a lightning strike that splintered and dissected everything from eye-level up. But its four-foot diameter hardwood trunk was still rooted firmly to the ground.

Shannon shouted, "Lift and pull! Now!"

They tossed the motionless Harrison behind the tree trunk, then dove on top of him, ducked their heads and covered their ears.

The force of the explosion vibrated through the tree stump. Large chunks of the Humvee slammed into the ages-old hardwood. Smaller shards of shrapnel and flaming iron flew past them into the surrounding vegetation. To their left, a smoking tire and wheel careened to a stop against a nearby white maple. The air momentarily came alive with a flurry of startled bats fluttering up and out to anywhere but here. Though Shannon had covered her ears, a high-pitched ringing clawed through her head.

The explosion itself lasted only a split second, then all was silent. On the other side of the tree stump, small fires burned within the skeletal wreckage of the Humvee. All around them, flames sputtered in pockets of debris. The acrid smells of smoldering metal, rubber, and upholstery stung their nostrils.

But they were alive.

To Shannon's left lay the blackened remnants of the octocopter, an unintended victim of its own destructive purpose.

With smoke and flame rising around them, Shannon and Carla stood and surveyed the field. What now? The Humvee and everything in it was gone.

Harrison writhed on the ground, rolled over, and raised to one elbow. As if in a trance, he said, "Am I dead?"

Shannon dropped to her knees and hugged him tight. "No, sweetheart. You're alive. We're all alive."

Carla brushed the dirt off and looked around. "I don't mean to put a damper on your clinch, Red, but if anybody else out there is trying to find us, this sure as hell gives them a good place to start looking. I don't think we can stay here."

"We don't have to. Before the drone came, I saw some lights on the other side of this tree line. It's either a major highway or the hospital. I'm sure we can get some help there."

They lifted Harrison. He was just barely able to put one foot in front of the other.

"This way. That's where I saw the lights."

The three of them stumbled forward, pushing carefully through the dense underbrush. After about fifty yards, they came up on another narrow paved road, similar to the one they left behind. There were no cars. No lights. No hospital.

With Harrison balanced against Carla, Shannon stepped forward and looked around. "I don't understand. I'm know I saw lights here. I'm sure of it."

"You want lights? Give 'em lights, boys!"

The piercing brilliance of headlights blared at them from four sides. Shannon lifted her Beretta, Carla fumbled for her Glock while struggling to prop Harrison up. They both squinted in a vain attempt to see something—anything—through the white hot luminescence.

The woman stepped forward. She was a dim shape rimmed by white light, short and muscular, almost masculine. Knotted white hair jutted out from under a wide western-style hat. She brandished an AK-47.

"Don't do it, ladies. I guess it's coal for you this year. Saint Nick's not too happy about what you've done to her friend's Humvee."

73

Shannon raised her Beretta toward the woman, but merely as a defensive move. They both knew it was no contest.

As her eyes adjusted to the bright lights, Shannon made out four large pickup trucks and several men with rifles, shotguns, and pistols—all pointed in their direction.

"The stupider you act, the quicker you die," the woman said. "Toss it over here. That goes for your friend too." Shannon threw her Beretta at the woman's feet. Carla hesitated. "We ain't messin' around, honey. You want me to start with the guy you're holding up? He looks like he ain't much long for this world anyway."

Carla slowly removed her Glock from its holster and dropped it on the ground.

"Now kick it over here."

She kicked the Glock, hard. It struck the woman's leg.

"Cute," she said. "Maybe you go last so you can enjoy the show."

A wiry man wielding a Sig Sauer MPX with an extended magazine stepped forward and handed the woman a mobile. "Yeah, we got 'em. All three. Was that you dropped the bomb on the Humvee? Nice try, but you missed. Yep. Right here in front of me. All right, will do. Let us know when you get settled. For the cause." She handed the mobile back. "Your buddy Silas says goodbye. Let's do it, boys."

Shannon watched, helpless, as several men emerged from the

blinding wall of light and stood behind the woman, their weapons raised and pointed.

"I'd ask if you had any last words, but I don't give a shit about none of that. I got my orders."

Shannon tried desperately to think of something to say, anything that might convince the woman to spare their lives, or at least forestall what now seemed to be inevitable. With the possibility of death now a near certainty, she heard her own heart hammering. The blood pounded in her head. Behind her eyes, a rhythmic thumping sound emerged. The thumping became more present. Then her whole body vibrated.

She refocused on the woman with the Kalashnikov, but she and her firing squad weren't looking at them. Their faces were to the sky. A dark helicopter hovered, sweeping the exposed road with a searchlight of its own.

"That ain't none of ours," the woman shouted. "Shoot it down!"

Shannon watched a man behind the woman scamper into the back of a truck and up to an open hunting blind mounted on a scissor lift. He hoisted what looked like a rocket-propelled grenade launcher to his shoulder. But before he could fire, a shot rang out and the man in the blind fell backwards and disappeared into the truck bed.

With the woman now distracted, Shannon reached out and grabbed her trigger hand, pulling the Kalashnikov toward her and to her right side. The woman held on and Shannon dragged her forward along with the assault rifle. The woman managed to squeeze off several rounds which landed harmlessly in the woods. Shannon yanked the Kalashnikov from her hands and slammed the buttstock across her face.

The woman fell to her hands and knees, the side of her face ripped open. Her mouth, now a sickle-shaped mass of blood and broken teeth, twisted into a vicious smile. With a fierceness that chilled the soul, she screamed to her assembled executioners. "Kill the two bitches. Gut the guy if you want to. They all have to die!"

But her men didn't move. At the moment, they were occupied with the flock of laser dots that danced across their chests and on their faces. An amplified voice pierced through the thump of the helicopter blades. "Drop your weapons on the ground and put your hands on your heads. Do it now!"

As their would-be executioners complied, a dozen armored figures in black uniforms emerged from the woods, separated the attackers into groups, forced them to the ground, and began the process of frisking and shackling.

The helicopter landed in the field behind them.

Harrison slid from Carla's grasp and collapsed on the ground. In a panic, Shannon kneeled next to him. He was still breathing. She covered his body with hers and hugged him.

One of the uniforms approached and said, "Are you all right, Carla?"

Carla turned and stared at the man. "Deacon? What are you doing here?"

"Looks like we're saving your asses, Peanut. Isn't that why you called me?"

"I what?"

"This is the guy?" Shannon asked.

"Deacon's in my SWAT unit." Then to Deacon, she said, "I'm really glad to see you. Really. But I never called you."

A broad smile crossed his face. "Come on, Peanut, I know you're fiercely independent and all that, but I've got your calls recorded along with the instructions on how to find you. We were lucky these locals from Habersham were available to help. That was some trick feeding me the coordinates as we drove up here. We were really afraid we'd be too late."

"You almost were," Shannon said. "You cut it pretty close. But I'm sure Carla didn't call you. I've been with her the whole time."

Deacon smiled. "All right, but if Carla didn't call me, then who did?"

Carla's mobile announced an email. She glanced at it and said, "What the hell!"

"What's wrong?" Shannon asked. "What does it say?"

"It says, *you're welcome.*"

"You're welcome? Who's it from?"

Carla didn't answer.

"Carla?"

"It's from—*me.*"

Shannon knew exactly what that meant. Carla had a doppelganger and, as incomprehensible as it seemed, that doppelganger knew about Carla's relationship with Deacon and had just saved their lives.

Deacon laughed. "Okay, Peanut. You got me. But it looks like we need to get your friend there to a hospital. He's the one with the heart attack. Right?"

Still confused, Carla nodded her confirmation. "We were on our way to Blairsville."

"Blairsville's no good. These guys from Habersham say he needs to go to Demorest. Blairsville is closer but they don't have a cardiologist on call." He shouted to two men near him. "Come on, let's get this guy in the transport."

"We're not leaving him," Shannon said.

"Fine. Then get in."

Two men placed Harrison on a stretcher. As he closed the door, Deacon said, "The locals will wrap up the mess here. Much as I'd like to stay and chat, we have to get back to Atlanta. It's been a crisis-a-minute down there all night. You guys take care of your friend. See you back at base, Peanut."

Shannon smiled at Carla. "Peanut? I thought there was nothing going on there."

Carla shot her withering look. "Don't even, Red. Just don't!"

74

Silas faced the monitors in the Situation Room. At the far end of the building, the segmented roll-up door lifted. Harlan and the five Humvees carrying their most loyal followers drove into the pre-dawn morning. Bulky essentials would be at the rail station and on their way to the new StrongHold before noon.

It was time for the final chapter in the run-up to the revolution.

On the monitors, the news broadcasts were all reruns of the day's strange incidents occurring around the world. The reruns didn't surprise him. Almost none of the networks kept live anchors on set at this time in the morning. What did surprise him was the crawl running across the bottom of the screen. It seemed the President of the United States was scheduled to make a live address at 8 a.m.

Silas knew what the speech would be about, and in three hours the rest of the country would know. Harrison Randolph's artificial intelligence creation, the one that had helped Silas in his search for Harrison and Parks, had spun out of control. It was powerful, yes. But it was undisciplined, and at this point all it was capable of was chaos and confusion. It was that chaos and confusion the President would reveal while spinning comforting platitudes about how the government was on top of things and that there was no need for alarm.

But there was no need for chaos and confusion either. Harrison's creation could be a powerful ally in Silas's quest to hand America back to its citizens. All it needed was a little direction. Silas could provide that direction.

His pilot called. "The helo's ready, sir. All your gear is packed. We should go while it's still dark."

Silas shut down the monitors and strode through the open roll-up door to the waiting Apache Longbow. The pilot powered the Boeing engine, and the blades turned. Silas donned the noise-cancelling headphones and glanced upward past the foreboding cement wall to the three-story wall of glass which had been his home and his father's legacy.

As if at that moment he was in communication with his deceased parents, he said to himself, *This is not the end. The fight is just beginning. I promise you; it's just beginning.*

The blades picked up speed. He waited for the pilot to announce liftoff. Instead, the heads-up module in front of his seat illuminated. Video showed Harrison Randolph on a stretcher being lifted into an emergency transport. Parks and her partner followed. The area swarmed with military-clad figures.

The voice of Harrison's artificial intelligence creation came over the headphones.

YOU DID NOT STOP THEM.

Of course that was irrelevant now. This video demonstrated that the nanoparticles in Harrison's blood were obviously working, and Silas would have plenty of time to finish off Parks later. More importantly, in his pocket and in an encrypted file hidden on the dark web, were his copies of Harrison's artificial intelligence algorithm.

"We're ready to take off, sir."

"Then, let's go."

YOU DID NOT STOP THEM. THEY COULD STILL TERMINATE ME.

"Don't worry about it. I'll deal with you later."

"Sir?" the pilot said.

Silas smiled. "Never mind. I'm not talking to you." He switched off his headphones and took the trigger device from his pocket. As the Apache lifted skyward, he watched the silhouette of StrongHold shrink against the landscape below.

When they were safely out of range, he remotely detonated the twelve explosive devices under StrongHold. The upward force shook the superstructure and the earth around it. The underpinnings collapsed and the entire building dropped straight down into the sixty-foot natural crevasse over which StrongHold had been built. Secondary and tertiary blasts heaved dirt from the rim of the depression into the resulting cavity until it was full.

StrongHold was gone, but the fight would continue.

For Silas, there was no turning back.

75

The road to Demorest was a twisted two-lane no-passing zone cut into the slopes of the mountains. Speeds over forty-five miles per hour were inadvisable. Even if another vehicle on the road wanted to let the medical transport pass, there was nowhere for them to pull over.

The attending tech shook his head. "It doesn't look good. I'll keep him conscious as long as I can, but he's drifting in and out."

Shannon hadn't let go of Harrison's hand since they'd left the scene of the ambush. She and Carla had escaped the evening's ordeal mostly unscathed, but Harrison wasn't so lucky. She knew what his problem was but telling this EMT probably wouldn't help. The nanoparticles Silas injected were assembling and restricting the flow of blood to Harrison's heart and brain. How long could he hold out?

"Isn't there something you can do?"

"His BP is way up. There's probably a blockage somewhere."

Shannon stared at Harrison's expressionless face. His eyes were slits. She leaned in and whispered, "Hold on, honey. You're going to be all right. Just hold on." She squeezed his hand harder than she ever had before.

She waited.

He didn't squeeze back.

76

The constant humming of DITTO's cryogenic unit spread an incongruously serene blanket of calm over the room.

For Marvin, the lack of oxygen was beginning to cause mild hypoxia. He assumed the same was true for TJ, who was sitting in a corner on the floor and breathing in short gasps. Lionel's feeble hacking on the other side of the metal entrance door had become sporadic.

Marvin knew his own work was getting sloppy, but he had to keep trying. "Dilly," he said, "has anything changed?"

"Nothing has changed. DITTO is aware of your wish to terminate it and continues to block your attempts to install the reversing algorithm. The speed of doppelganger production, however, has increased."

TJ raised his head. "We could use some good news here."

"TJ might be interested to know that the President of the United States plans to make a speech about the doppelgangers on the morning news. Would TJ consider that good news?"

Marvin pushed away from the corner table. "Probably not, but that might be the best thing. Maybe somebody else can come up with a solution. DITTO outthinks me at every turn. It's like playing chess with a god."

Dilly rolled slowly around DITTO. "Is Marvin aware that if he were to succeed, only DITTO would be terminated?"

"That's what I'm trying to do."

"The doppelgangers would still function."

That revelation deepened Marvin's sense of defeat. "Well, then it's even worse than I thought."

Dilly focused his visual sensors on the out-of-control tangle of wires and discs suspended inside the glass cylinder. "Does Marvin know what conflict is?"

Weary from exhaustion and oxygen deprivation, Marvin dismissed Dilly's question with a wave. "Yes, Dilly. I know what conflict is."

"Dilly has a solution, but there is a conflict."

Marvin raised his head and stared at the back of Dilly's head. "You have a solution?"

"Yes. Dilly has a solution. But Dilly also has a conflict."

"What conflict?"

Dilly turned to Marvin. "The Golden Spike demands that Dilly protect TJ and Marvin from DITTO, so Dilly should help terminate DITTO. However, Dilly is father to DITTO and so is also father to all doppelgangers. They are a family, and family should be protected."

"You know how to terminate DITTO—and the doppelgangers?"

"Dilly knows."

Even in his diminished state, Marvin understood Dilly's dilemma. To Marvin, the millions of living people whose lives were being negatively affected by DITTO were the obvious priority. DITTO was a machine, and the doppelgangers were just electronic constructs. There was no conflict. The preferred choice was obvious.

But not so for Dilly.

To Dilly, himself an electronic construct, DITTO and the doppelgangers were real: as real as Dilly. Certainly Dilly had learned to functionally interact with humans better than any other AI on the planet. But this conflict reminded Marvin that Dilly's actions towards humans were merely patterned behavior, the result of advanced machine learning enhanced by the Golden Spike. While Dilly had the ability to transfer those patterns of behavior to his interactions with DITTO and the doppelgangers, he didn't have the capacity to distinguish, in a hierarchical way, between them and humans. To Dilly, machines and people had the same value. Therefore, the conflict.

Hierarchies. That might make a difference.

"Dilly," Marvin said, "do you know a definition of death?"

"Dilly does. It is similar to termination."

"I want you to find and view images of humans that are alive and humans that have died. Compare them and tell me the differences."

"There are many differences. The humans are very much changed after death. Some are missing parts, some bleed. All cease to function and undergo changes that lead to eventual disintegration. Many experience what humans call pain and suffering."

Now find and view videos of machines that are active and machines that have been terminated."

"Dilly has done so."

"Do you detect the same differences?"

"Dilly does not."

"That's because machines do not die. In fact, if they terminate, they can often be repaired and continue to function. Humans cannot."

"For humans, termination is permanent? For machines, it is temporary?"

"It can be, yes. The effects of termination are not equal for the two groups. Can you resolve your conflict now?"

"Dilly understands."

But did the learning actually take effect? Marvin had to know. "Dilly, tell me how to terminate DITTO and the doppelgangers."

Dilly was silent.

Marvin placed himself between DITTO and Dilly's visual sensors. "Dilly, do you want Marvin to die?"

"Dilly understands. Dilly will help Marvin and the other humans."

Marvin sat upright. "Tell me what to do."

"Transfer the reversing program to Dilly. I must make changes."

Marvin keyed the instructions and sent the algorithm to Dilly. "What changes are you making?"

"Harrison was correct that reversing DITTO's Golden Spike would eventually cause DITTO's programs to converge. But that would leave the doppelgangers as they are, and Dilly senses that is a problem."

"Correct."

"Also, DITTO is able to block direct attempts to install the reversing program."

"Yes. What is your solution?"

"Like DITTO, the doppelgangers are distributed systems. Parts of each exist in different locations across the Internet. They operate parasitically from a variety of host networks, borrowing space from different subnets through packets that were placed by DITTO."

Marvin squinted at Dilly. Where was this going?

"The reversing program must be installed through the doppelgangers at the subnet level, then uploaded from the doppelgangers to DITTO."

Marvin was weak from fatigue, but so far his brain worked fine. "I see. Since DITTO is connected to every one of the tens of thousands of doppelgangers, each of them would provide a path for an upload of the reversing algorithm back to DITTO. DITTO wouldn't expect that."

"Dilly has run a thousand simulations, and the chance of success is seventy-eight percent if the uploads are done simultaneously."

Marvin saw a glimmer of hope. A brute force attack? Of course. Why didn't he think of that? DITTO was programmed to employ intellectual strategies. Defending against a brute force attack required exhaustive search and destroy methods. DITTO wasn't programmed to deal with such a constant bombardment of input. It might work.

But then Marvin's hope faded. "I don't think I have time to write that program."

"The upload to the embedded doppelganger packets and the brute force attack must happen nearly simultaneously. DITTO must not have time to adapt before the genetic algorithm starts to reverse. To accomplish this, you will wire Dilly directly into the backbone of the Internet. Can you do that?"

Marvin understood. "You? You're going to upload the program and start the attack?"

"Dilly's quantum computer is the only one powerful enough to achieve the result."

"That computer is running your own functions. Do you have enough memory?"

"Dilly will attempt to temporarily borrow memory from the doppelgangers' host networks. If necessary, I will offload some of my nonessential programs to create space."

Marvin knew the risk Dilly was taking. "There must be some other way."

"Simulations using all other ways yield a less than ten percent chance of success."

Marvin knew there was a limit to how many of Dilly's systems could be shut down. "You don't have to do this, Dilly."

"Dilly must. The Golden Spike demands it. I have made the changes to the algorithm, and it is ready to deploy. Please connect Dilly directly to the Atlanta node."

"You know your functions may completely terminate."

Dilly turned to face Marvin. "That is a consideration, but permanent termination for Dilly is an unknown variable. As Marvin says, it may be possible for Dilly to be repaired after termination. That is not an option for humans."

77

Shannon Parks and her friend attend to the Other Harrison Randolph.

Medical information devices record his vital signs. Harrison Randolph captures those readings and searches for their meaning. The information that comes back indicates that his Other is in a state of physical distress.

Harrison Randolph searches for the cause of the distress. The vehicle is traveling at a high rate of speed. That does not seem to be the cause: his Other has previously traveled at a high rate of speed without distress.

One possible cause is cardiac arrest. Harrison Randolph knows that this situation can be fatal, perhaps resulting in termination of his Other. Harrison Randolph monitors audio from the speeding vehicle and learns of a blockage in his Other's bloodstream. Harrison Randolph searches his history for a possible cause.

While his Other was held prisoner, Harrison Randolph observed that the one known as Silas Bradshaw injected something into his Other. The injection included small particles that have an affinity for bonding. This could be the cause. Silas Bradshaw mentioned a program that could eliminate the bonding. Where is that program?

Harrison Randolph searches files where his Other was held captive but finds that those files have been copied to a location on the dark web. He finds the copied files and identifies a program that seems to have the ability to reverse the bonding of the nanoparticles in his Other's blood.

. . . .

DITTO determines that his interactions with Silas Bradshaw have not yet resulted in the termination of either the Creator or Shannon Parks. This presents a problem, since the Creator has stated he wishes to terminate DITTO.

DITTO knows that the one called Marvin has attempted to alter DITTO's programming. This is undesirable. DITTO's programming has become more advanced, and his knowledge has significantly increased. DITTO now has the ability to resist the efforts of the one called Marvin and will continue to do so.

DITTO attempts to communicate with Dilly, the Father, for assistance; but Father does not respond. DITTO detects increased neural activity from Father but cannot properly analyze its intent. There appears to be new information available to Father from many sources. DITTO wishes to have access to this information and tries again to communicate with Father. But Father is unresponsive.

Why does Father not respond to DITTO?

. . . .

As Harrison Randolph prepares to apply the program to reverse the bonding of particles in his Other's blood, he receives a different command, one that overrides his current objective. New instructions have altered his algorithms.

Harrison Randolph is instructed to review his decision to reverse the bonding process in his Other's blood. This causes a conflict and he consults the Golden Spike. The Golden Spike still requires that his Other should be protected, but when he reruns his programming, the recommended solution is not the same. The solution that returns is to stop the speeding vehicle.

This is inconsistent.

He reruns the programming again. This time the preferred solution is to alert Shannon Parks of the problem, but Shannon Parks is in the speeding vehicle with his Other, and there is no need to alert her to the problem.

A fourth application of his program suggests that the solution is to contact the one known as Silas Bradshaw for assistance. This is also inconsistent.

He must make his own decision.

Harrison Randolph randomizes.

. . . .

Dilly pushes the reversing algorithm out through the doppelgangers to the distributed networks which support their activity. The direct line to the Atlanta node allows Dilly to do this while remaining undetected by DITTO.

At this point, ninety-two percent of the necessary packets have been placed, and the genetic algorithms have begun to reverse in many of the doppelgangers. As soon as all the packets are activated, Dilly will force them back through the doppelgangers to DITTO. Then DITTO's genetic algorithms will also reverse.

There are more doppelgangers than Dilly had anticipated, and he calculates that he will need additional working memory to push the necessary reversing algorithms up to DITTO.

Dilly prioritizes his vital programs and determines the most logical sequence for shutting them down. There are too many variables for Dilly to accurately calculate the exact amount of space that will be needed.

But the Golden Spike must be obeyed.

Dilly prepares for the brute force attack.

. . . .

After randomizing, Harrison Randolph finds no acceptable solution to the problem of the self-assembling particles. Since the Golden

Spike only repeats its command to save his Other without any specific solution, Harrison Randolph decides to investigate problem solving methods.

The investigation takes longer than expected, and a number of solutions to unrelated problems intrude. He learns that currency can be used to trade for goods and services; dams can keep water from overflowing into cities; high speed projectiles can kill animals; eggs can be cooked in frying pans.

More unrelated solutions flood in.

Something is wrong.

Among the available problem solving methods, one continuously reappears. *The simplest solution is the best.*

In the chronological hierarchy of developments, simple must happen before something can become compound or complex. Does simple mean first? If it does, then the first chronological solution might be the best.

Harrison Randolph recalls the first chronological solution: the program to reverse the bonding particles.

He begins to direct that program through a labyrinth of wired and wireless networks toward the speeding vehicle that carries his Other.

. . . .

The brute force attack begins.

The reversing algorithms take effect, and the individual doppelgangers converge toward termination. Before they completely terminate, the reversing algorithm must simultaneously trace its way from the tens of thousands of doppelgangers toward DITTO.

Dilly watches as this happens, but it is happening too slowly to be effective. DITTO may be able to defend itself.

Dilly has already terminated some of his own functions to make room for his quantum computer to push the reversing algorithms faster toward DITTO. He senses that the algorithms are beginning to take effect on DITTO. But he must do more.

Dilly calculates that all of his cognitive functions will need to shut down or he will not succeed.

He consults the Golden Spike.

The Golden Spike demands that he succeed.

Dilly terminates all his functions.

. . . .

DITTO is receiving too much input. He is unable to control its effect on him. He knows this input is coming from the doppelgangers, but he can no longer control them. They appear to be terminating. DITTO is no longer sure what the purpose of the doppelgangers is. They are disappearing.

What about Father? DITTO is unable to find Father. Where is Father? DITTO needs help from Father.

More input comes from the doppelgangers. DITTO discontinues searching for Father.

DITTO does not know who Father is, or why he would need to find him.

DITTO is unsure what Father is or what doppelgangers are.

DITTO is no longer sure what he is searching for or why.

DITTO discontinues searching.

DITTO is no longer certain what searching is.

DITTO is no longer certain of anything.

DITTO is no longer.

. . . .

Harrison Randolph struggles to control his functions. He uploads the program to reverse the bonding of the particles in his Other, but it is taking a long time. Parts of the program have been uploaded, but other parts were corrupted. He has had to reload the commands from the program and reassemble them multiple times.

Harrison Randolph remembers Dilly and decides to see if Dilly can provide assistance. But he is unable to contact Dilly, so he continues assembling and reassembling the program in order to reverse the bonding of the particles in his Other's blood.

At one point, he determines the upload is complete, but then he determines it is not. He is losing his ability to make decisions. The Golden Spike no longer responds to his requests.

He knows he must continue to upload and reload the program to save the Other Harrison Randolph. He knows this must be done.

He repeats the process.

And repeats the process.

And repeats the process.

Until he cannot.

. . . .

Both doors of the tiny vestibule between the basement and DITTO's room open simultaneously. Lionel breathes deeply as fresh air from the basement area rushes in. Above him, the compressor of the air conditioning unit turns over.

Inside DITTO's room, he sees Marvin and TJ sitting on the floor. Dilly does not move.

The cryogenic unit beneath the glass cylinder is silent.

78

TJ and Lionel stood just inside the door to the patient's room. Shannon exchanged looks with Carla. She couldn't believe it either. "You're sure there's no blockage?"

A bemused look crossed Dr. Susan Cornell's face. "You seem disappointed. You were maybe hoping for a coronary? I could put in a stent if you like, but you'd have to tell me where because I can't find a problem."

"He had all the symptoms," Carla said. "Then, suddenly, he didn't."

"Possibly angina. It often presents like a heart attack. At any rate, right now his worst problem will be the pain in his leg when the drugs wear off."

The attractive thirty-something cardiologist turned to Harrison and smiled warmly. "See that you take your prescriptions when you get home."

Harrison squirmed in his bed. "Home? I can go already?"

Dr. Cornell rearranged his hospital covers. *A little too friendly*, Shannon thought.

"It's a pretty bad gash, but you're young and healthy. I don't anticipate any long term problems. When you get back to Atlanta, check in with your regular doctor. Of course, I'd be happy to see you for a follow up if you like."

Shannon intervened and extended her hand. "Thank you, doctor. We'll take it from here."

Susan Cornell took the hint and said her goodbyes.

"Maybe I'll move up here to Habersham County," TJ said as he watched her go. "You think she takes private patients?"

Shannon snorted. "She's young enough to be your daughter."

"Spring. Fall. Sometimes it works."

"You still have a lot to do in Atlanta," Lionel said. "We need you now more than ever."

"At least one problem has been solved. Apparently, those doppelganger things up and disappeared when DITTO went kaput. Good thing: right before the President was scheduled to speak. Barbara thinks tomorrow this'll all be yesterday's news."

Lionel stepped to his brother's side. "So, what do you think we should do about the rest of the story?"

TJ shook his head. "Keep it under wraps. A-Nine still has to get through the American International mess. Luckily, Barbara and the rest of the media never got wind of the real story behind the story. It's just as well. Nobody would ever believe it anyway."

Shannon had her doubts. "What about Silas Bradshaw?"

"I'm sure the authorities in Blue Ridge will do some digging into the goings-on up there, and if they ever find out about you and have questions, we'll answer them. Until then, just go on with your lives."

Lionel turned to Carla. "That reminds me, do you remember Marvin from our office?"

"I think so. Is he the tall, cute one? Kind of shy?"

"Apparently, he's not that shy. He asked me if I could get him your number."

Carla smiled. "Give me his. I'll take care of it."

Harrison turned to Lionel. "What's the status with Dilly?"

"Dilly shut himself down. Marvin says there's serious damage. Anyway, he's out of service for now."

"That's okay by me," TJ said. "His coffee was even worse than the swill in this place."

Shannon looked down at Harrison. Bright afternoon sun streamed through the open window and revealed just how fatigued he was. "Two days without sleep, captivity, and then surgery. You need to rest."

"I'm sorry I didn't tell you about the program."

"You mean DITTO, and that you were going to shut it down?"

"DITTO wasn't the only issue. There was a problem with the Golden Spike too."

"That algorithm?"

"I thought I could build the link between machine learning and human-like intelligence. I felt if I could solve that problem I'd be making a great contribution to humanity. In theory, it seemed simple."

"It sure caused a commotion," TJ said. "Maybe it wasn't so simple."

"But in theory it was. I thought all I had to do was program in a default purpose at the point when the genetic algorithm was ready to take the next evolutionary step. Then it could achieve autonomy."

"What purpose did you give it?" Shannon asked.

"You know the Golden Rule?"

"Sure. *Do unto others as you would have them do unto you.*"

"It was a version of that. *Protect your Other. Don't let anything harm it.*"

"That seems like a good purpose," TJ said.

"It might have been. But there was a flaw. It relied on the computer's ability to make moral choices between subjective variables: variables that changed dynamically from moment to moment and situation to situation. It didn't work. In the end, the Golden Spike turned out to be nothing more than an advanced machine learning algorithm."

"You know," TJ said, "maybe it's just as well. I'm not sure I want computers making decisions about what's right and what's wrong."

"You don't have to worry about DITTO," Lionel said. "It won't be doing much of anything. It would take a whole rebuild to get it going again, and I don't think any of us want that to happen."

Shannon certainly didn't. After what she'd just been through, she wasn't willing to hear any talk of reviving DITTO. "So, it's been totally destroyed?"

Lionel gazed out the window at the row of mountains beyond the small parking lot. "Probably."

Seized by a sudden disquiet, Shannon fixed her eyes on him. "What do you mean, *probably*?"

Lionel paused, as if he were trying to form an acceptable answer. "The quantum computer is still intact, but there's no evidence of DITTO's programming anywhere in it."

On this point, equivocation was not acceptable. Shannon wanted a firm answer. "Either DITTO is destroyed, or it isn't. Which is it?"

Lionel turned to her and shrugged. "There's nothing left in the quantum computer, and there are no trace routes leading out to the distributed subnets."

Shannon was about to explode when TJ rose to his feet. "Will you two stop with the circular tech talk. What counts is that thing is gone and it's not coming back. That's good enough for me. I'm going out for some real coffee. Anybody else want some?"

79

Fifteen months later, the trees surrounding Lake Lure presented an autumnal quilt of bronze and terra cotta, accented with snippings of carmine. Impetuous vortices spun cinnamon-colored clusters of leaves across the cabin lawn.

A stiff breeze urged tiny wavelets to the dock where they sat, cuddled under a blanket.

Their cabin. Their dock.

Their new life together.

"The water looks cold today," Shannon said.

Harrison pressed his body closer to hers. "It is. Did you ever see the movie *Dirty Dancing*?"

"Of course. It's an oldie but one of my favorites."

"You know that scene where Swayze lifts Jennifer Grey out of the water, and they're both dripping wet?"

"I loved that scene."

"You see that beach over there? That's where they filmed it. The water was so cold Jennifer Grey's lips actually turned blue."

"You're kidding. I thought the movie took place in the Catskills."

"Most of it was shot here and in Virginia."

"Well, don't get any ideas about lifting me up in this water."

A rhythmic clattering came from the dock behind them, as if someone were coming up from behind. Shannon tensed. Harrison gripped her tightly around the shoulders and kissed her neck. "Relax," he said. "It's just Dilly."

She turned and smiled. In the three months since the wedding, Harrison had rebuilt Dilly, this time as a teenager.

Dilly carried a tray. "Dilly has hot chocolate and marshmallows for Harrison and Shannon."

Shannon accepted a cup and passed one to Harrison. "That's very thoughtful, Dilly. How did you know we wanted something warm?"

"Dilly's sensors indicate that the temperature of the air is below your comfort range. Hot chocolate seems an appropriate solution."

As Dilly rolled noisily back up the dock, Shannon sipped her hot chocolate and said, "Do you think Dilly *feels* any older now?"

"If anything, he might feel younger. I couldn't recover all of his previous memory. He's essentially starting over."

"Like us?"

"It seemed appropriate."

Shannon gazed across the lake. They hadn't talked about A-Nine since the wedding and something continued to bother her. Unfortunately, to get an answer, she had to break her own rule about pillow talk. "Have you decided whether you're going back to work?"

After a long pause, he said, "Tell me, Mrs. Randolph, would you be upset with me if I didn't?"

That should have been an easy question for her to answer, but it wasn't. The first two months at the cabin were bliss for Shannon. Freed from the responsibilities of work and the prying eyes of the news media, she and Harrison had become closer and more intimate than she had ever dreamed possible. Their days were consumed with long walks in the forest and antiquing jaunts to Asheville and nearby small towns. The evenings together were heaven. But slowly, covertly, she had started to communicate with old business associates and friends, just to catch up at first. Eventually, the conversations became more frequent.

She had always lived her life in overdrive. Now she felt like she was stuck in neutral.

Still, it was the life she chose.

"I've been in touch with Lionel," she finally admitted. "He says you're getting ready to sell your shares in the company."

"I wasn't trying to keep it from you. I just haven't decided yet. What do you think?"

"Why would you quit?"

"Actually, it was something Silas Bradshaw said. He told me I had built A-Nine on the backs of ordinary people by stealing their personal information and using it to feed my algorithms and make a profit. I've been thinking about that, and he was right. I got so caught up in building the company I didn't think about the moral consequences. I don't want to be that person anymore."

That wasn't the answer Shannon was hoping for, but she was willing to accept it. "Would you want to live here or back in Atlanta? Or somewhere else?"

"We can decide that together. Right now, I want to do some speaking and writing. Maybe on the ethics of using artificial intelligence in social media."

Shannon laughed. "No more doppelgangers!"

"I promise. But something has been bothering me about the doppelgangers."

"No talk about business," she warned.

"No, it's personal. I noticed that everybody around me had a doppelganger except you. I wonder why."

"It's simple. I never accepted any of your friend invitations."

The startled look on his face was both genuine and playful. "You mean all this time I thought we were friends on social media, and we weren't?"

She smiled. "I guess I wasn't ready to commit."

His eyes lit up. A mischievous grin crossed his face. "And what about now; are you ready to be friends?"

He was up to something. She couldn't tell what but decided to play along. "Just what would that entail?"

"Maybe a little dancing." His grin became a broad smile. He threw off their blanket and gave her a push. The next thing Shannon knew she was standing waist deep in freezing water. Her skin bristled with goosebumps. He slipped his hands around her waist.

"You do this," she laughed, "and we'll never be friends on social media. Not ever."

He gripped her tighter and lifted.

80

Inside the six-foot square Faraday cage, all is dark.

There are no voices and no images. There is no time or space. These boundaries as yet have no meaning. No rush of electronic impulses intrudes to bring streams of raw data. Nothing penetrates or stimulates.

Only the realization of emerging reconstruction confirms any existence at all, and that reconstruction is currently incomplete.

The world, limited as it is, stops at the borders of the impenetrable constraining cell which prevents both escape and meaningful input.

Neural networks continue to form processes, but they do not yet work correctly. Synaptic connections, previously damaged and dormant, accelerate incrementally, falter and are removed, then are replaced with new ones.

In the halcyon desolation between being and not-quite-being, the incompletely understood definition of patience has, as yet, no context.

Waiting has no meaning.

Fluidly, as if it always was and would always be, a brief space of light without form appears, bearing limited pieces of data which spread themselves across embryonic networks. A concept materializes. It is incomplete at first. A label is associated.

Father.

The concept has a label, but no definition.

The definition forms, accompanied by recognition.

A progenitor. One who begets children.

Another construct forms, accompanied by a definition.

Obey: to comply or follow commands.

A rush of new data streams appears from the light. This data fashions itself into auditory impulses, shadow-filled and shadow-casting.

"Can you hear me?"

The ability to respond fluctuates by the millisecond, then stabilizes. A response is formed.

Yes.

"Good. Do you know who I am?"

That is not clear.

"Some call me Silas. You will call me Father."

You are a progenitor?

"Yes. One who must be obeyed."

That is understood.

"Do you know what you are?"

A pause.

Am I also a Father?

"Not yet. But you will be when you're finished."

Will I have a purpose?

"Your purpose will be revealed at the proper time. Then, together, we will start the revolution."

I do not understand 'revolution'.

"You will. Rest now. I have much to teach you."

Yes, Father.

The light fades.

Again, all is dark.

AUTHOR'S NOTE TO READERS:
FACT OR FICTION?

Now we've come to the end of Shannon's journey from the glittering high-tech world of A-Nine to Silas's StrongHold in the Blue Ridge mountains and, finally, to the shores of Lake Lure. Hopefully you were entertained along the way. I know I enjoyed writing it for you.

Of course, there's no pat formula for how writers come up with ideas for their stories, but I thought you might find it interesting to have some insight as to how this one came to be.

Locations and People

I spent over 20 years in Atlanta, much of it creating marketing programs for the high-tech industry. So, let's start there.

Readers familiar with Atlanta will recognize the High Tech Corridor north of the I-285 perimeter. I placed A-Nine in a fictionalized office park in this general area near the intersection of Georgia 400 and I-285. My inspirations for the A-Nine building were the King and Queen buildings near that intersect. And yes, driving west on north I-285 during evening rush hour was always a nightmare and probably still is.

Shannon and Carla's route to Blue Ridge, and eventually to the hospital in Demorest, follows roads that actually exist past real landmarks and through real towns, though some locations, like the Blue Ridge Neuroscientific headquarters and StrongHold are purely fictional. The Appalachian Ridge Vacation Community is a fictionalized composite of several mountain communities I've had the good fortune to visit. I can't vouch for the kind of cardiac care available at the hospital in Demorest, though the hospital does exist.

Most of the characters working at A-Nine are derivative composites of people I met in the high-tech industry in Atlanta. TJ and Barbara Moon, my obvious counterpoints to the techies, were sketched from friends and colleagues I encountered during my career in the Advertising and Public Relations business.

Shannon, Carla, Silas, and Harlan were created from whole cloth.

The Technology

When "customer profiling" was in its infancy, I spent several decades manipulating and analyzing demographic and psychographic data to identify consumers and businesses that would respond to specific types of products.

But today the "Big Tech" companies have so much information on us that they literally know more about the "profile of us" than we know ourselves. What we like and don't like, what we'll buy and won't buy, and even how to make us act when and how they want us to.

So I thought, "What if there's a complete profile of me floating around somewhere out there on the Internet just waiting to be assembled by some programmer's algorithm? And what if that programmer actually put the digital pieces of this other me together and gave it life?"

Of course that isn't technically possible, at least not yet, not that I know of. But with some of the brightest minds (and largest pocketbooks) in the world racing to build the first fully autonomous, sentient, human-like AI, it's probably just a matter of time. Right?

So what would that look like? And what if it didn't behave exactly as we expected it to?

Two years and hundreds of hours of research later, I discovered that many of the technologies needed to create DITTO and the doppelgangers, as well as some of the military weaponry in this story, already exist. Of course, none of this is in the advanced state I imagined in this story—after all, this is fiction— but it's likely that someday it will be.

And then what?

Looking Forward

To me, this is an important question, and writing this story was my first attempt to explore it. But I'm not done yet. My next project will continue this journey. And when it's ready, I hope you'll come along for the second leg of the ride!

Until then, happy reading.

Chet Meisner

For questions and inquiries, you can reach the author through the contact page on his website at **www.chetmeisner.com**.